CW00433178

"War, politics and tragedy test the f(
... a thrilling story of loyalty and b(
in which there would ultimately be
—**Bruce Dennill,** *The Citizen*

"Cranswick's love and deep respect for nature is obvious in his admirable descriptions of the beautiful Zimbabwean bushveld and wildlife. He highlights a number of actions which were an important part of the Rhodesian bush war campaign. However, the real strength of this compelling story lies in its hope that good will eventually derive from the chaos that predominates in this country at present. It is a hope we all share"
—**General John Hickman** (former Commander Rhodesian Army)

"I could not stop reading this in-depth story; it was fascinating to read of those incredible incidents that actually happened. *Blood Lily* sends a clear message to all people on this continent that we should not allow our leaders to dictate and feed propaganda to the masses. It is a book that we can all relate to and it will touch your heart when you recognise what a great place Africa can become if only we communicate with and respect all cultures. *Blood Lily* brings back so many memories, both happy and sad. An enjoyable and easy read, I could not put it down. Thank you for allowing me to rekindle all those years in that wonderful piece of land called Zimbabwe"
—**Ray Mordt** (former Springbok and Rhodesian winger)

# blood
# lily

a novel

by Mason Cranswick

30° South Publishers

Published in 2009 by 30° South Publishers (Pty) Ltd.
3 Ajax Place, 120 Caroline Street, Brixton
Johannesburg 2092, South Africa
www.30degreessouth.co.za
info@30degreessouth.co.za

Cover image by Craig Bone

Design and origination by 30° South Publishers (Pty) Ltd.

ISBN 978-0-958489-19-5

The author has drawn on some factual events from
Barbara Cole's *The Elite*, which he would like to thank her for
and gratefully acknowledge.

*One generation passeth away, and another generation cometh: but the Earth abideth for ever ...*

**Ecclesiastes 1.4**

# one

*London, 2008*

Rays of sun burst through the branches of the mango trees at the end of our lawn over a family of guinea fowl scurrying past. A small herd of impala fed unperturbed from the rich green grass in the vlei behind them. As the early-morning mist melted into the air, our koppie could be seen in its full glory, glowing red with the fresh show of the spring msasas.

I turned and pushed the heavy teak front door to enter the lounge. The grandfather clock ticked regally against the wall as I walked past Dad's stone fireplace towards the passage. Kathy's bedroom door was shut. I knocked first, then stepped in.

*The sky was filled with crows beating their wings and screeching.*

*A defiant Mugabe shook his fist. "I will never, never surrender!"*

*Still the screeching. I held my hands over my ears.*

Wearing latex gloves, men in white overalls carried bodies wrapped in strips of black plastic. Above them, the crows circled, beating their wings like drums of war. I clasped my hands over my ears, but I couldn't block out the sound.

*"There is no cholera in this country!"* Mugabe bellowed, his voice straining over the cry of the crows.

A young African boy pushed a wheelbarrow. In it a girl lay on her back, her shrivelled, stick-like legs dangling over the side. Her deep, hollow eyes looked right through me.

*"We are not hungry … why foist this food upon us?"* Mugabe ranted, waving his fists.

Bagosora, the Rwandan colonel, stumbled past, his hands red with the blood of his people. His arms and legs were bound in chains. Behind him, protestors had gathered carrying placards: 'Mugabe is next'.

*More beating of wings, screeching of crows.*

*I ran for the door.*

*In the corridor, the baboons frantic. "Hold on, Bruce. The Hunters are coming!" I shouted, flinging open Mum's bedroom door.*

"Mum! Dad!" Standing before me on the lawn, war vets. In front of them a dead kudu, blood oozing from its slashed gut.

*The leader, Mugabe, one foot on the kudu's horns: "The land is ours!"*

*Crows circling over the kudu, beating wings and screeching.*

Dad looked straight at Mugabe, his voice calm. "For fifty years I have farmed this land." He paused to look up at the crows. "For fifty years I have helped feed the people of this country!"

*Drums of war … crows ripping into the flesh of the kudu.*

Mlilo's voice boomed: "You can't beat him, Peter. He'll do whatever it takes." Then the army trucks. One, two … ten, I counted as they roared into the driveway.

I ran for the door.

*In the corridor, the baboons, still frantic. "They're coming, Bruce!" A burst of gunfire. Desperate now, I dived for my bedroom door.*

Inside was calm. I looked up to see black granite koppies; above them the sky a bright comforting blue. On a mopane tree sat a black eagle. I stood still, taking in the beauty of the scene. But there was a strange smell in the air: rotting meat with a tinge of sweetness.

The black eagle with a distinctive white V-marking on its back swivelled to face me. Surging from its eyes were tears—red tears of blood running down the yellow markings on the cruel beak, down the black feathers in a waterfall to the ground below. Torrents of blood flowed from the waterfall to a mineshaft nearby.

*Antelope Mine.*

Then the drone of an army truck. I leapt behind a thorn tree as the truck pulled up at a makeshift loading bay on the edge of the shaft. Ten soldiers jumped into the back behind their leader, Mugabe. Each wore a distinctive red beret. Fifth Brigade.

Crows circled the mineshaft beating their wings. The stench was overwhelming. Human bodies, thousands of them, flung into the open hole. A light breeze blew towards me—and with it the dust from Antelope Mine.

I ran for the door.

*In the aisle, passengers—their heads between their knees, terrified.*

*"Mayday, Mayday, Rhodesia 825, help us!" cried the pilot on the radio as flames swarmed past the windows. The plane in a nose-dive. In front of me a man clawed at the window. Then a little girl. Everyone screaming as the pilot called out: "Brace for impact!"*

*"You have taken our land!" Gunfire. More screaming.*

*I ran for the kitchen door. Still screaming. Traders screaming at each*

9

*other across the trading floor. "It's collapsing! We're going down!"*

*TV blaring: "Turmoil grips the financial markets amid reports that Lehman Brothers, the fourth-largest US Investment Bank, may be in serious trouble."*

My eyes opened. I was covered in sweat. Anxiously, I peered across at my wife. Still sleeping. I climbed from the bed.

# two

Careful not to wake my wife, I crept from the bedroom to the study. I turned on my computer, opened an Excel file, *Dollar-Rand currency trades*, and pressed a green button at the front of the spreadsheet: *Profit and Loss*. My pulse raced as I waited. The figures flashed up.

I ran to the bathroom and threw up the last of yesterday's dinner.

Back at my desk, I clicked the Reuters icon. Headlines jumped out at me:

*Lehman announces $3.9bn third-quarter loss.* I scrolled down the page, but it only got worse:

*Lehman shares plunge by more than 90%.*

I walked from the study but stopped as I caught my reflection in the mirror. You sad, sad bastard, I muttered. Bags bruised the soft skin beneath my eyes. My face was pallid, my hair almost completely grey. I scarcely recognised myself.

"My goodness, you've done well for yourself, Scott," James Parker noted as he looked around my plush office, then out of the windows at a magnificent view of the Thames.

"What brings you to Lehman, James?"

"Your young man over there," he said, pointing at Hayden on the modern, open-plan trading floor outside. "He's been looking at restructuring one of my investments."

"What investment?"

"I've five million dollars with one of your special-purpose vehicles in a note, credit-linked to Russia."

"Why restructure?" I asked.

"Young Hayden out there can improve my return on the note simply by adding Lehman risk. The only way I can lose is if Russia or Lehman goes bust."

"Hold on, James. Have you done your research on us? We've had a tough few months."

"Come on, Scott, look around you." He pointed in all directions. "Will this giant ever fail? Also, if Hayden's your man, I know I can trust him."

I was about to respond when the speakerphone interrupted me. "Mr Carter, the Barclays team is here." I escorted James to the door and hurried across the trading floor to a large meeting-room. On the way I stopped over at Hayden's desk and left a message with his colleague not to execute the James Parker trade until he'd spoken to me.

I shook hands with the three Barclays suits as I entered the room, then sat across the table with two other Lehman executives.

The head of the Barclays team pulled a folder from his briefcase. I couldn't miss the large label on the front of the file: *Lehman: Distressed Debt.*

He opened it and looked across at us.

"Who the hell made the decision to invest in Sub-Prime?"

We looked at each other. If Barclays bought us, whoever

admitted responsibility could be out of a job the morning they took over. There was a long, awkward silence.

"It was my decision," I replied, looking straight at him.

He tossed the folder in my direction.

I picked it up and cast an eye over the schedule of our distressed debt.

"Without US guarantees," he continued, "it'll be extremely difficult."

I caught my breath. We needed Barclays.

He rose to his feet. "What news from the US?"

"In all our discussions with the Fed and the Treasury so far, they've been reluctant to bail us out," I told him.

Frowning, he led his team from the room.

I strode back over the trading floor.

Hayden jumped to his feet when he saw me. "Mr Carter—I didn't do the James Parker trade."

"Great!" I punched my open palm. "No selling Lehman risk without my permission. Make sure everyone knows," I said, pointing at the rows of traders tucked behind their plasma screens and Bloomberg terminals.

As I marched into my office Jamie, my PA, cried out: "Head of Credit, Evan from Legal, your banker and your wife all called. Messages on your desk—please call them back. Oh, and Head of Operations called. Please call him."

Ben, another high-level Lehman executive, was waiting for me in my office.

"Barclays or Bank of America are our only hope," he told me.

I nodded.

"But if they don't get US government guarantees, I'm sure they won't buy us. We'll hear from the US at three o'clock today."

"Understood."

He walked to my door, then turned. "Hey, how are those personal rand trades of yours doing?"

"Bloody awful. The rand's tanking with the market."

He smiled. "You're losing your touch."

I shook my head. "No, it's a great trade. When the market turns, the rand's going through the roof."

Quickly I closed the door and pulled out my banker's number.

"Morning, Mr Carter."

"You called?"

"Yes. I'm getting a lot of pressure from Head Office. They can't extend the deadline on your mortgage payment any further. Either the money is in the account by eleven tomorrow morning, or they take the house."

"Look, I'd been hoping to sell some of my Lehman shares, but the market's crashed. I've got to find school fees for my daughter—just give me one more week to sort things out."

"I'd like to, Mr Carter, but the deadline is from Head Office. Either the money's in your account by eleven tomorrow, or they start liquidating your assets."

I lowered the phone but almost immediately it rang again.

"You were up early this morning, Scott."

"Hi, darling."

"I know you're busy, but I was just calling to remind you about Sidney's play this evening. Please don't be late."

I put down the phone and rushed to the bathroom. I'd had no breakfast; only coffee, but it spasmed blackly into the open toilet below.

Back in my office, I pulled up the pricing on my rand trades. More losses. Again the phone rang. It was Jamie: "I have Evan from Compliance on one line and your mother on the other."

"Okay, put Mum through—tell Evan I'll call him back."

"Hello, Scott."

"Hello, Mum. Everything okay?"

"As well as things can be in Zim at the moment. Look, I've been thinking about your phone call the other day. If there's anything Dad and I can do to help, you know you just have to ask."

"I know, Mum. I really appreciate it, but we'll be fine."

"Have you told her yet?"

"No, Mum, and please don't you do it either. I'll tell her when the time's right." Telling my wife would be the final acknowledgement of defeat.

"Scott." Mum's voice was faltering. "Your Dad and I have always been very proud of you. Whatever's happened, you've always done the right thing."

She hesitated so I jumped in quickly. "Mum, I've got to go."

"Son, remember that cross-country race when you carried Bruce?" How could I forget? Bruce and I, two knock-kneed eight-year-olds, at the start of the Selukwe cross-country race. I was desperate to win and I knew I would be the fastest by some distance, but Bruce twisted his ankle on the final corner, so I picked him up and carried him to the finish line. We came third, together.

"Even before that day, I knew I'd always be proud of you."

"Okay, Mum, that's enough," I mumbled.

Ben poked his head around my door.

"Okay, I really have to go. Hi to Dad."

"The CEO is calling from New York," said Ben.

I ignored my ringing phone and followed Ben quickly across the trading floor to the meeting room.

In a few minutes we'd know our fate. Ben clicked on the speakerphone in the centre of the large room. "We're ready," he told the CEO's PA on the other side of the Atlantic.

We waited in silence, not looking at each other.

Finally the CEO's voice came into the room: "Gentlemen, I wanted you two to be the first in London to know. The US Treasury has confirmed they will not be providing any guarantees of our debt, nor will they be using any taxpayer money to bail us out. Barclays and Bank of America won't buy us. We're filing for Chapter 11 bankruptcy."

He kept on talking. I've no idea what he said after that. It didn't matter any more. My Lehman shares were worthless, my house in negative equity. Tomorrow we could be homeless.

I went back to my office, where my phone was still ringing. I packed my briefcase and slowly walked across the floor. When I got to the lifts, I turned for one last look. There'd been some tough times at Lehman, but I'd always imagined walking out a wealthy man.

I kept walking along the Thames until I reached the stairs above the Royal China restaurant. On a bench overlooking the river, I took out my cell phone to call my wife.

As I dialled, another call came through. My banker's private number.

"David."

"Well done, Mr Carter. I knew you'd pull through."

"What?" I wasn't in the mood for games.

"I'm sitting here looking at your very healthy bank balance."

"What do you mean?"

"There's enough cash to pay your mortgage, school fees, whatever—you name it. For years to come." He paused. "Who is this Mlilo who's bailed you out?"

"Mlilo sent me money?" My hands were shaking.

"Yes, and there's a message."

"What does it say?"

"It's in another language. I can't read it, so I'll spell it out for you." It took him a while, but I wrote it down as he laboriously spelled it out. It was in Ndebele:

*Inotho kanye lobungane kuyabunjwa kubuye kutshabalale.*
*Impi esayilwayo;*
*lokubulawa kwelizwe okwenziwa nguMugabe*
*... konke lokhu kuyaphela.*
*Umhlabathi kuphela yiwo ozasala,*
*ngoba okungapheliyo kuyahlola.*
*Ngumngane wakho uMlilo.*

# three

*Selukwe, Rhodesia, 1973*

"You okay, Simba?" He didn't look up; just stood, hands in his pockets, leaning on the mud wall of his hut.

"Hey, who did this?"

"*Baas* Miller's boys."

"Why on earth?"

"They called me a smelly kaffir." He leaned over and spat hard. Red blood pooled in the dry sand. "Man, I told them, *eh*, I said, 'Don't talk to me like that.'"

"So they did this to you?"

He nodded slowly, blood still dripping into the sand. Hell, they'd given him a beating.

"Bugger it. I'm calling the police."

He looked up at me now through two swollen eye sockets, one eye completely closed. A long gash on his forehead oozed dark red blood. "What's the point, Scott? Who they gonna believe—three white boys, or a little *piccanin*?"

He was right ... the police would laugh at him. We had to stand up for ourselves. But they were seriously big blokes. Farm boys, hard as nails. And we were half their size. I kicked at a stone lodged in the dirt.

"We've got to fight them, Simba."

"Are you crazy?"

"I mean it, man. It's the only thing they'll understand. If we don't, they'll thump you whenever they see you."

He was shaking his head.

"Look, if we train, I'm sure …" I bent down and picked up a handful of the dry red sand. Slowly, I let the light breeze blow it from my open hand. "I've got it! Dad! He can teach us to box."

He looked at me with his lopsided grin. "They'll never expect it."

"Exactly!"

I found Dad in his bedroom, putting on his veldskoens. There was nothing he liked more than telling his old boxing stories. His gloves were wrapped up under the bed with a pair of red and blue boxing boots. He began unpacking them.

"Bigger boys. Means nothing. Remember that. Joe Louis versus Primo Carnero? Size wasn't an issue." I could see that look in his eyes as he punched the gloves into shape and admired them. "Tell your pal we start at five o'clock tomorrow morning, and if either of you are late, we're finished. I don't need any softies on my programme. Got it?"

"Yes, Dad." I tiptoed from the room, leaving him to his memories. I couldn't wait to tell Simba and rushed outside, stopping briefly to pick up the rugby ball lying on the grass at the front of the house. I drop-kicked it over the makeshift rugby posts—the line of mango trees at the end of our long, rolling lawn—then walked quickly past the avocado tree and around the house to the back.

Our large thatched house sat on a long sloping hill. In front, the dirt road led from the lawn to the farm. Beyond the mango trees a vlei, and in the distance our favourite koppie, carpeted at this time of year in the distinctive amber and wine of the msasas' spring leaves. At the back a long, open vlei. About three hundred metres down the vlei was a dense thicket of acacia and msasa trees.

Two hundred metres beyond the thicket stood the compound where Simba lived with his mother, our maid, Anna.

I looked out towards his home, but could only see as far as the thicket that screened us from their huts. The Africans living there only ventured to our side of the thicket for work or on important business.

A narrow bush-path ran through the vlei from the house to the compound, and it was along this path I jogged to find Simba. After I passed through the thicket I heard raised voices—Anna was yelling at Simba, who was washing the blood from his face in a bucket of water outside his hut. I stopped running and walked quietly towards them.

She was still shouting at Simba in Ndebele, which I didn't understand.

"They just attacked me, mother," Simba replied in English.

Again she screamed at him in Ndebele.

"I know the whites run this country, mother. But it won't be forever."

Anna looked up as she saw me entering the compound. "Hello, *baas*," she bowed meekly, and slipped into her hut.

"Is everything okay, Simba?" I asked. He nodded his head without looking at me.

"Dad'll train us, starting five o'clock tomorrow morning on the lawn!"

We stood under the mango trees. Simba and I'd been there since four-thirty.

"What've you got on your feet?" Dad poked at my track-shoes with a stick. "Run in shoes, and you'll end up with soft feet. Do you want to be a cook in the army?" I certainly didn't and took them off immediately. He glanced approvingly at Simba's bare feet as we set off on our first three-kilometre run.

Dad led the way along Leopard Pass. I was ahead of Simba on the flat as we sped past the red spring leaves of the mountain acacia. Keeping my lead through Impala Vlei, I quickly admired the early-morning herds of impala gathered at the water hole. I knew Simba was catching up on me. As we began the final uphill leg through the msasas I started sprinting. But it was too late. He was already past me and held his lead through to the finishing post, the mango trees.

Dad gave us three minutes to catch our breath, then it was sprints on the lawn. Then press-ups, star jumps, squats ... all the time with Dad shouting at us. I'd never seen him this way before—it was like he'd been made for the role. After school he had us on the pads. First me, then Simba, firing punches at his padded hands while he shouted at us: "Left jab, straight right, left hook, right hook!" In the evening we sparred behind the tool shed so that Mum wouldn't see us.

After a week of Dad's training we were in great shape. And when we arrived for sparring, Dad broke the news. "All right, boys—tonight's the real thing." He patted us both on the back.

"Hey, Dad, you mean ... fight Simba?"

"Who else?"

"But ... he's my friend."

Simba looked uneasy. "Sorry, *Baas* Peter," he stared down at his bare feet. "I can't fight Scott."

Ignoring Simba, Dad bent down, his eyes level with mine. "Are you a man or a mouse?" I looked away.

"Well? Man or mouse?"

"A man!"

"Good! We can practise all you like, but there's only one way to learn to fight, and that's to fight."

Simba and I glanced at each other. I could tell he was thinking the same as me. We'd do whatever it took to win—at anything—whether it was playing rugby on the front lawn or riding bareback over the veld.

We shook hands before we gloved-up in the corners Dad had set up for us. He rang an old cattle bell to start the fight, then jumped into the ring to referee.

I marched forward, hurling punches at Simba's head. He met me in the centre of the ring and we swung furiously at each other, neither of us taking a step backwards or thinking to defend ourselves. Finally I caught him with a giant wraparound right, causing him to stagger against the ropes. Then I charged forward, flinging aimless punches in all directions. The bell rang again.

"Scott takes round one," Dad called. I should have been pleased—my opponent was already struggling and panting heavily, but I could hardly stand.

"Go, Scott, you can beat him!" We turned our heads. It was my little sister, Kathy, who must've been hiding behind the wall, watching.

"And what do you think you're doing, Miss Madam?"

"Just watching the fight, Dad."

"Yes, I realised that. You're not to tell your mother a word about this, okay?"

"Sure, Dad ... promise."

My legs were giving way under me as Dad rang the bell for

the second. Simba saw my weakness and took advantage, surging towards me. My arms couldn't even reach his jaw by the third round and, as the final bell rang, Dad declared him the winner.

"Okay, boys—a week to get your strength back, and we'll have a re-match."

I felt awkward as I approached Dad before dinner that night. He was sitting on the veranda blowing smoke rings into the dark night.

"Hey, Dad, I want to beat Simba. I'll need some extra coaching."

"Determination, eh?" he puffed, not looking at me. "I'll tell you, boy, you need to work on your tactics and fitness." He ground his cigarette under his boot and leaned forward in his chair. "Let's start with tactics. To win, you've got to fight to your strengths. Now imagine you and Simba are looking into a mirror. What do you see?"

I gave him a strange look.

"Come on, it's important. Start with Simba."

Describe my best friend? I had no words, just an uneasy guilt that I was going behind his back. I'd seen him almost every day of my life. Jeez, nearly fourteen years. I could mention the scar on his right thigh where he'd been bitten by Bruce's Alsatian—he never showed any emotion, never had—or those cold eyes, or the chipped front tooth he'd got falling from the avocado tree right in front of his mother. She'd beaten him with a sjambok. He didn't flinch.

"I said describe Simba. Five things."

"Tall, big shoulders, wiry … big nose … tacky lips."

"Now you. Four things, and quickly."

"Short, stocky, dark-brown hair, green eyes."

"Right. You're short, four inches shorter than Simba, and

probably shorter than any opponent you'll get. So you've got to fight at close range. How do you get close? Two ways. When you're experienced you slip punches, bobbing and weaving to get in. But you're not ready for that yet. So, what do you do?"

I looked at him blankly.

"You force your way in close, even if you take a punch on the way in. Rocky Marciano was the greatest heavyweight alive, and he was only five foot ten. Sometimes he'd jump to get close to his opponents. Right. Over here." I followed him onto the grass, the lights from the kitchen illuminating a small patch of lawn.

"Okay, pretend I'm you—let me show you what you've got to do. As I move in close, you hit me!" When he pushed forward, I held out my arm.

"I said hit me. Properly, not like a little fairy!" Again he drove forward. But this time I slammed a right into his cheek.

"That's better. Now look where I am." He held his fist in front of my face. "This is where you have to be—right up close."

He grabbed a branch from the mango tree and held it tightly. "Next thing to remember is you're stocky ... strong and muscular. So once you're close, throw your punches, hard and fast. Use your strength to drive him backwards. Crowd the taller boxer, keep him off balance and he won't be able to hit you. After you've thrown the punches you've got two choices. If your opponent's in trouble, knock him out. If not, move away and take a rest. Then you go in again."

He paused. "Now, I want to see you do it. Remember—power your way in, strike hard and fast."

I charged forward. Dad caught me with a left as I moved in.

"Now!" he shouted.

I unleashed a barrage of punches, driving him backwards.

"The second thing to sort out is your fitness," he explained.

"If you're fighting two-minute rounds it's anaerobic, like a four-hundred-metre race."

"Peter, Scott ... dinner!" Mum called from the veranda. Dad put his hand on my shoulder and led me inside.

I was in a confident mood when I went to bed that night. The Millers were in for a nasty surprise. But there were three of them and only two of us, so early the next morning I called Bruce.

"Hi, Kelly, is Bruce there?"

"He's out on the lands with Dad."

"Can you tell him we're going riding—to meet at my place at eleven?"

"Can I come with?"

"Sorry, Kelly. Another time, hey?"

By the time Bruce arrived, the horses were saddled and raring to go. My three-year-old kudu, Shoko, was bucking his way across the lawn. I paused briefly to admire his rich grey coat and the white stripes running down his sides. Two magnificent horns spiralled upwards and outwards from his narrow head. He loved running with the horses.

As I mounted my horse, I looked up at my two friends. "Boys, a swim at the Impali?"

"Sounds good," said Simba, spurring his horse into action. We set off at a furious pace after him, down a bush track, dodging guinea fowl as they scuttled off the road. Through Impala Vlei we raced. As we drew near the Impali I caught up with him and we galloped the last four hundred metres together. We tied our horses to a msasa tree and waited for Bruce and Shoko to arrive.

I took off my rucksack and pulled out three of Dad's Lion Lagers that I'd taken from the fridge. "It's ice-cold, Bruce," I said, tossing him a bottle. He got off the horse, sat down next to us on the banks of the Impali, and took a deep sip. Shoko nudged me in the back, so I poured some beer into my open hand and held it out for him. He put his nose into the beer, shook his head in disgust and walked away to drink from the river.

"Hey, Bruce, remember when the three of us found Shoko?"

"*Ja*, of course."

"And we all promised to look after him. We also promised to look out for each other."

"*Ja*." He looked at me suspiciously.

"You know Simba got nailed by the Miller boys?"

"*Ja*."

"Well Simba and I want to take them on, but there're three of them and only two of us. Will you help?"

"Scott, they're huge. They'll eat us for breakfast. Just drop it, man."

"We only need you to keep the younger Miller brother out of the fight—okay?"

He hesitated. "I'm not keen."

"Come on, Bruce, we have to. Otherwise they'll keep on bashing Simba."

"All right, all right, I'll keep the younger Miller out of the action, but that's all."

"Thanks, Bruce. You're a champion." I downed my beer, dived into the Impali and floated on my back as the powerful current pulled me downstream.

The next morning, I met Simba for our early run. But after we finished our workout that night, after the sprints and the press-ups and the sparring, I added Dad's new routine to my training. While Simba slept, I worked the bag, using a mielie-meal packet filled with river sand. I did hill-sprints in the darkness over and over, until even the dogs headed back home.

My fitness wouldn't let me down again.

I sat in maths class on the day of the re-match.

"What are you dreaming about, Carter?" shouted the teacher as he caught me staring out the window.

"My maths test results, sir," I lied. I had to win tonight's match. I couldn't lose twice in a row. When I got home from school, Kathy was waiting for me on the lawn.

"Why don't you wear dresses?" I frowned at her. "You're a real tomboy."

"What's wrong with this?" she asked, looking down at her rugby shorts and T-shirt. "I'm too young to wear dresses."

"Nonsense, you're eleven. That's old enough for dresses."

"Anyway, what time are you fighting Simba?" She picked up a green mango from the lawn and tossed it into the air. We both turned to watch it land in the open vlei beyond the mango trees.

"How do you know I'm fighting today?"

She didn't answer.

"It's at five o'clock."

"Good luck! I'll be watching," she grinned, flinging another mango into the air.


As Dad rang the bell I drove forward, hammering straight punches at Simba's head. The intensity of my attack took him by surprise and he staggered backwards. I moved to finish him off, and kept punching until he stumbled to the ground. Dad gave him a standing eight count. Then I was on top of him again, pounding blows to his head. But he survived.

"Scott gets round one," announced Dad.

I was breathing heavily, with two rounds still to go. I knew I had to pace myself, so I kept away from Simba in the next round.

He did all the work, and Dad declared him winner of the second. I had regained my breath and was starting to feel the benefits of my fitness training.

The bell rang for the third and deciding round.

Simba anticipated my tactics, and as I moved in at the start of the third, he caught me with a powerful right, flush on the nose. I hesitated before smashing a series of left-right combinations to his jaw. Then I moved out to take a rest, dancing from side to side like I'd seen Muhammad Ali do on TV. Knowing he was losing, Simba came after me, catching me with a heavy right to the jaw. I shook my head, took a step backwards, then attacked again, targeting a cut below his eye. As long as I was in close, Simba was off balance. So I stayed in close and kept punching, my legs strong under me, until the bell rang. Dad held my arm aloft.

"The re-match goes to Scott."

My friend patted me on the back. "*Aiee*, Scott—you got some legs on you, *eh?*" he gasped through hard breaths.

"We'll need a third and final decider, though, to find the real champ," Dad said. "Not now, eh? But you boys," he pointed at me and then at Simba, "keep up the training, and you'll make fine boxers. Both of you." Simba and I were finished. One-all would do for now.

The next morning Kathy and I went swimming at the Selukwe town pool. When I got back I ran over to find Simba. I stopped and looked around me as I entered the compound. Nine small huts were spaced out across a small clearing in the bush. In the centre of the clearing stood a large syringa tree, its pale-lilac flowers adding colour to the dull grey and brown of the huts. He was sitting outside his hut on one of our old garden chairs that Mum had given Anna.

"What's up, Simba?"

He didn't say anything.

"Hey, Simba, let's take a walk down to the Baboon Pool." He was in one of his moods again and not even the stunning Baboon Pool, nestled in the msasa-clad koppies, could lift his heavy spirits. We sat on the rocks at the water's edge, admiring the striking red of the surrounding msasa trees.

"Are you gonna tell me what's wrong?" I asked again.

"Ah, forget it. Let's talk about something else."

I had a pretty good idea why he was upset. "Is it because you can't come to the town pool with us?"

He didn't say anything.

"Look, Simba, I agree it's not fair, but you know why those laws are in place. They don't want blacks straight out of the bush, who haven't bathed for months, using the pool. But you're spotless, and those rules shouldn't apply to you."

"Then why don't they have other rules?"

"Simba, Ian Smith'll change all that. He's been saying for years now that he wants to get rid of segregation. As soon as you blacks are ready, he'll let you run the country."

Simba leapt to his feet, bent down, grabbed a stone and hurled it up into the koppie above. We both stopped to watch the baboons, sitting on the rocks above us eating *mahobohobos* and casually tossing the pips in our direction. At the back of the troop, perched on a ledge, was our favourite, Grey, so named after a deep grey scar on his right cheek, which he'd had since before I could remember.

"Look," I continued. "You spend far too much time reading your books and worrying about this and that. You'll just depress yourself. We've got far more important things to worry about. Like the Millers tomorrow."

That night I dreamed that Simba, Bruce and I were standing

at the edge of the Baboon Pool on a summer's morning. Among the rocks above us were the blood lilies with their green fleshy stems and red puff-ball blooms. It was comforting to see them back again. Every year they would explode into colour in the summer months before dying back in the winter. We looked down at the reflections of our faces and the blood lilies. Bruce's kind face broke into a grin as a fish eagle swooped down onto the water—he loved birds. She was striking. Her snow-white head, neck and upper breast offset the rich chestnut-brown of her body, flanked on either side by her powerful black wings.

Simba was next to Bruce, rattling off statistics on some new subject he'd been reading about. Not about how unfair things were for the blacks, but happy stuff like he used to talk about when we were younger. I couldn't see his reflection, but my own reflection smiled back up at me. Above us, on the rocks, Grey caught my eye, turned to face me and gave a short bark.

Up early the next morning, I was keen to get our showdown with the Millers over with. I watched Simba brush his teeth over the tin bucket outside his hut. "Best not to tell Dad we're fighting the Miller boys," I told him. "He trained us so we could defend ourselves. Not sure what he'd think about us going after them."

Mum picked up Bruce and dropped the three of us near the Selukwe municipal pool.

"If these guys carry on with this kaffir nonsense, then we make a stand," I said as we waited anxiously for the Millers to arrive. "But if they say sorry, then we shake hands and walk away. Okay?"

"Hey, guys, just remember I'm not involved in the fighting," Bruce reminded us.

The three Miller boys walked out of the pool buildings and onto the large lawn on the edge of the road. When they saw us they stopped. Jeez, they were big—bigger than I remembered. But there was no going back, so we moved in front of them.

Big Miller recognised Simba. "Kaffir, have you had a bath yet? Hey, you'll like this one—there's an Englishman, an American and a kaffir standing outside a cave. 'I say chaps, what do you think is in that cave?' asks the Englishman. So he goes in first and comes out clutching his nose, 'My dear fellows, there's a skunk in that cave—and, by George, he stinks.' Then the American walks into the cave." Big Miller paused and walked along the green grass to where Bruce was standing and stuck his face in front of Bruce's. "Now tell me, fatty, what does the American say?"

Bruce froze, his fists clenched. It was the first time I'd seen him really angry.

Big Miller continued. "He walks out the cave almost sick in disgust, 'Hey, dudes, there's a skunk in that cave—and man, he stinks.'

"Then the kaffir walks into the cave." Big Miller stopped and a grin appeared on his menacing face. He walked over to where Simba was standing. "Go on, kaffir, tell me what happens next." Simba turned his head away as Big Miller kept at it. "Well, the poor old skunk comes running out the cave clutching his nose and says to the Englishman and the American, 'Hey, guys, there's a kaffir in that cave—and hell, he stinks something terrible.'"

His brothers stood on either side of him, clutching their stomachs in mock delight, "Man, I love that! Typical smelly *munts*."

Big Miller let loose a loud, ugly laugh, then turned to Simba. "The only good kaffir is a dead one," he sneered.

Then he turned to me, "And the only good kaffir-lover is a ..." He stopped and spat at my feet. "No, there's no such thing as a good kaffir-lover, you short-arsed little runt."

I lunged at him. He tried to push me away but I broke through, ramming a left jab at his chest and crunching a right into his throat. I couldn't reach his jaw. As he staggered backwards I could see the astonishment in his eyes. And fear. He hadn't bargained on having to fight. Then he was on the ground as Bruce hit him with a flying tackle.

"No, Bruce I've got him—take the other one, quickly." To my left, Simba was struggling with the two brothers. But Big Miller was already back on his feet. I slammed a right into his belly. He buckled over. Then a left to his jaw. Down he went, and I was on top of him.

"Say sorry to Simba," I shouted.

"Never, you white trash," and he sank his teeth into my left index finger.

I shouted in pain as I yanked it from his mouth. Holding his hair with my left, I smashed a right into his nose. Blood exploded across his face.

"Say sorry."

"Never."

*Thump!* This time his left eye, then his right.

"Sorry, sorry!"

"No, say sorry, *Simba*."

He held his lips tightly shut and I slammed a right into his jaw.

"Okay, okay ..." he spluttered from his bloody lips. "I'll say it. *Sorry, Simba!*"

Simba looked up. He had a badly bruised Miller boy in a headlock. Bruce and the youngest Miller were involved in a frantic wrestling match on the floor.

"Now get outta here!" I shouted.

Wiping the blood from their faces, the three Millers slunk

away, looking back over their shoulders, muttering. We used a tap on the lawn outside the pool to wash the blood from our clothes. Then, on top of the world, we strutted up the road to meet Mum.

# four

It was still dark when Shoko and I arrived at Bruce's farm gate for our morning run.

"Today's got to be lightning-fast," I told Bruce. "If we're not super-fit, we'll never pass the SAS selection."

We pushed it hard along the bush path that wound its way through the untidy acacia-topped mountain range leading to the Impali, then ran along its banks. Shoko stayed close behind me.

Just after the bridge at our regular swimming spot, Bruce and I slowed down. I was hot and sweaty and the water of the Impali was cool and inviting. We ripped off our clothes and dived in.

"Come on, Shoko," I called as Bruce and I powered our way upstream against the strong current. Shoko jumped in and swam after me, his dark eyes and huge cupped ears poking out above the surface as he dog-paddled through the water.

A grey dove was perched on a big thorn tree overlooking the river and watched us closely as we swam past.

"Okay, Bruce, flat out!" We sprinted back to the house over the vlei, pumping our legs and arms all the way to the front lawn.

Shoko cantered easily alongside me, his ears pointed skywards.

After a hot shower we sat down with Mum and Dad and tucked into Anna's mielie-meal porridge.

"How are your mum and dad coping, Bruce?" Dad asked softly.

"Not great, Mr Carter."

I looked across at Bruce. It'd been almost two years since Kelly'd been murdered by Mugabe's terrorists. It had hit him hard. He didn't like to talk about it.

"Boys," said Mum, perhaps sensing Bruce's discomfort. "I've got you both a special treat for your last day of civvy life." She handed us each a stick of beef biltong, giving the fatty piece to Bruce.

Anna waited for Bruce to go before calling me from the kitchen. "Excuse me, *Baas* Scott …"

"What is it, Anna?"

"Your friend is here."

I ran over to Anna's hut. He was sitting on a tattered mattress, putting on a pair of old Bata takkies.

"Simba, what're they doing to you? You've lost even more weight."

"Scott, good to see you, *eh*. Are you well?"

All I had thought and talked about over the past month was the SAS selection course. "Great! I'm looking forward to the course." I stopped. "But hey—how about you? Are you enjoying the army?"

"Fine, all okay. The pay's great. As an African, you can't earn that sort of money doing anything else … and I'm trying to save up for university."

He stepped out of the hut. "I'm gonna take a walk down to Impala Vlei. You want to come?"

I nodded and we set off through the bush.

"I'm specialising on the tracking side. It's going well." He paused.

"Take a look at that," he said, pointing at a reedbuck as it bent over to drink from a watering hole about forty metres from where we were standing. I stopped to admire its black, forward-curved horns set against a pale grey-brown coat and white underbelly.

"Are you sure Bruce and I should go for the SAS?"

"Well, if you want to join Special Forces, then it's either SAS or Selous Scouts. I'd go for the SAS."

We headed towards the reedbuck. As we got closer he scampered into the thick thornscrub behind the vlei. At the watering hole Simba got down on his knees and scooped a handful of the clear water into his mouth.

"*Eh*, Scott, my mother was gonna make us some tea—let's go back." As we turned for home, he continued. "Also, if you join the SAS you don't have to put up with as much nonsense on the selection course. The pass rate in the SAS is about twenty-five per cent, but less than fifteen per cent get into the Scouts."

"Hold on ..." I stopped to extract a pebble that had found its way into my track-shoe.

Simba slowed down to let me catch up. "A friend of mine who did the Selous Scouts course was telling me they don't give them any food when the course starts, and run them into the ground. Three days into the course the instructor shoots a baboon, hangs it up in the camp but doesn't skin or gut it, so it goes rotten. Leaves it for a couple of days, then dumps it into a pot to make stew—green rotten meat covered with maggots. *Aiee*, but it must stink."

Anna was waiting for us at the compound, with two enamel mugs of tea resting on a broken table at the entrance to her hut.

"Thanks, Anna." The tea was sweet and warm, as always.

"Everything okay?" I asked.

"Yes, *baas*," she answered, as she left to go back to work.

"Anyway, nobody on the course gets any food for five days, except for one small rat-pack. And after five days everyone is so hungry they eat the stew."

"Ag, *sis*, man!" I crinkled up my nose in disgust. "Did your friend eat it?"

He nodded. "So I decided against the Selous Scouts."

"All right, Simba, I reckon it's the SAS for me. But why didn't you join them?"

"Well, the SAS doesn't take Africans."

Soon afterwards I turned to leave. There was a lot to do before I left the next day.

"Good luck with the selection course," he shouted as I headed down the narrow path towards home.

Early the next morning Bruce's parents arrived in their old Land Rover to collect me. Mum, Dad and Anna all waved from the lawn as we roared off in a cloud of dust. On the way to Llewellin Barracks we stopped to fill up at Insiza Garage. When Bruce and his dad stepped out of the car to get some Cokes, Mrs Thomas turned to me with her sad green eyes.

"Scott, I'm worried about him. You know how he looks up to you. Has done ever since you were little boys and you carried him in that cross-country race."

She put her hand on my shoulder. "Promise me you'll look after him. I just can't lose another ..." Tears welled up in her eyes.

"Ma'am, please don't worry. I'll keep him safe, I promise." I felt I had to say it to stop her crying. She was the most beautiful woman I'd ever seen, even on TV. Bruce used to boast that she'd been a top Rhodesian model before she met his dad. But she'd aged since Kelly's death, and her hair was now almost completely grey.

After preliminary screening at Llewellin they chose one hundred and sixty of us for the SAS selection course. Then on to Salisbury for six weeks' basic training: drill, PT, weaponry, map-reading, medics and signals. Bruce and I were excited. Not even the grey, military-style buildings of Cranborne Barracks, which would be our home for the next six weeks, could dampen our enthusiasm. They made us run everywhere and soon the months of extra training began to pay off.

A lot of time was spent practising shooting. Perhaps he was trying too hard, perhaps he was overexcited, but Bruce had a shocking first week on the firing range and was presented with the Shit Shot Bell award. Not only did he have to do a 'lap of honour' to the cynical cheers of the other recruits, but he had to wear the bell around his neck for the full week. It came in handy for me—whenever I needed Bruce, I simply listened for the bell.

Mike Conway, a city boy from Salisbury, loved teasing Bruce. "Hey, *okes*, apparently after he was given the Shit Shot Bell, Thomas confided in Corporal Jones: 'Corporal, I think I'm gonna commit suicide by shooting myself.'

"'By shooting?' asked Jones. 'Not a bad idea! But take as many cartridges as possible.'"

There was a loud burst of laughter from the troops. Conway grinned and whenever he saw Bruce he'd ring an imaginary bell, making a lot more noise than the real one. Bruce scowled; he'd been the butt of jokes all week and it was starting to wear thin. But his shooting improved, and by the end of week two he was consistently outshooting Conway. At the end of week six he was in the top ten. By then, with basic training complete, fifty-five of the original group had dropped out. We moved onto the second six-week leg of our course at Gwaai River Mine, north of Wankie

National Park. This is where the course got interesting. Now we'd be able to put all our new skills to the test: demolition work, map-reading, patrols, tactical training and canoeing. And still more shooting. I hated map-reading. Whenever I saw a map my eyes would glaze over, but Bruce was an expert and spent hours giving me private tuition.

In the last two weeks of this phase we were joined by five officers and NCOs from other units.

Instructor Corporal Jones called them into a large clearing in front of our tented-camp and made them introduce themselves. First up was a well-spoken Brit: "Lieutenant Waters, corporal! SAS Borneo."

"What the fuck is he doing here?" Bruce whispered to Conway.

"Moved here from Mud Island ... married a Rhodesian girl. He's already done two years in the RLI."

Next up was a tall, wiry man.

"Tough-looking bastard," I told Conway quietly.

"Sergeant Young, corporal! Green Berets, Vietnam."

"And him?"

"Bit of a nutter ... just enjoys the fighting. You get more action here than anywhere else."

After introductions I collared Conway. He seemed to know everything. "Do lots of foreigners join our army?"

"*Ja*, mostly *Slopes* ... but also Brits, Yanks, Kiwis, Aussies and Frogs."

When the six weeks at Gwaai were up, we knew the tough part was about to begin. Another twenty-five had dropped out. The eighty that were left transferred to Llewellin Barracks.

"Bruce, this is where they hammer us—physically—to try and break us down. Are you up for it?"

"Damn right I am."

As we entered the gates Jones barked, "Mud pit. Five minutes." When we got to the pit, he paired us up: "Two groups of forty. No punching, no biting, no kicking … First group, go!"

Bruce flashed me a smile. He'd been paired with Conway. It was time for revenge. He dive-tackled Conway and forced him on to his back. But Conway was a fine athlete, having played on the wing for Prince Edward First XV for the past two years. They rolled frantically in the mud, each trying to get a neck grip. Conway's superior strength was starting to count. I could see Bruce weakening.

"Go, Bruce, go!" I shouted. But Conway was on top, with Bruce tiring rapidly.

"One last kick, Bruce!" and he used all the strength in his legs to flick Conway over his head. Furiously, they wrestled in the mud.

"Okay, second group, go!" I had been paired with the Yank, Sergeant Young. I was tentative at first—Young was my senior by at least ten years, and a Vietnam vet who deserved respect. But he wasn't holding back, and when he smashed my face into the mud I dived forward and rolled clear of his grip, then leapt on him, curling my arm around his neck and forcing him to the ground. His lean muscular arms and legs strained to break free, but I had him. So he swung his left fist at my groin. I shouted in pain before smashing a right hook into his jaw. Jones turned to see Young flat on his back, while I clutched my balls in agony.

"No punching! Hundred press-ups. Now!"

"Good punch," Young smiled as we did our press-ups.

"Running track … five minutes!" Jones yelled.

Bruce fell in beside me as we jogged over, "Nice fight, Bruce."

"Cheers, Scott … I'm shattered."

"Me too. Keep at it … pace yourself."

Jones was waiting for us when we arrived. "Four-hundred-metre sprint. Last ten will get nailed." I sprinted to come in fifth behind Conway, then turned to shout for Bruce, who was struggling at the back. But no luck. He was seventy-sixth.

"Hundred press-ups. Now!" barked Jones.

"And again," he shouted to the last ten when their hundred was up. He worked us for another forty minutes, then screamed, "Boxing gym. Five minutes!"

Two of the group looked at each other. "Fuck this. I'm outta here."

"Me too," said another two, who also walked. I winked at Bruce who had a determined look on his face. Whatever they threw at the two of us, we'd keep going.

We stood in the gym waiting for Jones.

"How're those legs?" I asked Bruce.

"Numb."

"*Ja*, mine are so stiff," I told him. "Just keep it up. You're doing great."

Jones arrived. "Right. Two groups of thirty-eight. No kicking, no biting."

Much to his delight, Conway was grouped with Lieutenant Waters. "I say, old chap," he said. "Fancy a spot of biff-biff, good old Queensbury rules, what, like we used to do at Sandhurst?" Everyone laughed, except Waters, who actually had boxed at Sandhurst. So successfully, in fact, that he'd been chosen to represent the British Army.

"First group, go!"

Conway attacked with typical enthusiasm. But he'd no idea of what he was up against, and within seconds a left hook had him on the floor. Stunned, he rose to his feet. But only briefly. A straight right to the jaw put him on his back. Again Conway rose unsteadily to his feet and again he was flattened, this time with a left jab. Even Jones was grinning. Conway wouldn't be mocking Waters any more.

As he lay on his back, blood splattered over his face, both eyes closing rapidly, Conway must have been thinking, *What the hell can I do?* Then his damaged eyes lit up. He rose to his feet, dashed forward and rugby-tackled an astonished Waters onto the ground.

"Conway, two hundred press-ups. Now!" shouted Jones.

Bruce would've loved to have seen Conway's hammering. But he had his hands full, trying to deal with the rugged Earl Williams. Williams had been fighting in the back-streets of Bulawayo for most of his life. Bruce didn't stand a chance.

"You little pansy," he taunted. Bruce charged at him, rushing straight into a right hook that sent him crashing to the floor.

Fortunately, Jones intervened before Williams did too much damage, "Second group, go!"

Jones was pleased with Conway's thumping, and I heard him whisper in Young's ear: "Teach the little bugger a lesson." But Young was planning on that anyway, and nailed me with a left-right combination. I sank to my knees. Then a left hook, and I was on my back.

"Up, Scott! Up! Sort him out!" cried Bruce.

"On your feet, Carter ... hammer him," roared Conway.

But Dad had taught me well: *Move in close, throw your punches hard and fast. Use your strength to drive him backwards. Crowd the taller boxer.*

Jumping to my feet I did just that, and Young staggered to the floor. As he rose I was on him again. Down he went. He rose again, but this time slowly. I attacked, and as I came in he swung his elbow. I stepped backwards waiting for the 'Hundred press-ups, Young!' from Jones. But it never came. Instead Young threw himself on to me, raining elbows and fists to the side of my head. I went down, rolled backwards, got on my feet and charged at him. Each punch counted, and when he fell to the ground I was on top of him. Left, right, left. His nose was a mess.

"Time out!" bellowed Jones. "Get off him, Carter!"

I helped Young to his feet.

He held out his hand. "Good fighting. From now on we're on the same side."

"Two laps round the parade ground. Go! Last ten will be in trouble," shouted Jones. Sixty-six exhausted trainees set off around the parade ground. Another ten had dropped out. My legs were cramping, but I shut it from my mind and kept running.

"Right, time out! Go for lunch. Meet back here at two o'clock sharp!"

There was a loud cheer as we made our way to the mess hall. At last, some rest and good food.

But Jones had other ideas. "Right, here's your lunch." He pointed to some glucose powder, tap water and salt tablets. "Are you bastards hungry? Well then, pack it in. Give up and you can join them next door: steak and chips now, with ice-cold beer and biltong tonight."

"Fuck this, we're out of here." Another eight left.

"And one more rule," Jones continued. "No talking at meal times!"

Shoulders sagging, Bruce and I trudged from the hall.

"Hey, Scott, remember that fatty biltong your mum gave me? Hell, I'd kill for a piece of that now!"

It was painful even to think about it. "*Ja*, I'm fed up. Starving, exhausted and every muscle in my body feels like it's been beaten with a ten-pound hammer."

There was a light tap on both our shoulders. It was Sergeant Young. "Stick with it, lads. I want you in my troop on the other side."

And stick with it we did. Through the rest of the 'Rev' phase as they systematically tried to break us down … every inch of my mind and body ached. Through to the last phase of the selection course—the gruelling orienteering through the Matopos. And finally, as I was approaching breaking point, when my legs were refusing to go any further, through the twenty-five-kilometre speed-march.

There were only thirty-two of us at the end, and when they told us we'd passed, we couldn't believe it. There were three final things we needed to do to get our berets: a parachute course, a canoeing course and to prove ourselves on an operation. Rested and refreshed, we sailed through these over the next twenty days.

Our time had come—we were ready for war.

# five

"Tonight we party! It's not every day you get an SAS beret!" Conway was over the moon; we all were. Led by Corporal Jones, Bruce, Williams, Waters and I entered the Winged Stagger.

"Look at this, hey," shouted Conway as he balanced himself against the wall on his head, then downed a beer. He laughed, we cheered, so he did it again. Then a round of tequila. Next, the Prospectors bar in the Monomotapa Hotel in downtown Salisbury. Conway and Bruce settled themselves in a poorly lit corner of the bar, arguing about the Shit Shot Bell award. Leaning against the bar counter, Conway was enthusiastically ringing his imaginary bell. "Ding-dong, ding-dong."

"Hey, at the end I was in the top ten, the *top ten*! Were you even in the top forty? No!"

"Ding-dong, ding-dong," Conway yelled over his shoulder as he followed me to the toilet.

A bearded biker ducked through the toilet doors in front of us. Hell, he must have been one of the biggest blokes I'd ever seen. We stared up at him. His enormous arms were covered with thick muscle and grisly tattoos. Probably a Hell's Angel from Jo'burg.

They loved it here. Always fights going on somewhere.

Never one to pass up an opportunity for mischief, Conway mumbled, "I don't think you look like a baboon!"

I looked away. This was silly. Conway was going to have to deal with this one himself … he'd have to learn the hard way.

"What? What did you say?" The man-mountain glowered at Conway, fists clenched.

"What I said was, I don't think you look like a baboon."

The biker stopped.

"But my mate does—the oke at the far corner of the bar—five foot-eleven, bit chubby, dark hair, blue shirt … you can't miss him." The biker stormed into the bar.

Conway reckoned afterwards that he was so angry his hair was standing on end, despite all the grease. Anyway, he grabbed a wide-eyed Bruce in his right hand and smashed him with his left. Bruce went flying across the bar into people, tables, drinks, glasses. It was mayhem.

Conway must have been next on his hit-list, but fortunately for him, Waters was there. None of us even saw Waters' punches, they were so quick. The biker certainly didn't. Williams said he hit him five times before the biker dropped. Out cold.

The bouncers asked us to leave and we did, without a fuss. It was only when we got to the bar at the George Hotel that the truth came out.

We were all in stitches, including Bruce.

"I'll get you, Conway, you bastard," he laughed.

We arrived at breakfast the next morning hungover and tired, but excited at the prospect of four days R&R. Once we'd eaten, Lieutenant Waters called Bruce, Conway, Williams, Young and myself outside.

"I've been handed my first op. I want each of you on it—it's big. Make sure you get lots of rest. No binges, Conway. I need you fresh and raring to go."

"Yes, sir … what's the op?"

"Will brief you when you're back. Enjoy your break."

I woke with the sun peeping through the curtains. It was great to be home. After a bowl of cornflakes I went looking for Simba, and found him washing pots in a bucket of water outside Anna's hut.

"Simba, Laurel's coming this afternoon. Can I bring her over? She'd love to see you."

"Okay, I'll persuade mother to do guinea fowl and *sadza* for a late lunch. Are you sure Laurel's okay eating with us at the hut?"

"*Ja*, of course she is!"

He went off to find Anna and met me on the front lawn soon afterwards. "Ah, she says she's too busy. Why don't you ask her? She can't say no to you."

"Mum and Dad don't like me doing that."

"Come on, they're not even here."

I went and asked Anna, who quickly agreed, "Okay, you shoot guinea fowl, I cook. Simba can clean, *eh?*"

But before that we had to pick Mum up from her school. Kathy and Simba jumped into the front seat of the bakkie next to me, and we drove to town.

We walked across to Mum's classroom, stopping on the way to admire the sports fields and brand-new classrooms.

"You know, Simba, you moan about the blacks not being able to go to the white schools, but I reckon this school's better than the one I went to."

Simba didn't look up. "I don't know about that, Scott. But

anyway, this is one of the best black schools in the country. I got in here thanks to your mother."

Always quick to defend the underdog, Kathy jumped in. "Hey, Scott, Simba's got a point. An article in one of the overseas papers was saying that the amount spent in this country on education per black kid is tiny compared with that spent on us whites."

When we got to Mum's classroom we stood in the doorway, waiting as she wrapped up an O' Level history lesson. Her face lit up when she saw Simba was with us.

"Come in," she waved.

"Class, I'm sure you all remember Simba Ndlovu, our headboy from two years ago."

The kids looked up at Simba respectfully.

"Simba's a good example for all of you. He got first-class O' Levels, including an A for history." She smiled proudly at him. "He went on to get great A' Levels too, so after his army service, he'll be able to go to university anywhere in the world."

"Thank you, ma'am," said Simba, looking embarrassed as he stood in the middle of the classroom, the focus of attention.

"Why don't you pop into the Headmaster's office? He'd love to chat to you," Mum told Simba, then turned to Kathy and me. "You two sit at the back while I finish off."

We sat down as Mum continued her class on the white pioneers of Rhodesia.

"Now, who can tell me about the 1888 Rudd Concession?" Mum asked.

Immediately, a dozen hands shot into the air. Mum pointed at a girl in the front row.

"The Ndebele king, King Lobengula, gave Cecil John Rhodes mineral rights in Ndebele territory. In return Rhodes promised to pay Lobengula a thousand rifles, a hundred thousand rounds of ammunition, a monthly payment of a hundred pounds, and a boat on the Zambezi."

Mum smiled. "Well done, Rutendo. Rhodes sent the first pioneers into Rhodesia in 1890, raising the British flag in Salisbury in September that year." She looked around the classroom. "When did fighting first break out with the Ndebele?" Again, hands flew into the air. Mum pointed at a boy in the centre of the class.

"1893, ma'am. The whites under Jameson were too well armed for the Ndebele. They mowed them down with the Maxim gun."

Mum smiled. "Good. Then, in 1896, the Ndebele rose up against the white settlers for a second time; this time so did the Shona. Again the settlers suppressed them. After that the Ndebele and Shona fell under the Rhodes administration." Mum looked down at the pupils in front of her. "Any questions?"

Another round of hands went up. The bell rang to end the class, but still the hands were rising.

Mum answered another five questions, but still more questions.

"Class, I'll answer these questions," she said pointing at the hands already in the air. "Then, no more."

I drummed my heels impatiently on the floor as Mum gave a careful and considered response to each query. I couldn't believe it. At my school, we were out of the class as soon as the bell rang.

Finally she pointed at a girl in the front row. "Go ahead, Tapiwa. Last question."

"Ma'am, Rhodes tricked Lobengula into signing the Rudd Concession: Lobengula couldn't read or write. The Europeans arrived uninvited on our soil in 1890. So who really owns the land today?"

A hush fell over the classroom. I looked up at Mum. *Would she be angry?*

Mum stopped and looked down at Tapiwa. "That's a very good question," she said softly. "I don't have time to answer that one today, but I'll leave you all with a quotation from one of my favourite American writers, Willa Cather: 'We come and go, but the land is always here. And the people who love it and understand it are the people who own it—for a little while.'"

I stood up impatiently. But that wasn't the end of it. Four more kids had lined up at the front to ask questions.

I felt like shouting out: "She said no more questions. I've got to get back home," but decided against it and waited while Mum spoke to each of the kids in turn.

Outside the classroom I chatted to Simba and Kathy. After what seemed ages, Mum finally walked out.

"Mum, let's go!"

"Hold on, son. I've promised Tinashe a lift." She knocked on the classroom door next to hers. "Tinashe, we're going, if you want a lift."

"Thanks, Mary, I'll be out in two minutes."

I rolled my eyes skywards. Finally Tinashe staggered out of the classroom under a pile of books.

She greeted Simba warmly and Mum introduced her to Kathy and me.

"Your name means 'God is with us'," said Kathy as she helped Tinashe with her books.

"Very impressive," Tinashe smiled.

"How come your Shona's better than your Ndebele?" Simba asked Kathy as we made our way to the bakkie.

"Sorry, Simba, the Shona are about eighty per cent of our population, so I've gotta try and learn their language first. You

Ndebele are only about fifteen per cent." Then a big grin appeared on her face as she pointed at me. "Hey, but my Ndebele is a lot better than his."

"Yes, I gave up on Scott years ago," laughed Simba.

We reached the bakkie and Tinashe started to climb into the back of the truck.

"No, Tinashe, you'll ruin your dress. Get in the front with us," called out Mum. I drove and Tinashe gave me directions to her house. She had a bright face, and chatted with Mum about her biology pupils who were sitting their O' Levels that year.

"You can stop here, Scott," she said, calling me to a halt outside a run-down shack.

"She lives *here*?" I asked Mum as Tinashe opened her front door.

Mum was frowning. "Yes. She's one of our brightest teachers and she lives in this shack." As I turned the car around, Mum called out to Simba. "Come sit in the front."

I put my foot on the accelerator. Laurel was arriving that afternoon and we still needed a guinea fowl for dinner.

"Mum, I'm really impressed. Great school. The kids are so keen." I looked at Simba. "I never want to hear you complaining again about the blacks getting a raw deal in this country. Just look at that school."

"I've never heard Simba complaining," said Mum. "Anyway, you might want to see things from his perspective. There he is, fighting for us. For his country. Yet he's not allowed into the same schools, hospitals, bars and restaurants."

I didn't say anything. Mum sounded really serious.

As soon as we got home we grabbed the .22 rifle and set off for Python Corner on the western edge of the farm.

Simba broke the good news as we marched through the bush.

"You know I've been doing a lot of tracking in Mozambique? Well, two of us have been asked to work with the SAS around Cabora Bassa."

"Hey, that's awesome! Before we left I was told we'd be going on a big op. Let's hope it's Cabora Bassa!" We kept on walking.

"Over there, Scott."

Under a syringa tree, a flock of guinea fowl were feeding. I rested the .22 on a branch and took aim.

"Go-*why*, Go-*why*..."

The guinea fowl made a speedy exit, ducking and weaving their way through the bushes.

"Bloody Go-Away bird!" I swore. At the top of the syringa tree was a grey lourie feeding on the yellow berries, his crest raised with excitement as he cried out his warning.

"Shall I nail him?"

"No, leave him," Simba smiled. "It's his job to warn about hunters. Can't kill him for doing his job."

"Your turn," I said, passing Simba the rifle as we kept on walking.

"Our cave." I pointed to two massive granite boulders sheltered behind a row of msasas. Between them lay the entrance to our secret cave.

"Hey, Simba, remember when we tied Bruce to this tree and pretended to leave him? Man, he was upset, hey!"

We both laughed and I watched as Simba eased his way into the cave. Quickly, he swung the rifle and fired.

"Guinea fowl?" I asked and casually followed him into the cave.

"Jeez, man!" I leapt backwards in fright.

A black mamba. At least three metres long, its olive-grey body, lifeless on the floor.

"Great shot!" There was a round bullet-hole through the middle of the mamba's coffin-shaped head. Simba calmly moved the dead snake with a stick. His eyes were deadpan. Not a trace of panic. "Hell, you're an ice-cold bastard!"

He gently poked the snake. "Sorry, boy, it was either you or me." Then he turned to me. "Normally they don't attack; they're scared of us. He must have felt cornered."

He poked the stick in the snake's battered mouth. "It gets its name from this black patch here. If he'd got me, without treatment, I'd have been dead."

Simba was still holding the .22 when we came across a flock of guinea fowl crossing an anthill about a hundred metres away.

He cocked the rifle, "Mind if I have a go?"

"Take it away."

He raised the rifle and fired. I saw one of the guinea fowl drop.

Later, around the fire with Simba, Anna and Laurel, the guinea fowl tasted delicious.

"Anna, your hut's really cosy," said Laurel. "Who built it?" I looked up at my girlfriend. Her faded blue summer dress looked stunning against her bright-blue eyes and dark-brown hair.

"*Ngiyabonga*, Miss Laurel. *Eh*, Simba, tell Miss Laurel."

"No, mother—it's boring."

"Not at all, Simba. It's interesting. Remember, I'm a city girl."

"Okay, well … my mother and I built it."

"Hey, me too!"

"Sorry—Scott helped mix the cowpats and water to make the floor. Looks like concrete, *eh*? Then we put poles on the side and plastered on mud from the anthills to get the walls."

Anna patted the walls proudly, "Very good wall, *eh*?"

"Yes, looks great. What about the roof, Simba?"

"Dried elephant grass from the river."

"Fantastic." Laurel sat down again in front of the fire.

Shoko had wandered over and all eyes turned to him. He was looking longingly at my beans. "No, Shoko, not for you … unless …" I glanced across at Anna, who nodded her head with a smile.

"Go on then, boy," and he tucked in as I rubbed his ears.

Finally it was time to say goodbye. Laurel held out her hand.

"Nice to see you, Simba. Hope to meet up with you and Scott in Salisbury some time."

Simba shook her hand politely. Then a strange look came over his face. "Laurel, don't forget … I'm a black man. I'm not allowed into most of the places you go to in Salisbury."

There was an awkward silence as we turned to walk home. When Laurel and I got back, Dixie made a huge fuss of her on the front lawn and kept jumping up against her legs.

"Hey, what a cute little dog, Scott."

"Oh no he's not—come and look at this." I took her inside. Mum was busy mixing stewed meat and *sadza* for the dogs. We watched from the kitchen window as she handed out the dishes on the veranda. Dixie started eating and snarling, making sure the other dogs knew he was in no mood to share. He wolfed down half the food in less than a minute. That was it. He'd had enough. But instead of leaving his leftovers for the other dogs, he peed in his bowl.

Laurel put her hand over her mouth, "I don't believe it!"

"*Ja*, not so cute, hey?" I laughed.

We grabbed a bottle of wine, saddled two horses and rode to the Impali. Shoko and the dogs followed, with Dixie yapping at the heels of the horses. Sipping our wine, we sat on the banks of the river, enjoying the warm glow of the afternoon sun.

The impala were everywhere. And the baboons. A baby baboon edged curiously towards us until her mother grabbed her by the scruff of the neck and marched her out of range.

In the distance a herdboy and his cattle slowly disappeared from view.

"I'm going for a dip, Laurel. See you just now," I waved as I slid into the river. I swam crawl upstream, fast. Then breaststroke back, panting, looking to the bank for Laurel, but I couldn't see her. I was about to panic when I felt the water rush behind me and there she was, treading water. I turned as her body brushed past me, her bare skin soft and slippery. The curve of her waist nestled tightly in my hand. Her wet hair ran down her back, splaying into the water around her shoulders. I pulled her back to the bank and onto the warm grass.

The sun was going down as we walked the horses home, listening to the sound of hooves on the soft earth and the gentle snorts from their muzzles. We rode in silence, completely at ease with each other. Neither of us felt the need for conversation as we crossed the vlei, through the msasa trees and back to the stables.

It was Mum's turn for the Salisbury run on Sunday afternoon. First we dropped Laurel at her plush house in Borrowdale. An air of silence hung over us as we got out of the car together to say goodbye. But it wasn't the companionable silence of the weekend … more of a sadness to be leaving each other. I climbed back into the car and waved to Laurel as Mum drove out through the front gates.

"Boys, it feels like dropping you back at school," Mum said as we approached the dreary army buildings that were Cranborne Barracks.

"*Ja*, a bit Mum—but this place is different. It's exciting."

After Mum dropped us we dumped our kit in our barrack rooms and went looking for Lieutenant Waters.

"Full briefing at three o'clock," he told us.

I put one hand on Bruce's shoulder and shook his hand firmly with the other.

Our first proper op was about to begin!

# six

Waters had a big map on the wall. "Since it got independence from Portugal in 1975, the terrs have been pouring into Rhodesia from Mozambique." He pointed at the map with a stick. "This is where many of them are coming in—through Chinhanda, and on through the Tete Province into Rhodesia." He tapped the Mague, Daque and Chinhanda roads with his pointer. "We've got to nail them here." He paused. "And Mozambique's mickey-mouse army, Frelimo, are helping the gooks—we've got to sort them out, too."

He rapped the desk in front of him. "Now they'll only be expecting attacks from the Rhodesian side. But ..." he pointed to the map, "if we hit them from the Lake Cabora Bassa side, we'll catch them off guard. Twelve of us will be going in—we'll canoe in and set up base on the lake about sixty kays from the Rhodesian border."

"For how long, sir?" asked Young in his Southern drawl.

"Around five weeks." He pointed at the door. "Two days to get your kit sorted and canoes tested, so get cracking."

We started to file out.

"Oh, and one more thing," he called to us. "We'll be linking up with two trackers who've been doing the recce work."

I smiled, patting Bruce on the shoulder. Simba would be joining us.

The next morning we were on Lake McIlwaine, just outside Salisbury, testing our canoes. Stroking our oars purposely through the calm water, Bruce and I powered our two-seater canoe over the lake. It was a beautiful sunny morning, not a cloud in the sky.

"Last one to the boathouse buys a case of beers," shouted Conway and Williams, who were paddling nearby.

"You're on!" We paddled as fast as we could. I could see the sinews straining in Bruce's neck. He didn't want to lose to Conway.

"Faster, Bruce … faster …" But they held their lead to the boathouse.

"Okay, we owe you a case of beers," I muttered with a smile.

Two days was more than enough time to test our equipment. We trimmed our kit to a minimum, packed the trucks and climbed on. From Salisbury we drove to Musengezi Mission in the Zambezi Valley in northeastern Rhodesia. A long, painful drive. We arrived as the sun was setting, unpacked the truck and put on our green 'terr' uniforms. I tried to catch my reflection in the water. It was the first time I'd worn a terr outfit. But it was already too late to get any reflection other than a dark shadow.

From there we launched ourselves into the Musengezi River, which flowed into Cabora Bassa, and paddled firmly but quietly.

Leading from the front, Waters called a halt after thirty minutes' paddling. "Hippo. Go round him." He gestured us to the right of where a hippo was wallowing in a shallow stretch of river, about to venture inland for his evening's grazing.

"Hey, Conway, what animal kills the most people in Africa?" I could hear Bruce ask.

"What's this, a fucking quiz?" grunted Conway.

"It's got to be the hippo," I butted in.

"No, it's the mosquito."

"What about these buggers?" I pointed across at the silhouette of a crocodile gliding effortlessly through the water.

"They're probably in the top four: say, mozzies, hippos, buffalo, and crocs."

We kept a brisk pace through the night, finally arriving at our destination near Mague on the shores of Lake Cabora Bassa in the early hours of the morning.

"Get some kip, boys," Waters told us, once we'd unloaded our kit from the canoes. As I drifted off, snugly tucked up in my sleeping bag, I could hear Williams muttering darkly in the shadows on sentry duty.

Refreshed and recharged, I climbed purposely from my sleeping bag the next morning.

Bruce was already up. "Hey, what the hell is that smell?"

"It's the rotting mopane forests. Drowned when they filled this lake at the end of '74," Trooper Dixon answered.

Not even the rancid smell of the decaying trees could dampen my good spirits. Simba was there with another African tracker, finishing off a conversation with Waters.

"Great to see you," I told him, giving him an enthusiastic slap on the back. We ate breakfast together, sitting on the edge of our makeshift camp. Just the two of us, like we'd done so often as kids. He was in a bullish mood, having lined up a number of promising ambush sites for us.

After breakfast, Waters divided us into three operational units. Ours was headed by Sergeant Young and included Bruce,

Trooper Dixon and myself. For our first op—an ambush on the Mague–Chinhanda road—we'd all go in together. Simba had already found a good ambush spot, and led the way through the thick thornscrub.

"Over there," Simba pointed after we'd been walking for about an hour. It was a koppie shaped like Table Mountain and covered with shrubs, mopane trees and boulders. "That's where the early-warning group can position itself. They'll be able to see for miles. Then, over there," he pointed with his AK. "That koppie is where the killer group can set up. We can hit them from directly above as they slow down to cross the river. Great spot. Lots of rocks and trees to hide in."

"Perfect," said Waters. "We'll give them the full treatment—I want a landmine forty metres before the river." He turned towards the koppie above. "Now, let's see what's happening on Table Mountain."

We climbed to the top and hid among a group of rocks, noting everything that went past on the road. A steady stream of army vehicles as well as a few civilian cars and buses. It soon became clear that this was a regular route for both Frelimo soldiers and ZANLA terrs.

"Let's head back," Waters ordered in his crisp British accent. An hour later we were back in camp.

That night Simba led us to an open clearing for our supply drop. There was little moonlight so the going was tough as we made our way through the dense bush by torchlight.

Waters directed the Dakota pilot towards the flashing strobe lights held out for him. "Drop, now!" and a parachute with ammunition, cigarettes, powdered milk, tea, coffee, sugar, biscuits, cans of chicken and bully-beef, rice and cool-drink powder fell from the dark sky. We seized the supplies and hurried back to camp. Waters warned, "Enjoy it, lads. That's the last drop we get. We can't risk the enemy hearing the planes. From now on we've got to fend for ourselves." He pointed to the lake and then to the .303 fitted with a silencer. "Fresh fish and fresh meat."

Later, as we sat around camp eating baked beans and tinned sausages, I sensed Williams was out to cause trouble.

"Hey, Carter … you've been grinning like a Cheshire cat for three days now. Did you screw your bitch over the weekend?"

"What?"

"I said, did you thump your missus?"

"What are you wittering on about, Williams?"

"He's asking if you did the business with Laurel," volunteered Bruce helpfully.

"Yes, thanks, Bruce. I got that," I muttered.

"Listen, Williams, if I did you'd be the last person I'd tell."

He smiled, "Your china over there will tell us when you give her one."

Bruce jumped in, "Oh no I won't, Williams. Anyway, he tells me bugger-all about Laurel."

Williams's mischief wasn't over for the night. "Hey, you know Conway got his missus up the spout?"

Simba looked at me blankly—Williams had a language of his own. "Conway's got his girlfriend pregnant," I explained quietly.

"Wind your neck in, Williams," growled Conway.

"Is that true, Conway?"

He turned to face me. "Yes, I reckon it's gonna be a boy." His face broke into a big grin. "He'll be a champion. When the war's over, I'll take him fishing at Kariba. Every weekend."

There was a cough. We all looked at Bruce.

Lieutenant Waters called us in. "Boys, no coughing. You'll compromise our position. It's all in the mind, anyway. In Borneo,

if anyone coughed at night we made them sleep 400 metres away."
His voice was steady. "Well done, Simba and Phineas—you've
found us a good spot for the ambush." He turned to the rest of us.
"We're live at first light tomorrow. Young, I want your group to lay
the mine—as early as possible. Then you join the killer group."
Waters was meticulous, and briefed each of us on our exact roles
and positions in the ambush. "Conway, you take the RPG-7."

After the briefing Bruce sidled up to Conway. "They'd have
been better off with a blind man on the RPG."

"Ding-dong, ding-dong," came back Conway, ringing his
imaginary bell from side to side.

We were up at five o'clock, and I had a quick snack with Simba.
I was edgy as I mentally prepared myself for the attack.

"How come you're always so calm?" I asked him. "What does it
take for you to get excited?"

He chuckled, picked up his AK and led us through the dense
bush to the ambush site.

When we got to Table Mountain, Waters motioned us to a
stop. "Young, sort out the mine. We'll cover you from here."

As Young, Dixon, Bruce and I climbed down to lay the mine,
a Land Rover sped past in a cloud of dust. We dived behind some
trees and watched. Five ZANLA terrs in the back. The vehicle
roared into the distance and we moved forward.

In a low voice, Young called out the orders: "We've gotta move
fast! You know the drill. Carter, you guard this side of the road.
Thomas that side. Dixon, I'll dig, you prepare and lay the mine."

Dixon lowered the anti-lift device and landmine into the hole,
armed the mine, then filled the hole with soil. "Pack it down
here, over the mine, get rid of the spoor. Quickly! Take the extra
soil with us. Okay, let's get the hell outta here!"

We moved quickly to the ambush spot. As we arrived, Bruce

let out a nervous cough. Waters glared at him. Daylight was beginning to peep out through the koppies. I could see Bruce was tense. Waters had left four troops to man the early-warning point. The rest of us took up positions overlooking the killing zone.

The early-warning team crackled into life: *"Land Rover."*

"How many passengers?"

*"Two."*

"Ignore."

I waited calmly as the Land Rover passed without hitting the mine. To my left, holding the RPG-7 rocket launcher, Conway was sweating heavily. He patted my shoulder. "Good luck, Carter."

"You too."

I glanced over at Simba, immediately to my right. Crouched behind a rock with his AK, he was calmly looking out over the horizon. I thought of the black mamba he'd shot—he was a valuable addition to our team.

We waited forever. Must've been at least three or four hours. Then the radio came alive: *"Truck. Fifteen on board. Frelimo and ZANLA."*

"Let's hit it." Waters motioned to the others in the killer group and we leaned forward into firing position. Tense. Then turned to watch the truck approaching at speed. It slowed as it approached the river. And the mine! I waited for it, but no blast came.

"Nail it," bellowed Waters, and Conway fired the RPG-7. Bright orange flames leapt into the sky as the vehicle exploded across the road. Immediately, ten AK rifles burst into life. The terrs were flung from the vehicle. At least half of them died instantly. The rest fled for their lives, scrambling into the open vlei on the other side of the road. I swung my rifle, aimed, fired and saw one of them drop. Then another and another. They didn't have a chance as the bullets tore into them from above, until Waters called an end to the carnage.

Bruce fell in next to me as we made our way back to camp.

"Stop grinning, you smug bastard," I whispered. I couldn't help smiling either as relief and exhilaration swept through my body.

"Fifteen out of fifteen. It doesn't get better than that." Bruce's cough had disappeared.

As we sat tucking into our food that night, Young asked Trooper Dixon, "I hear you were a terr prisoner?"

"Ja, I was held in Mboroma in Zambia for three months."

"You got revved by Comrade X?"

"That's how I got caught. We ambushed his platoon. Thought they'd roll over and die, like the rest of these gooks. But no, they regrouped and came after us. Ended up killing my best mate and wounding me. They took me prisoner."

"Did you meet him?"

"Ja, ruthless bastard." I could see Dixon enjoyed the fact that he was the only living Rhodesian soldier who'd ever met the brutal X.

We crowded around, quietly asking questions. Comrade X was a legend, and we all wanted to find out why.

"Did he torture you?"

"No, thank God. He had to leave the day they caught me."

"So where's he based?"

"No one knows—that's one of the best-kept secrets in Africa."

Williams pointed at Simba, who was already tucked into his sleeping bag on the edge of the camp. "Hey, I don't trust that black bastard."

I grabbed him by the throat.

He took a step back. "Sorry, Carter. I know he's your mate. It's just the way he looks at us, when he thinks we're not looking. I'm glad we don't take blacks in the SAS."

As I climbed into my sleeping bag, Conway, who was on sentry duty, winked at me and pointed to Bruce.

"*Argh!*"

"Who the fuck was that?" growled Waters.

"Sorry, sir—spider in my sleeping bag," said Bruce. It was an enormous black spider with long hairy legs.

Waters was irate. "Thomas, one more peep out of you and I'll throw you out of camp. You'll get us all killed!"

"Yes, sir, sorry, sir." Bruce flicked the spider away with a stick.

It'd been a big day. I laid my head down. Conway was still giggling.

The next morning Waters called us for a briefing at our regular meeting point, a small clearing under a big mopane tree. We sat on sand, Simba to my left, Bruce to my right. I looked up at the butterfly-shaped leaves of the mopane, then at Waters.

"Tonight, as soon as it's dark, we paddle to the northeast corner of the lake." Waters indicated with a stick at a sketch he'd drawn in the sand. "We arrive at about one o'clock and leave our canoes there. Then a short three-kay walk to here," he pointed again. "Set up camp and get some sleep. Tomorrow we hang out, no one sees us. Then at night we hit the terrs, who are at this point."

He went on to describe the camp layout, where the guards were positioned, where the fifty terrs and twenty Frelimo soldiers were likely to be. He lowered his voice, "They're a competent, well-trained outfit. Not your regular ragtag gooks. We've got to be on top of our game."

I had an uneasy feeling in my stomach that evening as we packed our canoes to leave. We were about to go into action against dangerous opponents who outnumbered us five to one.

## seven

We set off as the sun edged its way down over the rugged mountains and dying mopane forest.

Bruce was craning his neck over the canoe. "Scott, look quick!" A fish eagle was perched on its nest, magnificently silhouetted against the bright-red sunset.

We paddled silently, anxious to avoid any attention. Four hours later we arrived, hid the canoes and promptly made our way to the overnight camp. I took guard right through the night. Sleep was the last thing I needed, I was so charged up for the attack.

After breakfast I found myself a sheltered spot and forced the war from my mind. I focused on peaceful thoughts—imagined I was with Simba and Shoko fishing for bream on the Impali. Bruce was there too. My breathing started to slow.

Bruce woke me at four that afternoon and we silently got ourselves ready. I felt like I was preparing for a big rugby match. But this was bigger, much bigger. If things went wrong in sport, you lost the match. Here, it was your life.

We walked together to the final briefing, picking up Simba on the way.

"Right … before I start," said Waters, "Simba is going to brief you on the target."

Simba stepped forward. "I've been watching this camp for several days. It's a Frelimo camp they use for housing Mugabe's terrs, ZANLA, en route to Rhodesia. At any time there are normally about seventy people in the camp, of which at least fifty are ZANLA." He grabbed a small branch from a thorn tree and drew us a sketch of the camp in the dark-brown sand. He pointed at the mess, not far from the guard posts. "Before six o'clock every evening, all the terrs gather here to eat. This is where they're most vulnerable."

Impressed, I watched Simba closely. He'd become a competent, professional soldier, always measured and in control.

When he'd finished, Waters pointed a stick at Simba's diagram: "Three elevated guard stations here. They're perfect for us to launch an attack from. Each is manned by two Frelimo guards. Young, your group take this station. Riley this one. Mine will take control of the third." He pointed again. "At eighteen-hundred we open fire on the mess—here." He gave us a detailed course of action for every possible scenario, his planning always meticulous. Finally, he rounded off his pre-attack briefing. "If you hear '*Toko*', we make our way to the canoes—back the way we came, and fast. But if we run into problems and can't make it back to the canoes, the call is '*Duzi*'." He pointed ominously with his stick: "Over here. This is the perfect spot to hide or draw them into an ambush if we need to stand and fight. Air support is on standby. They know *Duzi*'s location. Good luck, boys."

It was two kilometres to the camp. Simba joined our group, and with Bruce on one side and Simba on the other, I moved carefully through the thick bush.

On the way Simba motioned us to a stop. "*Duzi*," he said,

pointing at a thicket on the top of a small koppie about a hundred metres from where we were standing.

"Yes. Remember it," ordered Waters sternly.

I took a brief look and kept on walking. It was unlikely we'd need to use it anyway.

As we got closer we branched out towards our respective targets. Thirty metres from our station we ducked into the bushes and watched. I could hear my heart thumping. Bruce was next to me. I wondered if he could hear it. His face was drawn, tense. Our two guards were listening to Radio Mozambique, singing along with the music and drinking from a bottle. *Probably cheap Portuguese Rosé*, I thought. One of the guards left his post and walked towards us, still humming to himself.

Young signalled to me. I aimed my AK at his head and followed him as he came towards us. He stopped about ten metres from where we were crouching and undid his fly, relieving himself against a thorn bush. There was the sound of a twig snapping from where Bruce was hiding, and the guard turned. I fired. He dropped. A dull thud, the silencer working. Dixon was onto him, ramming his bayonet into the guard's temple until all movement stopped.

Silently we dragged the body into the bush and crept towards the other guard. Still enjoying his music and his wine, he was oblivious to what was unfolding around him. We lay still on the ground in cover, waiting. After five minutes he walked outside and called, "Luis? Luis?"

The silenced AK coughed once. Again I hit him between the eyes, and again Dixon was onto him with his bayonet.

It was ten to six, so we waited patiently in the bushes. Waters was right: the elevated guardhouse overlooking the main camp was the ideal position to launch an attack from. The terrs had already assembled in the mess. At two minutes to six we took up our attack positions on either side of the guardhouse. They would now be eating. I counted down the hundred and twenty seconds in my head: *Crocodile One, Crocodile Two* ...

"Fire!" Young called, and the dark night sky lit up as rockets smashed into the buildings, AK rounds punched through the windows of the mess and grenades were lobbed into the exits where the terrs were fleeing. The results were spectacular, and the few terrs who survived scattered in all directions. It was going to be a good night.

Then I heard the trucks.

"Oh, fuck!" I heard Young curse next to me. There must have been at least five trucks, all packed with heavily armed Frelimo soldiers. Reinforcements had arrived.

"*Toko,*" Waters' voice rang out above the gunfire. We turned and ran for the canoes. The reinforcements were jumping from the trucks and setting off after us.

"Shit!" It was Williams, and he dropped to the ground, blood pouring from his leg. Simba grabbed him and kept going, fast.

"Turn! Fire!" shouted Young. We stood our ground and let loose a few rounds as Young frantically called through on the radio. The advancing Frelimo troop ducked, giving us valuable seconds.

"Man down, need back-up fast, location *Duzi.*" He gave directions for the air force.

"*Duzi,*" Young screamed loudly so the other groups could hear. We turned and ran, in serious trouble.

"I'll take over, Simba."

"No," he panted. "Keep going."

Mortar and rocket fire were still flying over our heads. But we were motoring and gaining precious metres, which would be critical once we reached *Duzi*. I could see Simba starting to lag, so I grabbed Williams and sprinted the last four hundred metres.

*Simba, you champion,* I mouthed silently as we ducked through the heavy bushes at *Duzi*—the spot was perfect. It was on an elevated koppie with 360-degree views. Surrounding it on all sides was dense, thorny bush. The two other groups were huddled next to us. Riley had been shot in the arm.

Waters whispered. "At least eighty of the bastards are chasing us. Lynx and two choppers will be here in thirty minutes. We can't go any further with the wounded. We hide here, but if they find us, we fight."

We waited silently, even limiting the breaths we took so as not to make any noise. Simba was at my side, his face covered with Williams's blood. He was wiping his forehead to stop the blood dripping into his eyes.

Fortunately our pursuers had seen the damage we'd inflicted on the ZANLA camp and were treating us with respect, anxious to avoid presenting themselves as targets. From the shelter of a line of big boulders they were firing blindly, hoping we'd respond so they could identify our position. It was dark, the moon now behind thick clouds. We held our cover, watched and waited.

Young grabbed Williams, who was biting his arm to prevent any screams coming out, and warned: "Not a sound, or we're all dead!"

I thought of Laurel. *Would I see her again?* I thought of home: *Mum, Dad, Shoko ... I wasn't ready to die.* Still, the Frelimo soldiers came towards us. They were firing aimlessly, so they clearly didn't know where we were. But it was only a matter of time. We held our fire.

In the distance we heard the reassuring sound of the Lynx. It was well ahead of schedule.

"Only five more minutes, boys." Waters' voice was tense. *Could we hold our cover for another five minutes?*

A flurry of activity broke out below. Frelimo were pointing excitedly in our direction. Damn! They'd picked up our spoor, even in the darkness—now they knew where we were and aimed their fire directly at us.

The Lynx ground-attack aircraft was getting closer. "Four minutes, boys. Hold fire!"

But Frelimo were also getting closer, and eventually Waters had no choice. "Fire, nail the bastards!" It was a relief. All the fear and dread flowed out of us as we let rip with all we had. If we were going down, we'd go down fighting.

Three Frelimo dropped immediately.

Taken aback by the ferocity of our attack, they moved backwards, giving us a few more precious seconds.

"Only two minutes to hold out," shouted Waters.

A muffled scream rang out to my right. One of us had been hit. I didn't look, loaded another magazine and kept firing. Frelimo were creeping forward again. Then a sound erupted from above: the Lynx's machine gun. *Yes!* I wanted to shout out. There was hope. Frelimo's fire suddenly turned away from us to focus on the Lynx, behind which came the two choppers.

Young threw a phosphorus grenade to mark our position. The helicopters circled overhead and then came down fast to a clearing about twenty metres from where we were lying. I quickly took in the bush between the choppers and our position. Mostly thornscrub, with a few mopanes dotted between.

"Right, go!" Waters shouted, and we sprinted for the helicopters. Thank God for the Lynx. It was blasting Frelimo, keeping their fire away from us. We bundled the two wounded men into the choppers and jumped in. Soon we were roaring away to safety.

Riley was already dead by the time we boarded. He'd been hit at *Duzi*. Williams was in serious pain. At least now he could scream as a medic tended to his wounds. Bruce put his head on my shoulder and we stayed like that, unmoving, saying nothing, all the way through the refuelling stations and then on to Salisbury. We'd been delivered from death.

Williams went to Intensive Care, Riley to the mortuary, and the rest of us to the pub. We were all in a daze, grappling with the enormity of what had happened.

Waters bought the first round. "Boys, this is the closest I've ever been."

"Me too," agreed Young.

We staggered out of the pub later that night, our bodies pumped with alcohol, adrenaline, fear and relief.

Conway shouted out as we stumbled back to our rooms, "Hey, I'll pick you up outside the gates at two o'clock. Don't be late."

He drove us to the rugby the next day. Rhodesia were playing Western Province. I was still in a daze. It was like I'd woken from a deep sleep. All these happy people everywhere—safe. No AKs, no mortars, no rockets.

"Hey, I feel really strange, like I've just woken from a long dream," I told my friends.

"*Ja*, me too. Feels really weird," said Simba. Bruce didn't say anything. He looked jumpy.

Conway wasn't having any of it. "Come on, you bunch of sissies. We're alive, fergodsake. Beers all round."

Each beer that went down helped ease the stress of the past few weeks.

"Go, Rhodesia!"

Ian Robertson made a break down the blind side.

Conway nudged me, pointing at a short man in front of us.

"Hey, another dwarf—are you related?"

Simba decided to jump on the bandwagon. "Talking of dwarfs," he said, "well, Scott and Laurel are on holiday on Durban beach. And this Afrikaans guy, massive, about six foot five, walks up to them and pinches Laurel on the bottom. So Scott clenches his fist and shakes it at the Afrikaner and says, 'Hey, listen ... I'm not happy!' So the Afrikaner looks at him, puzzled. 'Well, which one are you, then?'"

Bruce and Conway were laughing so much, they almost fell over. I laughed too. Simba had become more comfortable with all of us, so much so that he was now cracking jokes with us. It felt odd, but I was pleased he was starting to join in.

We turned back to the rugby. Chris Rogers threw in at the lineout. Alan Sutherland jumped. Down to Bucky Buchanan, out to Ian Robertson. He broke through two defenders, then slipped to David Smith. And in the dying seconds of the game came the highlight of the afternoon. Ray Mordt, on his debut, made a powerful run from his own try-line to score under the Western Province posts. The win was sealed for Rhodesia. The crowd was delighted:

'Cos we're all Rhodesians, and we'll fight through thick and thin,
We'll keep our land a free land; stop the enemy coming in,
We'll keep them north of the Zambezi, till that river's running dry,
And this mighty land will prosper, for Rhodesians never die.

"My little boy's gonna play rugby for Rhodesia," announced Conway proudly. "In fact, better than that—he's gonna play for the Springboks."

"But he's not even born yet," pointed out Simba. "You don't know if the baby's gonna be a boy or girl."

Conway laughed him off with a wave of his right hand. "Details, details."

"All I can say, Conway, is that if he's got your girlfriend's looks and your charm ... well, then, at least he has your girlfriend's looks."

"Ha bloody ha," muttered Conway sarcastically.

Bruce wasn't going to be left out of any Conway-bashing. "He's probably gonna be a big drip like his dad, anyway."

"Well, at least he'll be able to shoot properly," retorted Conway before ringing his imaginary bell from side to side, "Ding-dong, ding-dong!"

After the rugby Simba told us he was leaving.

"Why?" we argued. "The fun's just starting."

"I'm not allowed in half the places you'll go to. It'll be awkward. See you guys tomorrow."

He had a point, and we couldn't persuade him otherwise. So we waved goodbye and went drinking at Salisbury Sports Club, the George Hotel, then Prospectors, and finally at around three in the morning we staggered into Club Tomorrow nightclub. As we entered I noticed a beautiful Spanish-looking brunette wearing a skin-tight pair of jeans and expensive black leather jacket. I couldn't keep my eyes off her. Neither could Conway.

While Bruce went to the bathroom, we compared notes. "See that bird over there, Carter? She's after me big time."

"Not a chance. She fancies me."

We strode purposely across the dance floor to see who she really liked. Fortunately, someone else swooped in before us.

She took a step back and looked at this guy, "Get lost, you fuckin' idiot!"

Conway and I stopped dead in our tracks and hurriedly retreated to the bar.

"Think we might've been safer with those Frelimo," laughed Conway.

When Bruce returned I pointed to the gorgeous girl in the leather jacket.

"Bruce, I hate to say this, but that beauty over there's been staring at you ever since we walked in."

"Really? Me?"

"Absolutely," jumped in Conway. "She wants you, big time!"

"Jeez, well she's really hot," said Bruce, a big grin appearing on his face.

"Hell, Bruce, you only live once," we told him.

Everything went into slow motion as Conway and I leaned back against the bar. We knew what was coming. Poor old Bruce—his innocent childhood on the farm in Selukwe hadn't prepared him for stuff like this. He stood up and confidently ran his hand through his hair. Then he casually walked over to her.

"So, what's a nice girl like you doing in a place like this?"

"Fuck off, you moron!" she shouted.

Crestfallen, Bruce made his way back to the bar, his shoulders hunched with the burden of the past weeks. I could see a shell-shocked expression on his gentle face. The same expression I'd seen as he watched Riley being taken to the mortuary.

Conway and I felt guilty. "Hey, Bruce, can we get you a beer?"

"No, thanks. I'm gonna call it a night. It's all catching up on me." We weren't going to leave him on his own, so we caught a cab back together.

After breakfast the next morning we met up with Simba and went to visit Williams at the Andrew Fleming Hospital. They'd just released him from Intensive Care when we arrived with five Castle Lagers stashed in our jackets. Once the nurse left, we passed him an open bottle and he swigged it down.

"Hey, Williams, you should have seen Thomas in action last night," said Conway, a naughty grin on his face. He told Williams about the beauty in Club Tomorrow and laughter rang out across the ward. Williams took another swig of his Castle.

"And what do you think you're doing?" We quickly hid our bottles from the nurse, but Williams was caught red-handed. She was fierce, a big buxom woman who was used to knocking soldiers into line.

"Sorry, ma'am—I just had a sip."

"Well, hand it over." She turned to us, "Any more of those, and you lot are out of here."

"Yes, ma'am."

She left, shaking her head. We passed him another beer and told him how Simba had saved him, carrying him at pace for nearly a kilometre.

"Thanks, man." He shook Simba's hand and took another swig of his beer. We told him about Riley and his face sank.

"Okay, out of here, all of you, now! You should be ashamed of yourselves. He's just been shot!"

"Thanks for coming, boys," Williams waved while the nurse shooed us from the ward.

As we entered Cranborne Barracks I noticed dozens of army trucks assembled near the parade ground. Soldiers were moving back and forth, loading equipment.

"Hey, Carter!" I turned at the sound of Young's voice. "I've been looking for you boys everywhere. There's something big going on. Briefing in fifteen minutes."

I got myself changed and hurried to the ops room. Major Doug Burton was briefing us. It had to be big.

"In thirty-six hours, every one of you and every plane in the country will be going on the biggest raid this country has ever seen.

We will be leaving for New Sarum Air Base at eight tomorrow morning. No one to leave barracks under any circumstances."

I took a deep breath and looked across at Bruce. Our next big adventure was about to begin.

# eight

At New Sarum Air Base, just outside Salisbury, the following morning I was immediately ushered into a hangar. I spotted Bruce's face among the two-hundred-strong crowd of men and slipped in next to him.

Bruce tapped me on the shoulder. "Hell, there's the commander of the whole Rhodesian Army."

Looking up, I saw General Moore sitting at the front. "Shit, this has got to be big."

SAS Commander Major Doug Burton and Air Force Group Captain James Hill took charge of the briefing. Burton pointed to the map. "Now, this is our first target. Chimoio Camp, ninety kays from the Rhodesia-Mozambique border. It's the headquarters for Robert Mugabe's war effort. There're nine thousand gooks at Chimoio. We're sending in one hundred and eighty-five, repeat, one hundred and eighty-five men." He paused to let the enormity of what we were going to do sink in.

Bruce whispered, "Why only a hundred and eighty-five?"

"Probably the max we can take in—not enough planes."

"But, we'll surprise the bastards," Burton continued. "And

you'll get a lot of support from the air: twelve Lynxes, eight Hunters, six Dakotas, six Vampires, three Canberras and forty-two choppers."

He pointed his stick towards the *papier-mâché* model of the camp. "At oh-eight-hundred every morning the terrs assemble on the parade ground here. At oh-seven-fifty tomorrow a DC-8 will over-fly Chimoio, as if it's a civilian airliner. We expect them to take cover and then reassemble on the parade ground. At oh-eight-zero-five the real bombers and fighter planes will arrive over the target area. Given that nothing happened with the first plane, they'll either not bother to run for cover, or do it slowly. By which time, for many of them, it'll be too late."

He pointed at us. "Now this is when you guys come in. The gooks will be running in all directions, away from the planes. You're going to box them in and nail them. At exactly oh-eight-zero-seven, ninety-seven SAS and forty-eight RLI troops will parachute from Dakotas, landing here and here. That's two sides covered. The third side over here will be covered by forty RLI men dropped by ten choppers. Finally, at oh-eight-seventeen, the K-cars will enclose the fourth side." He paused before stressing, "There may be Frelimo in the camp. Remember, our quarrel isn't with Frelimo, so stay away from them, and only shoot if you have to. There may be civilians in the camp. Leave them alone. But don't take any chances. If it could be a gook, you've got to shoot him before *he* nails *you*."

He continued to give us a detailed breakdown covering almost every conceivable eventuality. Towards the end of his briefing, he lowered his voice. "There is a good chance we will catch either Rex Nhongo or Josiah Tongogara in camp, and there's an outside possibility Robert Mugabe will be there. Good luck!"

"Hell, those are three important gooks. If we can nail any of them it'll be awesome," said Bruce.

Afterwards we broke up into our various sticks and were told exactly what our respective roles in the operation would be. We spent the rest of the day practising our drills and going through every potential scenario. We were in bed by seven that evening.

"Hey, Scott, you still awake?"

"*Ja*, what's the time?"

"Two o'clock. Just can't sleep. Too excited."

"Do you think any army's ever done this before—a hundred and eighty-five against nine thousand?"

"Doubt it … Israel, maybe?"

I was still tossing and turning fitfully when we were woken at four o'clock. Shortly after five we assembled outside, fitted our parachutes, strapped in our rifles and waited anxiously on the edge of the runway.

Conway stood at my shoulder. "You know there was a security clampdown last night—no staff or soldiers allowed out of camp. Well, they caught one of the black staff trying to crawl through the fence."

"I'm glad they caught him. There must be terr informers everywhere."

"Emplane!" shouted Waters, and we boarded the Dakota.

We sat in our group: Sergeant Young, Bruce, myself and Corporal Jenkins, impatiently checking our watches as we drew near the drop zone. It was quite a procession in the sky: five other Dakotas flew alongside, jets streamed past, and all the way we kept overtaking choppers. Then word trickled down from the front of the plane that the DC-8 had done its dummy run. The terrs had reassembled on the parade ground. In ninety seconds our air attack would commence. It was all going according to plan.

My stomach tightened. In less than four minutes we'd be dropping from the sky.

Waters nodded. "Green light on—go!" And I was falling over Mozambique. Then relief, always relief when my chute opened. I looked across and saw Bruce floating down next to me. So far, so good. Below me, carnage. Air strikes were smashing into the camp, and the terrs were fleeing like ants in every direction. They were moving fast, faster than we'd expected.

*Right … focus!* I went through my pre-landing drills.

*Landing spot.* Fine—no trees.

*Head tucked in … knees bent … elbows in.*

*Thump.* I rolled on the ground, released my parachute harness, then scrambled onto my knees, firing at terrs as they sprinted past. Most ran for their lives, AKs slung over their shoulders.

*Got him!* Another terr dropped. Then another—I hit him twice in the head. He'd virtually run straight into me, not even looking, he was so desperate to get away from the Hunters' bombs. As he lay dying, less than a metre from where I crouched, I noticed he was carrying a wooden gun.

Now that we were on the ground, the model made sense and we could see where we were.

"Take cover!" Young called, as we held our lines and fired at what looked like a never-ending procession of oncoming terrs.

Finally the signal to advance. "Let's go!" Young shouted, and we advanced towards our target, the eastern perimeter of the camp. Past the ZANLA warehouse, past the garage. All the way, nailing any terr that moved.

"Please no!" shouted one gook as Young blasted him backwards off his feet. Dragging his leg, the terr crawled into an open storeroom. There was lots of activity inside. Jenkins tossed in a grenade, and another and another.

Then screams. Women, children. Flying out of the storeroom. Body parts. Bloody mess. "Hell, no!" cried Bruce. More screams. A boy with an AK shouted, "Surrender!" Jenkins nailed him. In the head, three times. Another boy's head landed at my feet, blood gushing. The brown eyes looked up at me. Tucked against the wall, under more mangled body parts, was a girl.

"Die, you murderer!" she screamed as she came to life in a jerk, swinging her AK towards me. I didn't have time to move, but Bruce saved me with a burst from his rifle and she splattered backwards into the wall.

"Keep moving," shouted Young. We had to move on. Physically, we did, quickly. Mentally was harder.

As the day wore on, the air strikes subsided, leaving the troops to do the fighting. Also because, as we got closer to the main camp, the danger of being hit by our own planes was greater. We were wearing our caps inside-out to show bright orange Day-glo patches so that our planes would recognise us, but many of us had lost them, either in the heat of battle, or had purposefully ditched them to avoid being targeted by the terrs.

As the sun made its way down, Jenkins shouted to Bruce and me: "Cover me, boys," and he scaled a tree, putting a Rhodesian flag on top of it.

"Crazy bugger," laughed Bruce.

"Put it there, Bruce," I held out my hand. "We'll tell our grandchildren about this raid!"

He grabbed my hand and shook it firmly. "Yes, it's been a good one, though pity Mugabe wasn't in camp."

That night I didn't sleep either. Every time I was about to nod off, the vision of the women and children in the storeroom kept coming back.

At first light we set about finishing our mission. The rule was simple: if we couldn't take it back to Rhodesia, destroy it. Our group made its way to the ZANLA operations centre, where we were tasked with seizing any intelligence we could find. Once we'd loaded everything we could onto the helicopters we returned to Umtali, stopping en route at our Mozambique admin base and then Lake Alexander. As I looked back over Chimoio the fires cast a red glow over the dark clouds in the afternoon sky. We'd struck a huge blow against Mugabe.

Next was Mugabe's second most important camp, Tembué, northeast of Cabora Bassa and over two hundred kilometres from the Rhodesian border. Here four thousand terrs were waiting for us. With the exception of a chopper and a Vampire that were both seriously damaged, all the aircraft that'd been hit in Chimoio had been repaired overnight. We needed to strike quickly before news of Chimoio caused them to flee Tembué as well. The strategy was the same, and it worked. When we got back to Salisbury the following morning we were exhausted, relieved to be alive and staggered by the success of the raids.

Reports were filtering in that more than two thousand terrs had been killed in the two raids, with thousands more wounded. Only one Rhodesian soldier and one pilot had been killed, and eight wounded.

We went back to barracks and hit the bar. Bruce, Conway and I sat in the corner talking about the raid. I told them of the terr with the wooden gun.

"But they weren't short of weapons," pointed out Bruce. "They'd a huge store of weapons in the camp, a lot of which we've captured."

"*Ja*, apparently those gooks don't trust each other. They don't like to arm the trainees. Most of the guys who were armed were instructors," explained Conway.

Bruce was in a sombre mood. "I know they're terrs, but hell, shooting those women ..."

"Hey, Bruce," I cut in. "They're the most dangerous of the lot. In Mugabe's camps those female gooks are badly abused. Raped, you name it—so they're angry. You don't mess around with them."

Bruce clearly needed cheering up. "Hey, did you see superman's roll on landing?" I smiled, pointing at Conway. "One roll and he was on his feet, nailing gooks."

Bruce grinned. "*Ja*, our very own Audie Murphy."

"The hell with you, Carter," Conway laughed. "And as for you, Thomas, all I can say is, 'Ding-dong, ding-dong!'"

I woke up the next morning, went straight to the basin and splashed cold water over my face. Had it all been a dream? Had we really attacked two camps with thirteen thousand gooks in them? It was quite difficult to take in. I shook my head and opened the curtains. I had a lot to look forward to this weekend—it was Conway's birthday, and he'd planned an active schedule, starting with a social rugby match for Old Hararians Third XV against Alex Seconds.

Conway was captain for the match. He tossed Simba a number 14 jersey as we got changed in the dingy Alex changerooms. "Simba, you're on the wing. These Alex boys have been complaining about us playing a black guy, so you've got a point to prove." He looked at Bruce. "Thomas, I hope your rugby is better than your shooting. You're on the other wing." Then he tossed me a number 9 jersey, "Carter, you're scrumhalf."

We jogged onto the field and waited for the Alex team to run on. I could see Laurel up in the stands. On one side of her was her friend from Denmark, a stunning blonde. On the other side was Conway's girlfriend, looking heavily pregnant.

"Hey, kaffir! What are you doing on the field? This is a white man's game," shouted a scruffy-bearded spectator at Simba.

"Give him a brown-eye, Toolbox," shouted another voice from the crowd. The bearded man rose to his feet and dropped his trousers, to the cheers of the rest of the crowd. Simba stared down at his boots, shaking his head in disgust.

As we lined up for the kick-off I looked across at the Alex team. A rough-looking bunch. They kicked off to Bruce's wing. And he dropped it.

The ref blew his whistle. "Knock-on. Alex scrum."

"Good skills, fat boy," the Alex players jeered Bruce. Poor Bruce went bright red. He was hoping to impress Laurel's Danish friend, and the match had got off to a bad start.

It soon became clear that the Alex team were more interested in a good punch-up than a social runaround. It also became clear that Conway was in a league of his own. He'd played on the wing for Rhodesian schoolboys at the annual Craven Week festival, and whenever he got the ball he carved through the Alex defence.

After Conway's second solo try the Alex players gathered in a huddle behind the posts. Even after Conway had slotted the conversion, they were still crouching behind the posts. Then they rose to their feet, and jogged back to the halfway line. Their flyhalf kicked off, but instead of kicking to the forwards he kicked straight at where Conway was standing in the centre of the field. A high, floating ball.

Conway shouted, "My ball," and as he took it the entire Alex team descended on him. Boots, fists and elbows all went flying into a bewildered Conway. Bruce was first to Conway's aid. He sprinted in from the wing. I'd never seen him run so fast. He dived onto the Alex players, trying to pull them off. Simba was next to hit the battle scene and waded in, swinging his fists to protect Conway. The ref blew his whistle madly as players charged in from all directions. Finally he managed to stop the fighting. Conway got to his feet with a black eye and bloody nose. He wiped the blood from his face and took his position at flyhalf.

By half-time the game was effectively over. We were twenty points up, and even though Conway wasn't quite the force he'd been earlier in the game, he was still able to break through and score at will.

So Alex decided to focus on their next target: the black man. Their captain was at scrumhalf. With his scraggly beard, he could have been Toolbox's brother.

"Floppy one," he shouted as he was about to put the ball into a scrum in the centre of the field. Three of his backline moved to the right of the scrum.

"Watch backline move to the right," I shouted quickly.

But Toolbox's brother had no intention of any backline move, and when the ball came out of the scrum he picked it up and punted it high into the air, directly above Simba. "Nail the kaffir," he yelled.

"I've got it," called Simba, before leaping into the air and grabbing the ball with both hands. As his feet left the ground Toolbox's brother hit his legs and three others smashed his head into the ground, hammering their fists into his unprotected face.

I went sprinting towards the brawl. Enough was enough. We had to teach these guys a lesson. Conway and Bruce were on either side of me as I charged at the Alex thugs. I grabbed Toolbox's brother by his long greasy hair and pulled him off Simba, then smashed a right into his jaw. Down he went, so again I yanked him onto his feet and smashed him with my right.

Simba still had two on him. Bruce hit one of them with a

flying tackle. Conway took care of the other, wrestling him to the ground away from Simba. The ref's whistle shrilled repeatedly. But still we battered them. All the pent-up fear and anger from Chimoio and Cabora Bassa came pouring out of me as I lashed out at our opponents. Finally, I noticed that the Alex team had stopped fighting back, so I called out to the others: "Okay, boys, hold off!"

Three of our opponents left the field badly bruised and bleeding heavily. The fight had been knocked out of them. With their ringleader, Toolbox's brother, now off the field, they were well behaved for the rest of the match.

As the forwards got ready for a scrum in the centre of the field about forty metres from the Alex try-line, Conway stuck an elbow into my ribs, a big smile on his face. "Hey, we've got to make Thomas look good. Otherwise he's got no chance with that Danish bird."

I grinned, and when the ball came out of the scrum I grabbed it and sprinted down the field, running straight at Bruce's opposing wing. As I drew close I straightened up, drawing him away from Bruce. Then popped it up into Bruce's hands. Perfect—he had a clear run to the line with no one in front of him. He pumped his legs, straining every muscle of his body into action.

"Go, Bruce, go!" I screamed. Twenty metres to go, still in the clear, no one near him. I could see Laurel and the Danish girl shouting for him. Ten metres to go. He was going to do it. But the other Alex wing was powering across, and catching up on him quickly. Just three metres to go now.

"Dive, Bruce!" I bellowed. But he didn't, and the Alex wing caught him with a flying tackle and they went rolling into touch. No score.

"Thomas, you're a carthorse," shouted Conway.

Bruce got to his feet, shaking his head in disappointment.

We kept trying to get Bruce on the scoreboard, but with no success. Finally, with a minute of the match remaining, Conway jinked past the Alex flyhalf, sold a dummy to their centre and sped across the field to Bruce's wing. Bruce was on the far edge of the field with no one between him and the try-line.

"Thomas!" Conway shouted, and threw a long floating pass out to Bruce. It flew through the air, perfectly weighted, perfectly timed. All Bruce had to do was reach out, grab it and score. The Danish girl would be impressed, no doubt about it. He threw out his arms to catch it, but it hit his chest and bounced forward.

"Knock-on, Alex ball," shouted the ref.

"No, no, no," groaned Conway, and buried his head in his hands. Bruce went red again.

As we trudged off the field at the end of the match Simba teased Conway. "Hey, Conway, nice friendly social match you arranged for us. Thanks a lot."

Conway laughed, "Sorry about that, boys. I promise Vic Falls will be better." He paused. "Hey, Simba, why don't you come with?"

Simba looked at him for what seemed like ages. Then he smiled and nodded his head. I slapped him on the back. Vic Falls with my girlfriend and three best friends—it was going to be a fantastic weekend.

# nine

As we waited for our bags at Vic Falls airport, Laurel gave me a dig in the ribs. "Stop staring!"

"I was looking for my bag," I told her. We both knew I'd been gazing at Ida. A Scandinavian beauty with long blond hair and blue eyes, Ida had been Laurel's penpal since they were kids. Finally our bags arrived and we waited for Conway's uncle at the entrance to the airport building. Soon a thick-set middle-aged man dressed in khakis arrived, and greeted Conway with a slap on the back and a firm handshake.

Conway turned to introduce the rest of us, but before he could speak, his uncle waved at Simba. "Load the cases in the back of the truck."

There was a silence, then Conway spoke: "Uncle Warren, that's Simba, my friend from the army. He doesn't work for us."

Bruce and I quickly grabbed the cases and bundled them into the truck while Warren mumbled his apologies to Simba.

Simba didn't look up, his voice tight. "That's okay, sir. It's an easy mistake to make. When you see a black man in this country, the chances are he's either a cookboy or gardenboy."

Uncle Warren dropped us at Conway's luxurious holiday home. "I'll bring the spare bakkie and keys tonight so you have a car for the weekend," he shouted as he roared out the drive.

After a braai by the pool, we turned in early for the night. First thing the next morning, we crowded into Conway's bedroom to give him his birthday presents and sing *Happy Birthday*. Then, after a plate of bacon and eggs, Conway's girlfriend drove us down to Warren's stables.

"Are you sure you girls can ride?" asked Warren, a concerned look on his face. "These horses can motor, hey."

"Of course," nodded Laurel confidently, and we all mounted. Conway led the way, cantering through the mopane woodlands towards Batoka Gorge. Latching onto the saddle, her knuckles white from gripping the reins, Ida trailed at the back. I winked at Bruce and he rode alongside her, talking to her gently.

As we entered an open vlei, Conway gave his black thoroughbred a kick and all the horses broke into a gallop. Ida screamed, her face now an ashen white.

I sat back in the saddle enjoying the moment. It was a beautiful sunny morning. In the corner of the vlei an elephant bull was steadily flapping his ears against his shoulders while he grazed on the long green grass. A pair of warthogs darted in front of us, their tails sticking straight up in the air. I loved warthogs, so ugly with their grey pig-like bodies and two pairs of tusks sticking out from their mouths. But I didn't have time to stop and admire them. Our horses swerved and all of us moved with the swerve— except for Ida, who went flying off the saddle onto the green grass below. Immediately we reined in. Bruce leapt off to help while Simba chased after her horse.

Bruce picked Ida up and brushed her down. She was fine; just a few bruises, but now very scared. Conway grinned at me. "Hey,

Ida, I think it's best you ride with Bruce." I lifted her onto the saddle behind Bruce, and she grabbed onto him tightly. It was all going well for Bruce; we couldn't have planned it better.

A few minutes later Simba arrived back with Ida's horse, leading it by the reins as he rode behind me. Soon afterwards we turned our horses for home. Not far from the stables we came out of the mopane woodland into a clearing, and there, staring straight at us, was an African buffalo. A powerful ox-like animal with a thick dark-grey hide, he must have weighed at least seven hundred kilos. His heavily ridged horns curved downward from his head and then upward to form a U-shape with sharp points at each end.

Conway spoke quietly, evenly. "Turn around, walk slowly in the opposite direction." I gently squeezed my horse's side and eased him into a turn. The buffalo lowered his head and carried on grazing.

Back at home Uncle Warren had already lit up the birthday braai and Happiness, Warren's cook, had a tray of ice-cold beers waiting for us.

As we sat around the pool drinking our beers Uncle Warren shouted over to Simba: "Hey, Simba! I'm really sorry about the mix-up yesterday. But, hey …" he pointed at Conway, "they say my nephew's got a touch of the tar-brush, what with his dark skin, brown eyes and dark hair."

"Cut it out, Uncle Warren," snapped Conway.

But Warren was in full flight. "Simba, if you're my nephew's mate you've gotta have a good sense of humour. You'll enjoy this one." Conway knew his uncle and jumped in quickly. "Uncle Warren, what time are you cooking?"

"Later, my boy."

Laurel and Ida had gathered round to hear the joke.

"Anyway," continued Warren, "Sipho, a black Rhodesian on holiday, walks into a bar on Bondi Beach in Sydney, Australia, with a parrot on his shoulder. The barman says, 'That's awesome! Where did you get it from?' The parrot replies, 'Africa ... there's fuckin' millions of them!'" Uncle Warren collapsed with laughter at his own joke. I looked at Simba who was staring coldly at Warren. He turned and strode off.

"He's had a bad few days," I explained to Warren, before following Simba inside. He was sitting on the bed, staring out the window.

I put my hand on his shoulder. "Come on, Simba. Warren didn't mean any harm. He was just telling a joke."

"I know, but it never stops."

"Sure, I can understand your frustration."

"You know, at some point the black people of Rhodesia will have to make a stand against discrimination, or it will never change."

"You mean like the terrs are doing?"

"Well ..."

"For God's sake, don't be ridiculous, Simba. The terrs are murdering scum. We've discussed discrimination so many times—it's going to change, anyway."

"But unless we make a stand, how will we ever get the vote? Be allowed into the same schools, hospitals, restaurants ...?"

"Look, we're here to enjoy ourselves, not discuss politics. It's Conway's birthday. Let's go and have some fun." Simba's moods were starting to annoy me.

Outside, I was pleased to notice Bruce making progress with Ida. He had his arm around her shoulder and puffed out his chest as he told her about the farm in Selukwe.

Conway wandered over to them with his imaginary bell in his

left hand, a beer in his right, and a big grin all over his face.

"Hey, Ida, you should see this guy shoot."

Bruce immediately tackled Conway into the pool where they splashed about in the shallow end, laughing and trying to duck each other. I walked over to where Laurel was sitting with Conway's girlfriend, Claire.

"How long to go?" I asked.

"A few months," Claire replied

"And are you also hoping for a little boy?"

"Ja, I am—for Mike's sake. He's desperate for a boy."

I turned to Laurel. "We need to bring Conway down to size. Are you on for a down-down?"

"Ah, no, Scott ... you always make me do it."

"Please, it'll cheer everyone up—maybe even Simba." She reluctantly agreed, and I went to brief Simba and Bruce. They were delighted. "Come on, Scott, let's do it now!"

I banged my fist on the outside table. "Quiet! Quiet!" I called.

When all talking had stopped, I spoke loudly: "Okay, Conway, you're nineteen years old today. You're such a feeble excuse for a man that my sweet little girlfriend over here could beat you in a *down-down*."

Conway shouted right back. "Carter, you've been far too cocky ever since you got kicked out of dwarf-throwing competitions for being too short." He waited for the laughing to stop before carrying on. "I'm a racehorse, not a carthorse, like Thomas. I'll hammer *any*one, *any*time!"

"If you're so confident, why don't you put your money where your mouth is?"

"Sure—loser buys the winner a weekend for two at the Caribbea Bay Hotel in Kariba." I hesitated ... that would cost a lot of money, and I didn't have the same kind of money as Conway.

Claire jumped in. "Mike, that's a bit over the top."

Conway smiled and turned to me. "You see, even the girls are trying to protect you. You've gone all quiet—what kind of a man are you?" Still I hesitated. Then I looked up at Laurel. She was smiling confidently.

I walked forward and shook his hand. "Okay, Conway, you're on."

Simba, Bruce and I formed a huddle, chanting, "Laurel! Laurel!" Even Claire was shouting for her.

Simba got right into the swing of it and led an impromptu dance, which he'd taught Bruce and me as kids. He handed us bar stools to use as drums, then armed himself with a stick from the floor and a drinks tray as a shield. While we played the drums he stamped rhythmically on the lawn, making dramatic gestures from side to side.

At the end of it Conway shouted out to Laurel: "Come on, let's get on with it." We all watched her step forward in her black bikini. Her triathlons at university in Cape Town were paying off. It was difficult to keep my eyes off her legs, her tight stomach muscles and her pert breasts. Simba reckoned she was skinny and her boobs were too small. We'd argue for hours about Laurel as he preferred chunkier women.

I stepped forward and poured two full glasses of beer. "Conway, I'll be the judge."

"Oh no you won't," he said quickly. "My uncle Warren can do it."

I looked across at Warren. "No," I laughed. "The stakes are too high, I don't trust him. Let Claire be the judge."

I put my hands on Laurel's shoulder blades. "Hammer him, Laurel." She ran her hands through her now cropped dark-brown hair and kissed me on the lips, her eyes a bright excited blue.

"On your marks," Claire called out.

They lifted their glasses.

"Get set."

They leant forward over the glasses, their mouths wide open.

"Go!" and they were off. Conway flung himself at the glass and took an early lead. But Laurel was simply too good and opened her throat like a true professional. After two deep gulps she placed the empty beer glass on her head, and waited for a gasping Conway to finish. Conway was furious with himself. Probably for the first time in his nineteen years, he was at a complete loss for words.

Delighted, Simba, Bruce and I tore into another rendition of Simba's dance, with Bruce and me furiously beating on our bar-stool drums. Soon all the girls joined in, stamping rhythmically next to Simba. Uncle Warren grabbed Conway, tossed him into the pool, and pulled up another bar stool to join Bruce and me on the drums.

Conway lay in the water laughing, lapping up the abuse. He knew how to dish it out, but he could take it too. And we were laying it on.

I put on Scott McKenzie's 1967 hit, *San Francisco (be sure to wear some flowers in your hair)* at full volume. Bruce and I sang loudly along with the tape, substituting the words "If you're going to San Fran-cisco" with "If you're going to Ka-ah-riba…" And Conway just lay in the pool, laughing.

Then the dancing started, and I took Laurel onto the dance floor. Bruce was quick to follow, pulling Ida towards him. Claire led Conway by his hand and the two softly danced together, leaving Simba and Uncle Warren by the pool, but Ida sidled over to Simba and gently coaxed him onto the dance floor. He finally agreed as she took him by the hand. *What a nice girl*, I thought, *making sure Simba feels involved and happy.* Bruce grabbed her by the other hand and pulled her towards him. But she sidestepped him and danced back to Simba.

"Tequilas all round," shouted Conway after the dance. He had regained his composure. As we grabbed our tequilas the sun was setting over the horizon, a bright red ball making its way down over the rugged bush.

Laurel licked the salt from her hand, downed the tequila, bit down on the lemon, then ran and dived into the pool. Ida followed her, but, on the way in, threw off her bikini panties and top. Simba and Bruce dived in after her.

"I wouldn't kick her out of bed," beamed Uncle Warren.

I passed him and Conway a stick of biltong and stood with them at the bar, peering into the pool.

Laurel climbed out of the water and stood next to Claire while she dried herself, leaving Bruce, Simba and Ida in the water. We couldn't keep our eyes off Ida, who was gracefully swimming from one end to the other, her long muscular legs kicking out from side to side. She seemed to be paying a lot of attention to Simba. I was pleased. It was good that he felt involved, and he needed cheering up.

I walked over to the fridge to get a round of beers. When I got back to the bar Conway and Warren were staring at the pool, their mouths agape.

"What's wrong, boys?" I asked, turning my head to look at the pool.

"She's kissing the *munt!*" said Uncle Warren in horror. Ida's tongue was dashing in and out of Simba's mouth. He was trying to pull away, but her naked legs were wrapped tightly around his chest, and she was holding him firmly against her body.

At first I was fascinated; it was the first time I'd ever seen a white woman kissing a black man. But the fascination was soon replaced by a feeling of awkwardness.

"You've got to stop them," demanded Warren.

Conway looked at me and shrugged his shoulders. "Look, Carter, Simba's a great friend and all the rest, but this makes me uncomfortable. I don't know; it's not natural."

"Okay, well it's not Simba's fault. He's trying to get away. I'll talk to Laurel."

I walked over to Laurel. "Sorry to interrupt, Claire, do you mind if Laurel and I have a chat?" She shook her head, and I led Laurel by the hand to the bottom of the garden.

"Did you see Ida and Simba?" I asked her.

"You mean kissing?"

"I was hoping Bruce would score with her."

"No, she prefers Simba."

"Look, Laurel, I don't think it's natural for her to be kissing him like that."

"What? I didn't think you were a racist."

"I'm not. I mean Simba's probably my best friend … but it just doesn't feel right. It's making everyone feel awkward. Why don't you have a word with her?"

"And what am I meant to say to her? 'Please stop kissing Simba because he's black and my myopic friends are feeling uncomfortable.'? Do you know how ridiculous that will sound?"

"Well, she's also embarrassing Simba!" But I was wasting my time: girls like Laurel who'd been to multiracial private schools often had strange ideas on these issues. She simply didn't understand what I was trying to explain, so I turned and went back to the bar.

Uncle Warren excused himself and left. Conway, Bruce and I drove down to the Victoria Falls Hotel.

None of us spoke as we sat on the veranda drinking Castle Lagers.

Uncle Warren arrived to pick us up the next day, loaded our bags and took us to the airport. Then he said goodbye to Conway and drove off without looking back.

We quietly boarded the plane. Laurel grabbed my hand, holding it tightly as we sat in silence all the way back to Salisbury.

# ten

"You boys, stop wittering on like a pair of old women." It was Conway. "Sergeant Young needs to talk to us, urgently!" I emptied a lukewarm cup of coffee down my throat and followed Conway and Bruce out of the canteen.

Young was pacing impatiently up and down when we walked into the briefing room. "Eight of Mugabe's terrs hit the Evans farm west of Karoi. Father and son are both dead. We'll be doing a follow-up."

"Why us, sarge?" asked Bruce. The SAS was largely used for external raids. Follow-ups were generally carried out by the RLI or the Territorial Army.

"It's an important one, boys. That's why you've been chosen. There's an extremely effective bunch of terrs operating in this area. It's likely they're behind these murders. Comops High Command want the best team on this op. That's you."

There was a knock on the door and Simba walked in. "Sorry I'm late, sarge."

"Boys, you know Ndlovu ... he's coming with, as our tracker."

Young straightened up, a serious look on his face. "We suspect these gooks are operating out of the Urungwe Tribal Trust Land. We'll need to go in undercover, so you've got to look like terrs. All of you to put on that *Black is Beautiful* cream and wear scruffy civvy clothes."

"But, sir, what if we run into our own troops?" asked Conway. "They'll think we're terrs."

"It'll be designated as a Frozen Area. That means there'll be none of our troops there. The Selous Scouts do this all the time. Before they go into an area as pseudo-terrs, they make sure the entire area is designated as frozen." He went to the door. "A chopper will be waiting in twenty minutes. Get yourselves ready, quickly!"

I packed my kit: AK rifle, webbing, magazines, grenades. It was good to be going on an op without the stress of a parachute. I covered myself with the *Black is Beautiful* cream and put on a scruffy pair of longs and long-sleeved shirt, as instructed. A *proper gook*, I thought, as I looked at my reflection in the mirror.

"Good to have you with us," I told Simba as we waited on the edge of the parade ground, but he seemed to be in one of his moods again.

Conway gave him a friendly slap on the back. "Hey, no Danish girls on this trip. We need you to focus on the terrs." We all chuckled, but Simba looked away.

"Conway, after your pitiful effort in the *down-down*, I think we might be better off leaving you behind," said Bruce, and we both started humming, *If you're going to San Francisco, be sure to wear some flowers in your hair* ... Even Simba smiled.

"Thomas, you're very chirpy after your pathetic performance in the rugby. A blind penguin could've caught those balls you dropped."

We turned to the sound of roaring *chukka-chukka* chopper

blades. It landed right next to us, so we jumped on board and immediately took off. Then sat peering out as the helicopter powered its way towards Karoi.

"Over there, take us down," said Young, pointing at a farmhouse in the distance. The chopper swooped and approached the front lawn of the farmhouse fast and low, cutting its speed as it drew nearer. It hovered about two metres off the ground as we jumped out. Then, like a giant dragonfly, it turned and roared away into the sky, gradually climbing until it was gone.

The farmer's wife was in intense discussion with the police on the veranda in front of the house when we arrived. She looked at us suspiciously, then turned back to the policeman. He pointed at us and must have told her who we were, because she greeted us as we approached her, Young leading the way.

"Please, ma'am ... can you tell us what happened? We've got to get after them quickly." The farmer's wife took us to the security fence, with the policeman following behind. Lying on the lawn were two dead Alsatians, froth hanging from their open mouths. "Must have been poisoned meat. This is where they cut through the security fence," she explained, pointing at a gaping hole in the fence.

We walked back to the house. "It set off the alarm, just before they started firing at the house. Alan grabbed the FN, and I radioed for help on the Agric-Alert."

She winced. "Then he started screaming ... my little boy. They'd shot him in the stomach. I grabbed him and we hid under there, in the cellar." She pointed at a trapdoor in the floor. "He was bleeding so much." She burst into tears. "I couldn't keep him alive."

A policewoman who'd been following us led her gently away.

I looked across at Bruce. He'd a grim look on his face, and

I realised this must have brought back memories of Kelly's murder.

The policeman continued. "Mr Evans was firing at them from the bedroom window. The terrs' firing suddenly stopped. Mrs Evans thought they'd gone and was about to open the trapdoor, when a series of explosions went off. Probably petrol bombs."

He pointed to the burnt interior of the house. "Mr Evans must have tried to run for air or to get away from the flames. They were waiting for him at the back door."

"How many of them?"

"From their tracks, it looks like there were eight."

"Anything else we should know?" asked Young quickly. "We must go."

The policeman looked at his notepad. "They were shouting to each other in Shona, so definitely Mugabe's lot, ZANLA. I'll take you to where their tracks led." Young waved goodbye to Mrs Evans, as the policeman took us at a brisk pace to the tracks.

"They've made a very poor attempt to cover their spoor," Simba told us. "Must be confident."

"Boys, we have to move it … two hours to make up," said Young. We set off at a fast trot after Simba.

"What's the point of murdering an innocent little boy?" growled Conway as we ran through the thick bush. I didn't say anything. Neither did Bruce, who was staring forward, his jaw clenched.

After twenty-five minutes Simba motioned us to a halt. "I've lost their tracks, but from the direction they've been moving in, I'm certain they're heading for Urungwe TTL." He turned to Young. "Sergeant, we're about three hours from Urungwe. I suggest we keep going now till we get to the edge of the TTL. I've got a good spot where we can hide out till evening, then we move in."

We followed Simba at a fast walk.

It was early afternoon when we arrived at Simba's hiding spot. He indicated to Young and we crawled on our hands and knees for about twenty metres through a dense thicket of acacia. I smiled as we came out into a clearing. Completely screened by the acacia on all sides, it was an excellent position.

I nudged Simba in the back. "Well done, man. You always come through for us."

Young called us together. "Find some shade, get some rest. You've got a big night ahead of you. I want you all back here at four when Simba will give us a full briefing."

I lay down in the shade of a tree and pushed the little boy, the farmer and the terrs from my mind. I thought of Laurel and our trip to Kariba, imagining I was lying between the sheets of a Caribbea Bay Hotel bed. Cool and comfortable, a world away from where I was now. Then I imagined I was fishing in the Impali with Bruce, Simba and Shoko. I could feel my breathing easing, and soon I was fast asleep.

"Scott, wake up! It's four o'clock." Bruce was shaking me. I followed him to where the others had gathered at the edge of the clearing under a large acacia.

Simba was standing in the front. As soon as we were all gathered round he started his briefing. "A lot of Mugabe's terrs are trained in China. Since the early seventies, in true Mao Tse Tung fashion, they've done an impressive job of politicising and indoctrinating the Rhodesian blacks. They send in their political commissars with a group of terrs, and they move around holding political rallies, which they call *pungwes*. They pump the blacks with propaganda, promise them the earth when they get independence, and destroy anyone who crosses their path."

Young then cut in. "Once these bastards have won over

and subverted a specific area, they bring in the gooks from Mozambique." He hesitated before continuing. "You know we laugh and joke about how useless these gooks are, but this strategy has really worked for them. Most of the locals support them for political reasons or out of fear." He sat down again and nodded at Simba to continue.

"In each area, they appoint a contact man for the gooks. Normally an important man in the population, like a chief. He looks after everything for the terrs in the area: food, women, intelligence, messages, security procedures, all that sort of stuff."

I waved my arm at Simba, interrupting him. "This is interesting, but what's it got to do with us? We're on a follow-up."

"We need to go through a contact man in Urungwe to find the gooks who murdered the farmer," he explained. "He's a cunning old bugger, by the name of Moses."

I shrugged my shoulders. "*Ja*, but if Moses is worth his salt, he's not going to believe we're terrs."

"That's what I'm getting to. They have an elaborate system of passwords and code words. I've got all the current passwords for this area."

"How did you get those?"

"We got them from Special Branch and Selous Scouts intelligence," interrupted Young. "They got them from captured terrs. You must remember that one of the key jobs of the Scouts is to pretend to be terrs. They go into these areas as pseudo-terrs, find out where the real terrs are, and then call in the fire-force, typically RLI, to wipe them out."

I looked around at the others. They were all staring at Young, fascinated.

"Will this contact man really believe that us whiteys are gooks?" asked Conway.

"You'll have to stay in the background when I talk to him," explained Simba. "Even with this *Black is Beautiful* cream, you guys still look different. Your hair, eyes, body shape, mannerisms and so on all give it away—even your spoor isn't the same. Obviously, none of you should speak."

He looked around. "Any more questions?"

We shook our heads and rose to our feet. I was excited. This was going to be a new challenge, and I couldn't wait to get hold of the gooks who'd murdered the little boy.

We arrived outside Moses's village just as the sun was going down. Simba called out to a child who was playing with a toy car made from fencing wire. I turned to watch his skinny legs and little pot belly as he ran barefoot over the sharp stones to Simba. I thought of Dad, and how he'd always made me and Simba run barefoot. Simba spoke to him in Shona, and he hurried off to find Moses. We sat outside the compound under a big baobab tree, waiting. Fortunately it was dark by the time Moses appeared.

He greeted Simba, a stern, suspicious look on his face. My grip tightened on my AK. Then Simba, speaking quickly in Shona, rolled out the passwords. Immediately Moses's demeanour changed, and he treated Simba like an old friend. They chatted away in Shona for about fifteen minutes. I didn't have a clue what they were saying, but it was clear they were getting on well.

Finally they shook hands. Moses waved goodbye and went back to the village.

"Let's walk," said Simba leading us away from the compound. When he was certain no one was in earshot he spoke quickly. "The ZANLA terrs who nailed the little boy have been operating in this area for about three weeks. They're holding a *pungwe* at a compound about two kays from here in forty-five minutes. We should be there—if we get an opportunity to nail them, we should take it." He stopped, a look of concern on his face. "A group of ZIPRA terrs have been around this region for a few weeks."

"Shall we take them out as well?" suggested Young.

"No," said Simba, firmly shaking his head. "It's Comrade X's lot. We'll need a lot more men."

Young didn't argue. We all knew X's reputation. "Well, let's get cracking, Simba. Take us to the *pungwe*."

We walked quickly, the full moon lighting up the bush and cloudless sky around us. Conway pulled in next to me. He put a hand on my shoulder. "Carter … just like the movies, hey?"

I nodded. It was going to be an interesting night.

The *pungwe* was about to start as we arrived at the compound. Simba led us to an elevated piece of bush about a hundred metres or so from the event. Well covered with boulders and thorn scrub, it enabled us to observe without being seen.

Eight terrs were gathered in front of a large crowd of at least two hundred people. Their leader was shouting loudly in Shona.

"What's he saying?" I asked Simba.

"He says that they are here to fight against the evil white government. And promises that when they come to power, the people will be rewarded for supporting them. No segregation, no taxes and they'll get back the land that the white men stole."

The crowd broke out cheering.

I nudged Simba and he quickly explained. "He quoted Nehanda before she was hanged: 'My bones will rise again.' She was a spirit medium …" He stopped mid-sentence as the crowd started screaming "*Pamberi ne Chimurenga, Pasi ne Smith*,"—*Forward with the War of Liberation, Down with Smith*—again and again. The terrs were roaming through the crowd and anyone who wasn't singing got beaten. But I could only see six terrs now. *Where were the other two?* I let my eyes wander over the crowd, then the bush around them, but still no sign of the other two.

Then I heard it. The dreaded metallic *clack* of AK rifles being cocked. Two of them. About five metres behind me.

They spoke in Shona.

"On your feet. Hands above your head!" translated Simba.

Slowly I rose to my feet.

# eleven

Simba was talking to the terrs in Shona. I'd never heard him speak so quickly. But passwords weren't going to help us out of this one; they'd caught us with our guns trained on their comrades. One of them swung the butt of his AK into Simba's cheek and pointed at the *pungwe*. We all headed towards the gathering: Simba, Conway, Young ... but no Bruce.

*Where was he?*

I took a pace forward, and another. Then the thud of two silenced shots behind me. When I turned, both terrs were lying on the ground, with Bruce standing anxiously over them.

Young grabbed one of the bodies. Simba took the other, and they dragged them to our hiding place.

"Now we wait and choose our moment," said Young. "Needs to be soon. It won't be long before they wonder what's happened to these boys."

The chanting of slogans had stopped, the crowd gathered in a circle. A woman was dancing around the fire in the centre. The terrs were chanting as she danced, all of them standing around the fire.

"She's a spirit medium," Simba explained. "They're asking her what they should do."

The spirit began to take possession of her. Her body started to sway and she screamed—a shrill, high-pitched wail. Everyone leaned forward as she delivered the verdict.

"Kill the white snakes," Simba translated.

The crowd grew wild with excitement and the terrorists took up the chant: "Kill the white snakes ... death to the white man ... give us back our land. *Pamberi ne Chimurenga.*"

Young tapped Simba on the shoulder. "Now?" The terrs were still standing around the fire. We could nail them quickly.

"No, let's wait."

Her job done, the spirit medium walked off to loud cheers from the crowd. The terr leader made the crowd shout out the slogans: "*Pamberi ne Chimurenga. Pasi ne Smith.*" Then he turned to harangue the crowd.

I looked at Simba.

"He's asking them to bring forward any traitors or sell-outs. This is where it gets nasty."

The crowd started dancing around an older woman, soon beating her to the ground. Then the terr leader walked over to her, grabbed her by the hair and dragged her to the front of the gathering. As he screamed at her, he swung a heavy boot into her head, sending her flying across the sand like a rag doll.

"Her son's in the Rhodesian Police," Simba explained.

Another terr picked her up, took her to one of the huts on the edge of the clearing, threw her in and bolted the door. Grabbing a jerry-can, he doused petrol over the thatched roof, grabbed a burning branch from the fire and tossed it at the hut. It burst into bright orange flames. *Bloody savages*, I thought as I watched in horror. I couldn't believe what I was seeing.

"Take up firing positions," ordered Young.

I lay forward and pulled the AK into my shoulder.

"Aim."

I took aim at the terr who'd set the hut alight.

"Fire!"

A burst of AK gunfire lit up the night sky.

*Got him*, I mouthed to myself as I saw my terr drop to the ground. Another one fell next to him, but the rest of the group disappeared into the darkness along with the crowd.

"Let's go," called Young. We ran in a half-crouch towards the dead terrs and burning hut.

"Take cover," he ordered as we got to within forty metres or so of the hut. We slid in behind some rocks and watched for any movement. There was no movement, no sound, only the screams of the burning woman inside the hut.

Conway jumped to his feet and sprinted for the hut; fast, his arms and legs pumping.

"Get down, you idiot!" screamed Young, but Conway was already at the hut. He kicked open the door, grabbed the old woman, put her over his shoulder and dashed back to us. Her clothes and her body were wreathed in flames. As he dumped her on the ground all I could smell was burning flesh, burning hair. We grabbed leafy branches and beat out the flames, but it was already too late.

"No more heroics, Conway. You'll get us killed," barked Young angrily. "Straight ahead," he called and we moved forward. It didn't look as if the terrs were hanging around to ambush us. No one had fired at Conway. We'd nailed two of them and wounded at least one other. Quickly we followed Simba and the trail of blood at a fast run through the bush. We had unfinished business. There were still four of them alive, and after what they'd done to the farmer, his son and the old woman in the hut, we wanted all of them.

There was a lot of blood; it looked as if our terr was badly wounded. Finally we found him, near an anthill. He wasn't going anywhere—there were two fresh bullet-holes in his head. They'd obviously decided they didn't want him taken prisoner, nor did they want him leaving a trail for us to follow.

Young spoke with Simba, then called us together.

"With no blood to follow it'll be very difficult tracking these guys at night. We'll camp about half a kay from here, then set off after them at first light."

Simba found us shelter at the foot of a koppie, and we pulled in together. Fascinated by what we'd seen, we were firing questions at him.

"Keep it quiet, boys. Nothing more than a whisper," Young warned.

"So who is this Nehanda they were cheering about?" I asked.

"She was a spirit medium behind the 1896 Shona uprising against the white settlers—they killed 372 of you whites. The terrs called that uprising the first *Chimurenga*, or liberation struggle. They call this war the second *Chimurenga*."

"But talking to the boys on the farm, I thought this Nehanda was still around," cut in Bruce.

"Yes, that's right … they say the spirit of Nehanda lives in the body of a spirit medium today."

"But, Simba … surely you educated blacks don't believe in all this mumbo-jumbo do you?" asked Young.

"Yes, of course we do!" snarled Simba. "My Ndebele tribe has slightly different spiritual beliefs to the Shona, but it's very important to us, too."

"Hey, Bruce, you're a bit of hero," I said, changing the subject quickly. "Thanks, man, we owe you big time."

Bruce smiled smugly. "Oh, it's nothing, don't mention it."

"Where the hell did you go to?" asked Conway.

"I sensed something wasn't right, so I shifted back a bit."

"Bullshit, Thomas, you went for a piss."

"Hell, you're an ungrateful bugger, Conway," Bruce said with a quiet chuckle.

I could see a big smile break out on Conway's face. He put a hand on Bruce's shoulder. "Just joking. Thanks, man."

I was first on sentry duty, and kept guard while the others tried to catch some sleep. Conway came over and sat down next to me. "I'll keep you company. Can't sleep. I'm still too charged up."

Deep in thought, we sat in silence for ages. Finally Conway spoke. "Do you get scared before a contact?"

"Sometimes. Not tonight. And you?"

"Never used to. But now, with a child on the way, I do. I've got to be there for him."

Again we sat without saying anything.

Conway broke the silence. "He left home when I was two."

I looked up at him questioningly.

"My dad. He ran off with his secretary."

"I'm sorry, man."

"After that, mum always had a point to prove. She took over the business, made lots of money, but all she did was work. It wasn't her fault, but she never had time for me. Esther, our maid, used to put me to bed at night."

"Did you ever see him again?"

"No. I wrote to him. All the time. But he never replied. Then, when I was chosen for Craven Week, I wrote to him again. Thought he'd be proud. Again, he didn't reply. So I tracked him down, phoned him ..."

"And?"

"I heard them telling him I was on the line. He wouldn't take the call. Never tried to get hold of him again." There was an uncomfortable silence, before he spoke again. "I've got to be there for my boy."

I put my hand on his shoulder. "You will … he'll be a naughty little bugger, just like his father."

As the sun was rising, we set off. Simba picked up their spoor quickly, and we ran at a fast pace after him.

We kept up our speed for a couple of hours, until Simba brought us to a halt. "That's where they're waiting for us," he said, pointing ahead.

Young called him aside and while the two of them spoke I looked at the area in front of us. There were four large granite koppies, set apart from one another like the four points of a crudely drawn rectangle. Each of them was covered with rocks, trees and thorn scrub, except for the one closest to us on the right, which had a steep granite cliff face that was completely bare. The area between the four koppies was an excellent spot for an ambush, and they could be waiting for us on any of the four.

"Over here," called Young, and we gathered together in a small circle. "We're going up that one." He pointed to the nearest koppie on the left. It was well covered with trees and rocks. "Conway and I will climb the left flank. You three take the right. We've got to be quick—and quiet."

We crawled silently through the thick bush on our hands and knees. At any moment I expected the gooks to open up on us. When we got to the koppie we split up into our two groups and climbed quickly to the top, where we set up an observation post behind a rocky outcrop.

There was no movement anywhere, so we sat and waited. Still

no movement. After ninety minutes or so we went across to meet Young and Conway. They'd seen nothing either.

We waited and watched for another ninety minutes. Young began to grow impatient. "Follow me," he said quietly, and led us through the bush down the side of the mountain.

About halfway down, Simba stopped us. "Shit, over there! Look at that." We stepped up behind him and looked to where he was pointing. In a small cave at the bottom of the far koppie, three limp bodies hung from ropes.

"Hell," said Young. "Looks like our three gooks came to a nasty end. Who would have done that?"

Simba shrugged and, being careful to keep our cover, we made our way to the far koppie. Once we reached the edge of the cave, we sat hidden in the bush for at least thirty minutes, watching and waiting for any sign of life. There was nothing, so we crawled into the cave on our hands and knees. There, swinging slowly from side to side, were the three remaining terrs. All eight of the terrs were now dead. The farmer and his little boy, the old woman who'd been burnt alive at the *pungwe*—they'd all been avenged.

*But who'd killed these three?*

I looked up at the corpses. Their backs were liberally covered with deep wounds, like holes, through which you could see right into the body: the bones, the sinews, the muscles. Blood dripped onto the cave floor. There were no bullet wounds. They must have been beaten to death.

I looked across at the others. Bruce and Conway were staring at the bodies in grim fascination. Young was pacing up and down the cave, looking for clues. Simba was anxious.

"What's up?" I asked him.

"We must go." He waved to the others and they came over.

"Sarge, we're in danger!" he warned Young.

"Why?"

"I'll explain later. Let's go!"

He set off through the bush at a furious pace. We sprinted after him, with Bruce straining at the back to keep up. We ran for a good half-hour before he slowed to a three-quarter pace, and I could hear Bruce heave a sigh of relief. After another two kays Simba pulled us into a thicket of trees. Now all of us were panting.

Simba got straight to the point. "That was Comrade X's work. No doubt about it."

"How do you know?" asked Young.

"It's his trademark torture. The beatings on the back. I've seen it once before on an op in Zambia."

"Shall we call in back-up?"

"Sarge, I think they're long gone. I was worried they were still around. But they're not. If they were, they'd have come after us."

Young radioed for a chopper while the rest of us caught our breath and drank from our water canteens.

"Why would Comrade X kill his own terrs?" asked Bruce, still panting.

"That's exactly the point," explained Simba. "They're not his own terrs. Comrade X is ZIPRA, Nkomo's lot, backed by the Russians. These terrs are ZANLA, Mugabe's men, backed by China. There's often friction between ZIPRA and ZANLA."

"Evil bastard, this Comrade X." Bruce looked perturbed. I think we all were. Even Simba was tense.

As we flew back to Salisbury, the mood began to lighten. Back at barracks we briefed Lieutenant Waters, then later that afternoon he bought us all beers in the Winged Stagger.

"Good job, boys. Eight out of eight."

Ever the stickler for detail, Simba pointed out that we had Comrade X to thank for three of the gooks.

"*Ja*, I get the feeling we haven't heard the last of this Comrade X," said Waters.

I stood up, raised my glass, and spoke directly at Waters. "Sir, I'd like to propose a toast to someone who embodies the spirit of generosity and camaraderie we have in our team. Someone who's not afraid to spend money on his friends. Someone who, this very weekend, is paying for me and my girlfriend to spend two nights at the luxurious Caribbea Bay Hotel. To Mike Conway."

"Bugger off, Carter!" Conway grinned. "You're the cockiest little dwarf I know. And as for you, Thomas," he said, turning to a delighted Bruce: "Ding-dong, ding-dong …"

That was the cue for me and Bruce to start singing. We grabbed our imaginary mikes and sang loudly to the tune of, *If you're going to San Francisco, be sure to wear some flowers in your hair.*

"*If you're going to Ka—ah—riba, be sure to say, that Conway's gonna pay …*"

Simba wasn't going to be left out of it and led us in a lively performance of his dance. Waters helped Bruce and I hammer out a noisy beat on our bar-stool drums, while Young joined Simba stamping on the floor, gesticulating from side to side.

"You're a feeble bunch of goons," Conway told Bruce and I as the dance came to an end. He picked up a bar-stool and tossed it at Bruce. "Catch this, butterfingers!"

Bruce held out his hands and caught the stool as it came flying at him.

"Now, why is it you can catch a bar-stool but not a rugby ball?" laughed Conway.

We stayed for another round of beers. Then another.

Finally I waved my goodbyes and, as I left the bar, I punched the air in delight.

A weekend in Kariba with Laurel! Conway paying!

It couldn't get better than that.

# twelve

"For God's sake, Laurel, that's bullshit. The blacks'll never run this country—they're just not up to it. You know that as well as I do." Neil was shouting as he towered over Laurel.

"Take your head out of the sand, Neil. It's not a matter of if, but when. It's been obvious they're going to take over—ever since Smith's talks with Kissinger and Vorster back in 1976. While it's a great life for us whites, you can't have a minority ruling a majority."

"Oh, nonsense, woman! Look at South Africa," argued Neil, throwing both his hands in the air in frustration.

"I'm telling you, they'll change too." She walked across the deck of the houseboat and gazed out over the lake. "The rest of the world is making us do it first. I mean we're not as big or important as South Africa. But, sure enough, they'll be next." She walked back to the centre of the deck, where she stood looking up at Neil.

"If that's the case, my girl, then why the hell are we fighting this war?"

"Exactly!" said Laurel triumphantly. "There's no point!"

He turned to me, shaking his head in despair. "Hell, Scott, this bird of yours is a bloody communist. You must keep her under control."

I stepped in. It was getting heated and their argument was starting to annoy me. I didn't like it when Laurel criticised our war. "Come on, that's enough arguing for one day. There're more important things to take care of." I handed them both a tequila, a slice of lemon, and a sprinkling of salt.

"How about some tigerfishing?" I asked after they'd downed their tequilas.

Neil laughed, "No, too much like hard work," and put both hands on his huge belly to steady it.

"I'd love to," Laurel smiled, her eyes still an angry blue.

"Sanyati Gorge, please," I shouted out to Tickey, our houseboat driver, cook and guide.

"Okay, *baas*, I take you lots and lots of tiger. Very good place." We cruised through the water, enjoying the wind and bright afternoon sun. I got up to fetch some Castles from the fridge.

"Hey, take a look at that!" said Laurel, pointing at a fish eagle, its powerful black wings fully stretched as it swooped down to catch a bream.

I brought back two beers and sat down next to her on the edge of the boat. "They reckon the tiger is the best pound-for-pound fresh-water fighting fish in the world," I said authoritatively.

"Ah, *boring*," she said, giving me a gentle shove off the side of the boat. Caught off guard, I went tumbling into the water. She dived in over me, giggling, and gave me a hefty slap on the top of my head as she flew past.

"You're gonna pay for that," I laughed, and tore through the water after her. I was conscious of shouting from the boat, probably Tickey, but I didn't care. I was focused on catching Laurel. I got to her quickly and ducked her under the water. She turned to face me, wrapping her legs around my stomach. I liked the feel of her stomach against mine, warm and smooth through the cool water, and I pulled her closer. But she was grabbing my shoulder urgently, pointing to the surface. We rose to the top—Neil and Tickey were motoring straight for us, shouting, "Hippo! Hippo!" I spun around to see a massive hippo about twenty metres away, snorting loudly as its grey, barrel-shaped torso rose above the surface like a giant pig. It opened its mouth, baring an enormous set of teeth.

We swam for the boat where Neil and Tickey were waiting to haul us aboard. Fortunately the hippo wasn't interested in us. Neil and Tickey were shaking their heads, while we sat panting for breath and dangling our legs into the water.

A little further along, Tickey pointed to the bank, where a herd of about ten buffalo grazed. In the distance a couple of elephants were pulling down leaves from a tree. He brought the boat to a stop and cut the engine.

"This very good spot, *baas* ... very good for tiger."

I turned to Laurel. "Competition time! Are you on?"

"You're on!"

Tickey helped us bait our lines, and soon they were in the water. Almost immediately, a tiger hit her line. She struck, successfully, her rod bent.

I shouted needless advice: "Play with it! Let it run! Keep the tension! Feed it more line!" The tiger leapt from the water, fighting furiously, its orange fins and black-and-silver scales glinting impressively in the late afternoon sun. Laurel calmly let it run, giving it as much line as it needed. Eventually she landed a six-kilo tiger on the boat.

"Great stuff, Laurel," I smiled, aiming my camera.

"Take a look at that," I shouted, proudly pulling my first from the water soon afterwards. "And the winner will be ... Scott Carter."

"We'll see about that," she grinned as another tiger took her bait. The afternoon flew by.

As the light began to fade, I turned to Laurel, "Are you going to accept defeat graciously?"

"Not a chance. I've won." She pointed to her keep-net packed with tigerfish.

"No ways—let Tickey be the judge."

I turned to him: "Look, Tickey, these are my fish, and these are Laurel's ... who's the winner? And remember who pays your tip!"

But Tickey was above bribery. "*Eh, baas*, it's the *medem* ... she is the winner."

I laughed, shaking my head at the injustice of the decision. But I accepted the result and my penalty for losing: a shot of tequila, followed by a bottle of Castle Lager, which I downed in four deep gulps. I took Laurel by the hand and we watched as the sun edged its way down over Matusadona, casting a red glow over the horizon. A pair of young bull elephants were sparring on the bank.

But Neil was getting bored. He shouted out from the top deck, "Laurel, Karen tells me you want to teach the *munts*. You're off your head, you'll never educate those *zots*."

Laurel's eyes lit up.

"Just pretend he's not there," shouted out Karen. She'd been Laurel's friend for years, and we were her guests on the boat.

But she couldn't, and went marching up to the top. "Yes, Neil, not only am I going to be teaching the Africans, but I'm also going to be paying for their education."

"Oh, and how the hell are you planning to do that?"

I smiled. She always rose to the bait. "He's only teasing you, Laurel. Just ignore him." But that was impossible for her.

"All right, let's settle this feud over a beer," I suggested. "A *down-down*. Winner of the *down-down* wins the argument. Are you on, Neil?"

"I'll do it."

"Laurel?"

"Why not?" She was smiling now.

"On your marks, get set, *go!*" I called. And they were off. Within seconds, Laurel had an empty beer glass on her head and was casually waiting for Neil to finish. He finished a good two seconds behind her, and we let him have it.

"What kind of a man are you, Neil?" I teased. "I mean—letting a girl hammer you like that." He didn't say anything, and after Tickey's delicious fresh-baked bream and boiled potatoes, he turned in for the night.

Laurel and I celebrated with a series of tequilas, and danced with Karen late into the night to the Beatles. When Karen said goodnight, it spurred Laurel into action.

"Skinny-dip! Let's go!" She ran and dived from the top deck straight into the dark, deep water below.

"I'm coming!" And I sprinted after her. But I lost my balance, and instead of a dive ended up doing a belly-flop, much to her delight.

Tickey came onto the deck and shook his head gravely, before turning back to his room. "*Aiee*, no, no … very dangerous … crocs, hippos. Very dangerous."

But Laurel was undeterred. She climbed back onto the boat, downed another tequila, and dived gracefully into the lake. This time I watched, clapping, from the top deck.

"Okay, one for the road," I insisted, grabbing two more beers from the fridge. We sat on the deck chatting and laughing, drinking our beers. This was definitely my last drink for the night. The tequilas were getting to me and my head was starting to spin. I looked across at Laurel, her taut calves and thighs glistening in the dim light of the top deck. Her lips curled into a smile as I pulled her towards me. She pushed back and leapt to her feet.

"Oh no ... I'm sorry ..." she said, and rushed to the side of the boat. It all came flying out into the lake: her dinner, the beer, the tequila. Lots of tequila.

"I'm terribly sorry, this is so embarrassing." Her head was still hanging miserably over the side. It stayed there for most of the night.

We must have looked a sorry sight as we made our way back to the Caribbea Bay boathouse the next morning. I was sitting on the top deck, head buried between my knees, when Neil joined me.

"When are you guys going back, Neil?"

"I'm putting Karen on the plane tomorrow and I'll drive back the day after."

"Why don't you drive back together?"

"It's safer to fly. The road to Salisbury is dangerous. Landmines, ambushes ... you name it."

I got up to make myself a coffee. Hell, my head hurt.

Back on shore, before we checked into our hotel room and slept, I booked Laurel on the Air Rhodesia flight the next day.

Laurel was still fast asleep when I woke up. I opened the curtains, took a step onto the balcony, and looked out over the bare *Kariba* trees against the glorious orange-and-black skyline as the sun made its way slowly down. It was a beautiful Rhodesian spring evening; the air warm, but not too hot. Down at the boathouse the fishing boats were coming in, laden with bream and tigerfish. An elderly couple walked hand in hand along the shore, barefoot on the light-brown sand. And almost everywhere I looked was the gorgeous pink of the bougainvillea. I savoured the moment. Holding a big glass of water to Laurel's lips, I gently shook her awake.

"Oh, I feel terrible," she complained. "My head is aching." She placed her hands on either side of her head. "I'm so sorry about last night."

I put my finger on her lips. "Don't say sorry. We had a fantastic time. Listen, tonight's our last night. Have a shower. We've got some serious dancing to do."

Laurel was such a bundle of sudden energy that within minutes she'd forgotten about her hangover, as together we strode into the Caribbea Bay disco. Immediately she brightened up the dance floor with her lively rock-and-roll.

When we took our first break, she slid her hand into mine. "These last few days have been very special."

As if on cue, Kansas' *Dust in the Wind* started playing, and I led her back on to the dance floor. Neither of us spoke as we swayed gently to the music. I held her close, and as I nestled my head into her hair I caught the faint scent of warm honey. It was my favourite song, but I didn't wait for the end. I took her hand and led her from the dance floor, over the lawn and back to our room.

As we entered the breakfast room the following morning, Laurel steered me to the far corner. "Away from him," she pleaded, pointing across at where Neil was sitting.

I smiled. "Talking about Neil, what's worse than a male chauvinist pig?"

"I don't know. What?"

"A woman who won't do what she's told."

"Ha, ha, ha," she said cynically. Then she burst out laughing; we both did. It was our last day, and we made it a good one. Bream fishing in the morning, then drinks around the pool in the glorious spring sunshine.

We were both quiet when I dropped her at the airport later that afternoon.

"Scott Carter, thank you so much for the most incredible four days of my life. I love you." She hugged me tightly.

I wanted to tell her how happy I was. How much I adored her … well … loved her, I suppose. But it would have sounded silly. We were only kids. So I picked her up and wrapped my arms around her. "Can't wait to see you in Salisbury!"

She turned and walked across the runway, chatting all the way to Karen. I was still waving when she boarded the Viscount.

I shouted over to Neil, "See you in the casino!" and drove back to the hotel, singing *Dust in the Wind* all the way back, and in the shower. It'd stuck in my head from last night.

Tonight was going to be my lucky night. So I set myself a limit of a hundred dollars—almost a month's salary—and hit the roulette wheel first. Five dollars a bet.

*Black 29!* The first throw. I'd won a hundred and sixty-five dollars. I leapt up and yelled with delight, much to the amusement of the onlookers, including Neil, who'd just arrived.

I greeted him with a round of Castles and tequilas. "Tonight's gonna be huge!"

He was a bit tentative at first, so I thought I'd get him warmed up. "Come on, what's your lucky number?"

He looked at me blankly.

"Okay, when's your birthday?"

"Today."

"What? Fantastic! The third of September. Now we win big." I put fifty dollars of chips on three.

We roared with disappointment when it didn't come up, and ordered another round of tequilas. Neil was well into the swing of it, and soon we were tunelessly belting out *Dust in the Wind*.

Finally the manager came over and politely asked us not to sing any more. We moved on to the blackjack table.

"Hey, Scott, I'm going to call Karen from the room. I'll be right back," promised Neil. He was gone for ages, and I had a miserable run on the blackjack table while he was away. Eventually I was down to my last ten dollars of chips. *The hell with it*, I thought. I'll put it all on Neil's lucky three. So I loaded it all onto three and waited. As the croupier spun the wheel I saw Neil come walking in through the casino door. I shouted over to him, "Hey, Neil! It's gonna be your lucky three."

But he didn't look up as he approached me.

*Black ten!*

*Damn!* I cursed silently, shaking my head at my own stupidity as I got up to greet Neil.

"Hey … Neil … you look like you've seen a ghost, man! What's up?"

"The Viscount's missing."

"What do you mean, missing?"

"Missing. Disappeared!"

## thirteen

They didn't find the plane that night. I didn't sleep at all, waiting and hoping for word of Laurel. In the morning the papers and radio carried news of the missing plane, but nothing more. I went with Neil to the Kariba Police Station and waited for reports. By mid-morning the police were certain there'd been a crash. By midday we heard the plane'd been found. We dared to hope. When word came through that there were survivors, our hopes rose.

I sat in silence outside the briefing office. Neil was next to me, sweating heavily, as we stared at the door. Finally it opened and I walked in quickly.

"Laurel Bevan," I told the young policeman behind the desk. Nervously he reached across and picked up a piece of paper.

"Laurel Bevan," he repeated.

"Yes, L-A-U-R-E-L- B-E-V-A-N," I spelled it out for him.

Then he opened his top drawer and pulled out a pair of black-rimmed glasses. I could see his hands were shaking as he put them on. He must have been looking at the list of survivors. Her name had to be there. *Please God*, I prayed. I could feel her tight up against me as we drifted across the dance floor to *Dust in the Wind*. *Please God*, she's too young to die.

The policeman sneezed. "Excuse me," he said politely as he turned his head away.

"Fergodsake, man, is she alive?"

He turned back. "My apologies." Then he looked down again at the list of names in front of him. "I'm afraid she didn't make it, sir."

"That can't be right. I was with her yesterday."

"Sorry, sir—I'm so sorry," he said softly. He was only a young fellow, my age.

I walked out in a daze. *How could Laurel be dead?* It was impossible. She'd too much life in her. I'd never see her again. I drove back to the hotel.

First I called her mum. Perhaps Laurel would answer, perhaps this had all been a horrible dream. But her mum picked up the phone. She told me she knew already, and I could sense she didn't want to talk. I didn't blame her—after all, I had put Laurel on that plane. It was my decision.

Then I called home. "Mum, Laurel was on the Viscount." My voice was cracking.

"Oh, my God … I'm so sorry, son. Come home as soon as you can."

I packed my belongings and drove off in the hired car. When I arrived in Salisbury late that night, I checked into the Meikles Hotel and slept. A deep, troubled sleep, right through the night.

When I woke late the next morning I buried my head in my pillow and shouted out loud, "It's only a dream … it's only a dream!" Then rushed to the door. Outside was a copy of the day's *Herald*. Splashed all over the front page were stories of the Viscount. It wasn't a dream.

I drove to barracks. I needed to know what happened.

At the gates I bumped into Conway who put his arms around me and hugged me. "Carter, I heard about Laurel. Hell, I'm sorry man."

"Thanks, Conway." *I could still see Laurel and Conway lining up for the down-down, her blue eyes bright with excitement.*

"Hey, Waters was looking for you."

Waters was on the parade ground. He put his hand on my shoulder, "I'm sorry, Carter. How're you feeling?"

"Fine, sir."

"Do you need some time off?"

"No, sir, that's the last thing I need. I just want to keep going."

"Good. That's what I wanted to hear. I've got an exciting op for you. One that you'll want to be on—there's briefing early afternoon. But first you need a full update on the Viscount business. Speak to Thomas."

I found Bruce in the canteen and we walked back to his room.

"Are you okay, Scott?"

"No, it's terrible; I can't stop thinking about her."

"Hell, I'm sorry, man." He put his arm around my shoulder as we walked.

"How come you know all about the Viscount, Bruce?"

"You'll see why just now."

I sat down on his bed as he looked at me gravely. "Scott, this is going to be really difficult for both of us." He took in a deep breath, got to his feet and started speaking. "It took off from Kariba airport shortly after five o'clock. Then five minutes out of Kariba it got nailed. By this." He passed me a photo of a Soviet-made SAM-7 heat-seeking missile. "Shoulder-fired by ZIPRA gooks. The Viscount was an old civilian plane. It had no chance. A National Parks plane heard the Mayday call."

"Hell, those poor people," I murmured. *Laurel would've seen it all from her seat at the back of the plane. I couldn't bear to think about how she must have felt as the plane plunged from the sky.*

Bruce buried his head in his hands and sat down on the bed next to me. "Yes, the passengers were ... well, you can imagine the scene. Anyway, the pilot, Captain Hood, was fantastic. He kept the plane more or less under control and aimed its nose at a cotton field in the Whamira Hills, about eighty kays west of Karoi, in the Urungwe TTL. As they came in for landing he kept his cool and told the passengers to brace themselves for impact. It looked like it was going to be a perfect landing. But it hit a ditch in the centre of the field, and the plane disintegrated ... flames everywhere."

Bruce paused as I took in the full horror of what he was saying.

"Now, Laurel was sitting at the back, right?"

"*Ja*, right at the back. Why?"

"Well, the survivors were all sitting at the back."

"You mean she could still be alive?" I got to my feet.

"No, I'm sorry, man. She's dead." He looked down at a photo on his desk and then quickly tried to hide it. I leaned over the desk and grabbed it. There was no mistaking; it was Laurel.

"But ... these are bullet wounds!"

"I'm afraid so. Can I keep going?"

"No, Bruce, tell me what happened to her!" I had the photo in one hand and I paced up and down, his small room suddenly feeling tiny.

"It's important you get the full story first. Please, it'll only take a few minutes." I nodded, reluctant as he continued.

"Eighteen of the fifty-six people on board survived."

"Hold on, there were only eight survivors—right?"

"No, eighteen survived the crash."

"And Laurel was one of them?"

"Yes, she was."

I slowly sat down again.

"Straight after the crash-landing, two of the men carried the other survivors to a spot about seventy-five metres from the plane, in case it exploded. Then a group of five went to find water from a nearby village. They brought the first lot of water back to the survivors. On their way back with the second lot, they heard voices. African voices. ZIPRA."

"Ah … no!" I was horrified. I could guess what was coming.

"*Ja*, apparently when the gooks first arrived they were friendly, and promised help and water. They got the survivors who could walk to carry those who couldn't. The passengers were chuffed, and were even thanking them." Bruce stopped, got to his feet and stared out the window. He turned his head to face me. "Then one of the terrs called out, 'You have taken our land!' They opened up with their AKs … mowed them down, women, children … the bastards."

"And Laurel was one of those they shot?" I buried my head in my hands.

"Yes, I'm sorry." He stopped, sat down next to me, put his arm around my shoulder and we sat in silence for several minutes.

"Please keep going."

"So, three of those thirteen passengers managed to escape. They and the group of five who fetched the water managed to hide from the gooks all night. They were rescued when our troops arrived the next morning."

I shook my head. What a nightmare for them … for Laurel.

*Hell, I hoped she'd gone quickly, with no pain.*

Bruce stood up, grabbed some photos from his desk. "Do you want to see these? They're bad."

I nodded without looking up, and he showed me the pictures of the passengers who'd died in the crash. Burnt, crushed bodies, wrapped untidily together in blood and dirt. And the charred bodies of children.

I saw him pick up a photo and shuffle it to the back of the pile.

"Let me see that," I said firmly. He reluctantly handed over a shot of the ten people who'd been gunned down. They were each about ten to fifteen metres apart, probably scattering as the terrorists opened fire.

I recognised the body of Karen, lying close to Laurel. *I wondered if Laurel had found any comfort in being near Karen at the end.*

"Savages," I muttered.

"Well, we're fairly certain who was in charge of this. The head gook who ordered the plane shot down and personally supervised the murders."

"Who?"

"Comrade X."

Young ushered Bruce, Conway, Dixon and me into the briefing room where Waters was waiting.

"We've been following the Viscount incident very closely and we're absolutely certain Comrade X is responsible. Every single Rhodesian alive wants revenge for this atrocity. The good news is that I've been asked to get together a team of six."

Waters stood up and looked at each of us in turn. "This is the team." He turned to me. "Carter, we're all grieving with you. But you're going to have to prove to me that you're in good shape mentally for this op. Otherwise you're not going. Okay?"

"I'm fine, sir," I said quickly.

"X spends a lot of time in the bush in Rhodesia, but he does have a permanent base in Zambia. Special Branch have been trying to track it down for ages." He stopped. "Well ... they've just had a breakthrough."

Waters started pacing the floor. "Lads, obviously you don't mention this to anyone outside this group—it's top secret, but the Scouts caught Moses Maduma two weeks ago, one of the senior ZIPRA intelligence officers. It's probably our best capture in the war so far. He's told us everything," he broke into a big grin, "including where Comrade X is based—not far from the Zambian border, a secret spot two kays from Kavalamanja camp, near Feira on the Mozambique-Zambia-Rhodesia border."

"Hell, that's a result." Young couldn't hide his excitement.

"Yes ... he's given us precise locstat details. Exactly where X is based, numbers, sentries ... everything."

He pointed at Dixon sitting in the front. "This is the only living member of the Rhodesian army who's ever seen X. So he and Simba, a tracker whom you all know, will be doing a recce of the camp next week. We need to confirm everything Maduma told us is true. Then ..." he pointed to the rest of us, "there's a meeting planned with some Russian bigwigs at the camp in fifteen days. X will be there, guaranteed. We'll be going in as a hit-team ... in and out, no fuss. We don't lay a finger on any of the Russians. The only one to nail is X."

He sat down next to us, leant forward and lowered his tone. "Lads, this is gonna be one of the most important operations of the war. If we nail X, it'll strike a huge blow for us—both Mugabe's and Nkomo's lot idolise him."

The memorial service for the Viscount passengers was held at

the Anglican Cathedral of St Mary and All Saints. Dad wanted
to come but he had a cattle sale on, so I persuaded him not to
miss the sale. Mum and Kathy sat on either side of me, Kathy
holding my hand supportively through the service. Bruce and
Simba were there in uniform. So was Conway, and next to him,
his girlfriend, Claire.

The Anglican Dean of Salisbury led the service. A tall, bearded
man, he cut an impressive figure in his long, flowing white robes.
His sermon was powerful and emotional. In it I remember him
questioning the lack of condemnation from the outside world:
"Are we deafened with the voice of protest from nations which call
themselves 'civilised'? One listens, and the silence is deafening."
As we walked out of the cathedral at the end of the service, the
Dean's words kept ringing in my head. "The ghastliness of this
ill-fated flight from Kariba will be burned upon our memories for
years to come."

Outside the church a group of demonstrators had gathered.
One held up a message for Ian Smith, "PM Smith: Give Nkomo
a message next time you meet him secretly: 'Go to hell, you
murdering bastard.'" The mood in the country was a mixture of
numbed disbelief, anger and outrage, particularly when Joshua
Nkomo appeared on a BBC interview and proudly claimed credit
for the disaster.

"Where to now?" asked Mum. I looked around the church for
Laurel's mother, but couldn't find her. I don't think she wanted
to see me, anyway.

"Scott, can we chat?" It was Conway.

I asked Mum to wait as I walked through the church gardens
with Conway and Claire.

"We're both really sorry about what happened to Laurel."

I looked at Conway, surprised. His tone was compassionate.

Claire spoke. "We were both very fond of her. She was a special girl."

Conway put his hand on my shoulder, "If there's anything we can do to help, anything at all, please let us know."

"Thanks, Conway, you're a good friend." I shook his hand firmly, kissed Claire on the cheek and turned back to find Mum.

Simba was leaving the church. "Thanks for coming, Simba," I called out, "and good luck for the recce in Zambia."

Still dazed, I drove home with Mum for the weekend.

Home was too peaceful. In the afternoon I sat with a book under the mango tree and tried to read, but I never got past the first page. *How could any human being, no matter how evil, shoot down a plane packed with women and children? Was she scared as the plane crashed from the sky? Was she thinking of me?*

The sound of crashing glass jolted me from my thoughts.

"Scott, Peter, quick!" Mum was calling from the front lawn. Shoko was standing on the veranda. A window pane lay shattered around him, and he was quivering in shock. Bits of glass clung to him, with splashes of blood all over his beautiful grey coat.

"He wanted to get to the dogs and came right through the window," Mum explained. "But I can't get near him."

I approached him with my hand out and comforted his muzzle. "Sorry, my boy, sorry, Shoko." Once we'd cleaned and de-glassed him, I gave him his favourite horse cubes as a treat. Gradually he started to calm down.

"Remember when we brought him home?"

Mum smiled, "Yes, such a cute little buck."

Dad had walked onto the lawn and stood next to us. "At some point in the future we're gonna have to let him back into the wild. They're not meant to be pets."

"Not now, darling!" Mum gave Dad a look.

"Yes, Mary, I said some time in the future."

They were obviously worried about upsetting me. I didn't know if I could handle losing him right now.

I sat with Shoko on the veranda for hours, gently stroking him and whispering in his ear.

Later that afternoon, I snuck out while the dogs weren't looking. Shoko was excited. His own private walk. I hadn't done this with him in years. First we headed for the Baboon Pool. The brilliant red leaves of the msasas were always an eye-puller in spring. And the game. Guinea fowl, pheasant, duiker, impala and stembok, were all out in force. Shoko would dart into the bush and then come galloping back towards me, making sure I was still there. I stopped at the tree where we'd found him: a big mountain acacia also sporting impressive red spring leaves. He'd been so small. Simba'd picked him up first. I did a quick detour to pass the spot where we'd buried Shoko's mother. But he was unenthused by my trip down memory lane and pranced around impatiently, pushing a wet nose into my back.

When we arrived at the Baboon Pool I sat at the water's edge, stroking his forehead. "Shoko, my boy, where do you want to live?" He butted me on the arm affectionately and I carried on stroking him. "Come on, boy, you've got to let me know."

He waded into the water, trying to tempt me in for a swim. *Laurel had loved the Baboon Pool. The last time we'd come here together, she'd swum. If only I'd stopped her from getting on that plane, let her drive back with me instead ...*

*Hell, it's nice at this time of year,* I thought, trying to force Laurel from my mind. The surface of the Baboon Pool was a hazy red from the reflection of the msasas. Above us on the rocks were Grey and the other baboons, carrying on with their afternoon activities—grooming each other, scratching their bottoms as though we weren't there. We made our way home as the sun was setting. Shoko grew increasingly frustrated at my slow pace, and continued trying to chivvy me along. In the distance I could see a massive duiker. No ... I looked closer ... the light was fading fast. It was a kudu, an adult female. I looked at Shoko to see what he would do. To him, kudus were unfamiliar animals, not like dogs. But today he wasn't concerned. He snorted at me and went galloping towards the female. She waited for him to get near, and then the two of them went running off together, through the msasas and over the koppie. Out of sight.

I leant back against a *mahobohobo* tree and waited so Shoko could find me when he got back. Five minutes passed: no Shoko. I always got uneasy when Shoko went off on his own. Stray dogs, even wild dogs, could get him. The sun had almost completely disappeared behind the koppies when I heard a noise to my left.

"Jeez, man, Shoko. I was worried about you. Let's get home quickly."

Shoko was really pleased with himself, excited, like a kid who'd found a new friend. When we got home, I fed him horse cubes, which he gobbled up.

"Thanks, Shoko. I asked you to tell me, and you did." After he'd eaten I held my face close to his, like I used to when he was a baby. But he grew bored and ran off to play with the dogs. I went inside for dinner. Anna had cooked my favourite: peri-peri chicken.

I tucked into the food. "Dad, what did you have in mind for releasing Shoko? I'm a bit worried he won't be able to handle the bush."

"I think we may be able to rehabilitate him. But not now. There's no rush. Sometime next year will be fine. Jim Brook's place at Mopane Park near Gwelo will be perfect. Drive out and meet Jim on your next R&R ... you'll like him."

I drove out the next day and found Jim in the lion pens. He also ran a lion rehabilitation programme. "Hi, Jim ... nice to meet you. I'm Scott Carter." He held out his right hand and shook mine firmly. I noticed his left hand was missing. Dad told me later that it'd been bitten off by one of his lions.

"Jim, I've got an adult kudu that I want to release into the wild. He won't last a day in the bush now. Can you rehabilitate him?"

"Sure. This park over here." He pointed at a strip of bush to my left, then saw my anxious look. "Don't worry, I'll keep him well clear of the lions. It's about three hundred acres. All game-fenced. He'll get used to the other animals here and become aware of his predators. Then, when he's ready, we can release him into the wider park. It's a wildlife park, also game-fenced, no poachers or snares, but he'll obviously have to deal with the predators. You know ... the big cats, mainly lions and leopards."

"How will you decide when he's ready for the big park?"

"I've been doing this for years. I'll know."

I returned to the bakkie, confident I would be leaving Shoko in capable hands, then climbed in and started the engine.

Jim spoke through the open window. "Oh, and one more thing—once we take him, it's better that you don't come back to see him. He needs a complete break."

"Okay, Jim. Hell, I'm gonna miss the bugger. When can you take him?"

"Sooner the better. Anytime in the next month."

I caught the train back to Salisbury at the end of the weekend, then a cab to barracks.

Bruce was in his room, rifling through his kit. "Scott, good to see you. Hey, I've got some great news. Take a seat," he pointed at the bed. "We're leaving for an op tomorrow."

"Good," I replied. The busier I was, the less time I had to think about Laurel. "Where to?"

"I spoke to one of the officers this morning. They've been doing drills over the past few days. Where we're going is confidential. We haven't been officially briefed yet. You won't say anything, right?"

"Of course I won't, Bruce … now, where are we going?"

He put his hand on my shoulder and looked directly into my eyes. "If you could make a wish to take out two people in this world, who would they be?"

I gave him a strange look.

"No, seriously, Scott … who?"

"Well, it'd be the two people responsible for Laurel's death: Comrade X and Joshua Nkomo."

He broke into a big grin. "Put it there," he said, holding out his hand.

I hesitated. "You mean we're going after Nkomo tomorrow?"

"Damn right we are!"

## fourteen

Forty-two of us drove to Kariba in seven Sabre Land Rovers. On the way we stopped in Karoi to get a drink and a bite to eat. I looked around me at the passers-by as I ate my meat pie on the side of the road. If only they knew we were going to Lusaka to nail Nkomo—next to Mugabe, the most hated man in white Rhodesia. A little boy carrying a pellet gun walked past.

"Hey, would you mind teaching my mate Thomas over there how to shoot?" Conway called out to the boy.

"That's what I like about you, Conway," said Bruce.

"What?"

"Absolutely nothing!"

I loved the banter, although since Laurel's death I noticed the others had toned down somewhat.

About five kays from Kariba airport we turned off to Charara and drove to the secluded Selous Scouts camp at Wafa Wafa. Away from prying eyes, the op was top secret. As we drove into the camp I turned to Conway and Bruce. "This is where the Selous Scouts recruits have to eat rotten baboon meat on their selection course."

Bruce screwed up his face and spat out the back of the truck. "*Ja*, I'm glad we didn't have to do that."

While we unloaded our kit from the Sabres, I took a quick look around me. The camp was basic: no barracks, just a few tents and grass huts. But it was beautiful … wild, remote and with stunning views over Lake Kariba. Soon after unloading, they assembled us into groups for the briefing. Bruce and I were together, but Conway was in a different group.

"This is the A team—the elite," claimed Conway, pointing at his new group. "At last I've been separated from you jokers."

Our group was called into the ops tent after Conway's.

Major Curtis took care of the briefing. "As you probably know by now, we're going to Lusaka. Our target is Joshua Nkomo. Why?" He paused and looked at each of us before continuing, "Two reasons. Firstly, the bastard shot down the Viscount. Secondly, he is now a serious threat. Our recent capture of Moses Maduma from ZIPRA Intelligence has revealed Nkomo is planning a major military offensive. To date, Nkomo has only had a few thousand terrs in the country. Mugabe's ZANLA terrs have been the major threat. But Nkomo has strong support from the Soviets, and he's planning a conventional military op against us."

"Sir, surely he's not strong enough to take us on in a conventional battle?" asked Lieutenant Waters standing at the front.

"Well, he's got twenty thousand regulars in Zambia now. With Soviet backing, he has a very strong army. His plan is to seize control of airports at Kariba, Vic Falls, Wankie and Salisbury using armoured columns. As soon as they've got control of the Wankie and Kariba airports they'll fly in conventional troops in Libyan transport planes. Salisbury would be taken within twenty-four hours."

"Hell," said Waters, a worried look on his face.

"And so confident is this fat bastard that he's already training immigration, customs and police officers in Zambia to be ready for when he takes over."

We stood there in silence, staring at Major Curtis. This was amazing stuff he was telling us. If I helped nail Nkomo, not only would I be getting revenge for the Viscount and Laurel, but I'd also be helping prevent a large-scale military invasion.

"Any questions?" asked Curtis. He looked around again, then carried on. "There'll be forty-two of us going, in seven of our Sabre Land Rovers. Each Land Rover will be painted green to match the colours of the Zambian army vehicles. The first and last vehicles will be wearing Zambian number plates. A commercial ferry will drop us near Siavonga on the Zambian side. Six men will be there to secure the landing spot and they'll be there to ensure your return trip is safe. From Siavonga we drive for about eight hours, through Kafue River Bridge, where you can expect trouble, straight through to Lusaka."

*It can't be as simple as that*, I thought. Driving unchallenged through a country with whom we were effectively at war.

"In Lusaka, you have three targets," Major Curtis continued. He got to his feet, walked to the opening of the tent, then back to where we were grouped.

"The first and most important target is Nkomo's house. Sixteen of you will be involved in that raid. Next is the Liberation Centre, which includes the offices of ZIPRA, the South African ANC and SWAPO, the South West Africa People's Organisation. The third and final target is ZIPRA's main armoury to the west of Lusaka."

"Any more questions?" We shook our heads. "Grab a quick bite to eat, then I want you to split up into your smaller groups for a detailed briefing." He stopped and looked intently at us. "We have a CIO agent based in Lusaka who has Nkomo's house under surveillance. When he gives the signal that Nkomo is back home, we go in immediately. Good luck!"

Waters approached Bruce and me. "Boys, this is Sergeant Grobler. The four of us are going to be working together. Meet back here in twenty minutes."

Bruce and I grabbed a plate of food and sat down next to Conway.

"I can't wait to find out which target we're getting," said Bruce.

"You boys will be on the armoury raid. The elite group, my lot, will be going after Nkomo," announced Conway authoritatively.

"Have you been told already?" I asked.

"No, but it's obvious I'll be getting the important role," he said with a smile.

"*Ja*, whichever role we get, this is gonna be the op of a lifetime," added Bruce as we quickly wolfed down our food.

I got to my feet. "Good luck, Conway. Hope your role's a good one." I turned to Bruce. "Let's go."

Waters and Sergeant Grobler were both sitting outside the ops tent.

"Which team are we on, sir?" I couldn't wait to find out.

He looked at me, then at the others, then back at me. "The four of us have been chosen to take out the fat man."

"You mean Nkomo, sir?" He nodded, and I punched Bruce's shoulder in delight. Bruce broke into a huge grin and looked around for Conway.

"Carter, we've discussed this before … I'm assuming you're not carrying any mental baggage after the Viscount."

"I'm fine, sir. Won't let you down, I promise, sir."

It was incredible news. I was on the team chosen to take out the man responsible for Laurel's death. Waters produced maps showing Nkomo's house and the important sites in the vicinity. He pointed out the Zambian Army base at Arakan, two kays from the house. We didn't know how the Zambians would react to the attack. It was a risk.

He showed us President Kaunda's State House on the other side of President's Lane. The armed state guard posed a threat, particularly as we were to launch our attack from President's Lane.

Then he produced detailed photos and maps showing Nkomo's colonial bungalow, which was surrounded by a green hessian screen. He also showed us the guard house, the guard post and the location of the vehicles.

After our briefing we went looking for Conway, who was throwing stones at a mahogany tree and cursing.

"Hey, Conway, what'd you get?" Bruce shouted out. He was dying to tell Conway we'd been chosen for the Nkomo hit.

"Third prize—the bloody armoury. What about you guys?"

"Just guess."

"No, what'd you get?"

"Come on, guess."

"The hell with your silly games, Thomas. Carter, what'd you get?"

"First prize," I answered.

"So you're doing the raid on his house?"

"No, even better than that. We're in the group of four going into his bedroom to kill him."

Conway was at a loss for words and stood staring at me, open-mouthed. "I get the armoury and you bastards get the hit on Nkomo. How did you manage that?" He scratched his head, then looked at me. "I know how you did it. One of you clowns is nailing Waters' daughter." He turned to Bruce. "And after your hopeless effort with that Danish bird, it can't be you."

Bruce hit right back. "They probably heard about your performance in the *down-down*."

Conway glared at him and immediately Bruce turned to me. "Hey … sorry, Scott, didn't mean to mention that."

This was my chance to set them straight and I took it. "Fergodsake, stop worrying about what you say in front of me."

They both looked away.

Finally Conway broke into a relieved grin.

"Listen, Carter, the reason why I'm upset about not being on the Nkomo raid is that I want to nail him for you. What happened to Laurel has hit us hard. She was lovely; so much energy. Only a few months ago we were all together in the Falls."

"Thanks, Conway, I appreciate that."

"And the other reason I'm pissed off I'm not on the Nkomo raid is because you boys *are*, and how an opinionated little dwarf and a blind penguin could be chosen ahead of me is beyond comprehension."

We all laughed and went back to our groups for rehearsals. Over the next few days, as we waited for the go-ahead from our CIO agent in Lusaka, the vehicles were painted, the kit and explosives were prepared and our drills were rehearsed. Over and over again. Waters was typically meticulous and after three days I felt I knew Nkomo's house better than my family home in Selukwe. At one of the briefings, Waters announced that two members of the Selous Scouts would be joining us on the raid. "One of them's a black guy who can speak the local Zambian dialects," he explained. "He'll do the talking, and he'll be dressed in a Zambian army captain's uniform. The other one will be our guide. He's a senior white guy, a captain, and was involved in an unsuccessful earlier attempt by the Scouts to take out Nkomo."

That afternoon the signal came through. Our agent in Lusaka had seen Nkomo going into his house. As I put on my kit—*Black is Beautiful* cream on my face, my Rhodesian Army combat-camouflage uniform and regular NATO-pattern helmet—I thought of Laurel. She'd have been proud of me. I'd been chosen to take out Nkomo. It didn't get much bigger than that.

We boarded the commercial ferry and, as the sun made its way down in a bright orange ball over the lake, we pulled up on the Zambian side.

"What time is the attack on Nkomo's house?" asked Conway as we climbed off the ferry.

"Eight hours from now: oh-two-hundred," I told him.

"Good luck, boys." Conway shook my hand, then Bruce's, and jumped into his Sabre.

Bruce, a medic, Grobler and I climbed into our Sabre, after Waters. In addition to our AK-47 rifles, our vehicle had an RPG-7 rocket-launcher and two machine guns, each with fifteen hundred rounds.

We headed off along the dirt road. After a couple of hours Waters briefed us that Zambian police messages had been intercepted—they'd seen our ferry. Immediately our troops on the Rhodesian side launched a diversionary attack on a fishing camp to make the Zambians believe this was our main target. It worked.

"Sir, a problem with the vehicle behind us," Bruce called out to Waters as Conway's Sabre ground to a halt.

Everyone crowded round the open bonnet of the Sabre offering mechanical suggestions, but nothing worked. It was dead.

Major Curtis checked his watch, shaking his head. "Sorry, boys. Got to get moving, we're already late."

"Shall we get into those?" asked Conway, pointing at the other Sabres.

"I'm afraid there's no room. Sorry, we can't risk overloading the other vehicles. We'll pick you up on the way back." He turned and headed back to his vehicle.

I tapped Conway on the shoulder as we left. "Sorry, man." He was furious.

After we'd climbed aboard our Sabre, Bruce raised his hand to give Conway a mocking wave.

I stopped him. "No, Bruce, don't. The poor bugger's gutted."

We continued along the dirt road. By the time we got off the dirt track onto the main tar road we were over an hour behind schedule. The later we were, the less chance we had of making our escape while it was still dark.

My grip tightened on my AK-47 as we drew near the Kafue River Bridge. A large Zambian military presence was expected. But the bridge was deserted; tonight was going to be our lucky night. We drove on through Kafue town into Lusaka, arriving in the outskirts of Lusaka at zero-two-forty. Waters briefed us that the attack on the armoury had been cancelled. Six of the team of twelve, including Conway, had been left behind. The spare armoury vehicle would now provide back-up at Nkomo's house.

I nudged Bruce as we drove through Lusaka, making sure to keep within the speed limit and stop at each red traffic light. "It's amazing these guys don't seem to notice us," I whispered. "I would have expected a convoy of six vehicles, armed to the teeth, driving through the middle of Lusaka would attract at least some attention." I suppose they were used to seeing ZIPRA and Zambian army trucks, and at night the *Black is Beautiful* cream was effective.

Two of the vehicles broke away from the main group and drove off towards the Liberation Centre. The remaining four kept on towards the main target. The tension was building. At the junction of Nyerere Road and Speakers Lane we stopped, and Curtis gave us our final orders.

The plan was simple. Two vehicles under Curtis's command would break through the two main gates on the Nyerere Road side of Nkomo's house. They would hammer that side of the house with rockets, firearms and bunker bombs. At the same time, our team would force its way through the security wall from President's Lane, then into the house to take out Nkomo. Opposition from the thirty guards was expected to be tough.

Our vehicle sped down Speaker's Lane, then turned into President's Lane. As we drew near the house a burst of gunfire shattered the night silence. We were under fire. Bruce immediately hit back from the rear machine gun, firing a volley at the guards in the security huts. The raid had begun!

## fifteen

Waters jumped from the vehicle and sprinted to the fence, using his wire-cutters to cut a hole for us to get through. I rechecked my equipment to ensure it was all in order: AK-47, nine-millimetre pistol and five grenades. Then I jumped from the Sabre. My feet had barely touched the ground before I heard Grobler cry out and fall to the ground in pain. The medic took care of him while Waters led me and Bruce into the house, our assault team now down to three men.

We moved quickly after Waters—only fifteen minutes to find and kill Nkomo. His bedroom window was barred, so we blew our way through the back door to be greeted by dust, smoke and darkness. We stormed into his bedroom, but no activity, no sign of life. Only his general's uniform.

Then the storeroom and bathroom. No Nkomo, no one. By now the flames were starting to reach us and it was difficult breathing. There was one room left to check. We burst in, willing him to be there. We were fired at, so took a step back as Waters and I both threw in grenades. Then we charged into the room, and Waters shot one of the guards hiding under the bed. I let rip at the cupboard, where the other guard was hiding, and watched him drop to the floor as the bullets tore into him.

Waters radioed Curtis and then shouted out to us, "Let's go!" We quickly made our way back to the vehicle, which had been hit. It started, and we drove around the block. But it was badly damaged, so we stripped off the equipment and set it alight. We climbed into the other Sabres and started to move out of town.

"Did you get him?" asked one of Curtis's team.

"No, wasn't there," I answered.

"We cleared out the other rooms and he wasn't there either," he told me.

On the way, we waited for the two vehicles from the Liberation Centre. They came speeding into view, accompanied by the sound of wailing sirens, which were now starting to blare all over Lusaka. As Curtis organised the kit to be distributed evenly among the five remaining vehicles, we watched our explosives tear into the Liberation Centre.

Then we were on our way. Back through Kafue town, over Kafue River Bridge, then onto the dirt road back towards Conway's vehicle. At about ten o'clock, just before we reached Conway's vehicle, we made a stop, cut a landing zone in a clearing in the bush and called in the choppers to collect our three wounded.

"How'd you go?" asked Conway as soon as he saw me.

"He wasn't there," I told him. "But we took out most of his guards, destroyed his house and blew up the Liberation Centre."

They towed Conway's vehicle and it roared into life almost immediately. Conway and his group were swearing furiously. They could have come.

From there we drove quickly back, and by midday were at the beachhead near Siavonga. Still no sign of any retaliation from ZIPRA or the Zambians. Soon the ferry was pulling up in front of us, and the vehicles drove on board. We were on our way back to Rhodesia. I looked out over the lake, sparkling in the midday sun. There above us was the welcoming sight of a Rhodesian helicopter, with a crate of beers. I grabbed three, which Conway, Bruce and I sipped as we ploughed through the Kariba waters.

I was disappointed at not having been able to get Nkomo. It would have made Laurel's loss easier to bear. She was constantly on my mind. But we'd struck a big psychological blow against the terrs in their own backyard. Also, I now had a chance to hit back at Comrade X, who'd been directly responsible for her murder. I couldn't wait.

After breakfast the next morning Waters called Young, Conway, Bruce and myself aside. "Well done, boys. Glad to see you're all in one piece. Dixon's back. He'll be briefing us on Comrade X at ten. See you then."

Dixon was upbeat. "While you lads have been sunning yourself in Lusaka, I've been doing some real work. Everything Maduma told us is one hundred per cent accurate. I'll be working with Intelligence to prepare a model of the camp, which'll be ready when you get back from R&R."

Waters wrapped up, "Okay, lads, enjoy your break, get a good rest. We meet back here in five days, eight o'clock Wednesday morning. This is gonna be big."

Conway drove Bruce and I out to his plush Glen Lorne home, where Claire was cooking lunch.

"Shame, Claire, you shouldn't have worried to cook for us." I pointed at her stomach. "You've got much more important things to worry about. When's he due?"

"A week from today," she said. "It's no problem cooking, Scott. Also, Mike and I wanted you round."

She looked up at Conway, as the four of us strolled across the lawn and sat down next to the small dam at the bottom of the garden. "We think about you and Laurel a lot," she said kindly.

Conway spoke next. "Well, I was going to take leave to be with Claire for the birth of the little one. But we want you to know that we've decided that I should go on the Comrade X raid instead. That bastard's got to pay for what he did to Laurel."

"Thanks a lot, guys," I said, then quickly changed the subject. "Hey, have you decided on his name yet?"

Claire smiled. "You're as bad as Mike, talking about him as if he's a boy. Remember, we still don't know its sex."

Conway laughed. "Of course he's gonna be a boy." He turned to me. "Still haven't decided what we're gonna call him. We have a shortlist of five names, and we'll decide when we see him."

That evening Bruce and I hopped onto the overnight train. Mum met us in Gwelo.

"How's it going, boys?" Mum asked as we drove home.

I opened my mouth to speak. *Awesome, Mum. Already we've ambushed ZANLA terrs, nailed Frelimo, escaped death by the skin of our teeth in Cabora Bassa; defeated nine thousand terrs in Chimoio and four thousand in Tembué, had a crack at Nkomo and done so well that we've been chosen to take out the most famous gook alive.*

"Fine, thanks," I replied.

"And you, Bruce?"

"Yes, fine, thank you, Mrs Carter."

We dropped Bruce off first.

"Scott, come and say hi to mum and dad. They'll be pleased to see you."

Mrs Thomas was almost too pleased to see Bruce. She got up from the breakfast table and hugged him, wouldn't let him go. "My darling boy, my darling boy."

"Mum, mum, please … say hello to Scott."

Bruce finally made his escape, and she turned to give me a welcoming hug. "How's the war going, Scott?"

"Fine, thanks, ma'am." I could smell the cane spirits on her breath.

"Morning, Mr Thomas."

"Good to see you, Scott." He shook my hand and I could smell the cane on him too, although it might have been brandy.

"All okay on the farm, sir?"

"Not great, it's been better," he shifted uncomfortably. "Are you enjoying the SAS?"

"Yes, thank you, sir ... it's a good experience."

I said my goodbyes. "Bruce, come round for beers tonight," I shouted as I ran for the car.

It was great to be back, to be alive. A large welcoming committee was on the front lawn: Shoko barking and bucking, Dad, Anna and Dixie. I got out of the car, hugged Dad and shook hands with Anna. Shoko started butting me with his head until I said hello. Even Dixie wasn't going to be left out and grunted until I patted him.

Anna called out to me as I carried my bag into the house, "*Eh, Baas* Scott, your friend is here."

"Now? He's here?"

She nodded.

"That's great, Anna, I'll be over as soon as I can."

I joined Mum and Dad for morning tea. Dad listened open-mouthed as I told him of the Nkomo raid.

"Well done, my boy, that's some effort."

After tea I excused myself and dashed over to Anna's compound. Simba was waiting for me.

"Good to see you, Simba. Dixon told us you had a good recce of Comrade X's camp. How was it?"

"Went well ... we'll give you all the details when we get back to barracks."

"Does he look evil?"

"No, just an ordinary-looking guy."

I was sure Simba was keen to get a break from his work and enjoy his R&R, so I didn't probe further. "Let's take a walk," I suggested.

First we walked to our secret cave where we'd played war games as kids, where Simba'd nailed the black mamba. Then to Leopard Pass, where we'd learnt to ride bikes for the first time.

"Remember that, Simba? Hell, you were a tough little bugger. Falling all over the place ... there was no skin left on your knees, but you kept at it until you could ride." Then to Impala Vlei, where Simba'd first ridden bareback, and on to the big acacia where we'd found Shoko. Next was our favourite spot, the Baboon Pool, where we'd spent so much of our youth.

"Still the same old troop ... Grey and the others," I said affectionately, looking up at the baboons. "Almost like family now." They knew us so well; we'd been coming here since we were tiny. Normally they'd stand on the rocks observing us from above while they feasted on the *mahobohobos*.

But today something was up. *Wahoo, wahoo*, Grey barked, and they all scampered away.

"That's strange ... he's never done that before," I told Simba.

We walked along the running track we'd trained on for the Miller fight and then back to Anna's hut, where we sat under the syringa tree and drank sweet tea from old enamel mugs.

"Did you go on the Nkomo raid?" he asked.

"*Ja*, it was amazing."

I went on to give him a detailed account of our attack on both Nkomo's house and the Liberation Centre. He was so engrossed that his tea went cold and he tossed it into the bush on the edge of the clearing.

When I got home I went straight to find Shoko. He was lying on the lawn, next to Dixie.

Mum came out and sat down next to us. "We don't need to let Shoko back into the bush just yet," she said gently.

"I know, Mum. It's just that ..." I wanted to tell her that I'd started to have a bad feeling about the Comrade X raid, that I wanted to make sure Shoko was released before I went on the op. But, again, I didn't want to worry her. "It's just that he needs to be free."

Today was our last day together. I was going to spoil him like he'd never been spoilt before.

I brought him horse cubes, then the best carrots from the garden. A walk to Impali River. And finally a walk to the Baboon Pool.

I didn't sleep at all that night. As soon as the sun peeped its head over the mango trees I was up, and we sat together on the front lawn watching the sun rise. Mum allowed Shoko to join us at the breakfast table for the first time. He stood to one side eating carrots while Bruce, Simba, and I tucked into Anna's bacon and eggs. After breakfast I hitched the horsebox onto the bakkie.

"Come, boy, come, boy." I led him gently towards the horsebox, tempting him with cubes. Then climbed in with him and sat in the box, gently stroking him. Bruce and Simba jumped in with us. Still fragile after the Viscount incident, I was glad they were there. Saying goodbye to Shoko would hit me hard.

When we arrived at Mopane Park, Jim opened the gate, and I led Shoko in.

"Hold on, Jim. I don't know if I'm ready for this." I didn't want them to see me crying, but what the hell, I didn't care. Shoko meant so much to me.

Dad was following behind. He spoke calmly. "Scott, we've got to do this. For him, now. He needs a proper life."

Simba scratched him gently on the forehead. Bruce stroked him, then walked away wiping his cheeks. We'd found him together, and in a funny sort of way he symbolised the friendship between the three of us. I wrapped my arms gently around Shoko's neck. "I'll miss you, my boy."

Jim put his good hand on my shoulder. "I'll look after him, he'll be fine, I promise."

As I made my way back to the car, Shoko stood at the fence, looking at me expectantly.

"Shoko, I'm doing this for you. I've got to do it. Please understand ..." I turned to Dad. "Let's go."

He started the bakkie and we drove away. I hung my head out the window and looked back at Shoko. He was running now, alongside the fence, after the car. He knew I wouldn't desert him. I'd never let him down. So he kept on running, knowing I would turn back and fetch him. But I couldn't. I would never see him again.

Back home I sat in the lounge listening to Elton John, with Kathy.

"Hey, that's Tinashe, the teacher from Mum's school," said Kathy, looking out of the window at two smartly dressed African women walking up the drive. I got up to open the door.

"Nice to see you, Scott and Kathy," Tinashe said in her clear, well-spoken voice.

"This is Tendai."

We both shook hands with Tendai.

"Is your mum here?"

"She should be back in about fifteen minutes," I told her. "Please come in."

Kathy went to make some tea while I invited the women into the lounge. They looked uncomfortable as they sat down in the spacious lounge chairs.

"I love your lounge. There's so much space and light," said Tinashe softly.

Dad had done a great job in designing the open-plan lounge and dining-room. My favourite feature was the imposing stone fireplace in the centre. Around it were large cream armchairs, from which you could look out through the enormous windows covering most of the front section of the house. At the end of the room was an impressive Rhodesian teak dining-room table.

"Tendai was one of your mum's pupils," explained Tinashe. "She's just qualified at the Teachers' Training College in Bulawayo."

"Congratulations, Tendai," I said politely.

"Thank you." She had a quiet voice. "I wanted to come and thank your mother for everything she did for me. She did so much for all of us at the school."

"I know she'll be pleased to see you," I said. "A lot of former pupils stop by, and she really appreciates it."

Kathy arrived with a pot of tea and poured us each a cup.

"I also wanted to tell her," continued Tendai, "that I'm going to be a history teacher, like her."

"That's great." We chatted for a few minutes until I heard Mum's car pull into the drive. Kathy and I politely said our goodbyes and went outside.

"Let's go say goodbye to Simba," I suggested. We walked round to the back of the house, down the path through the vlei, weaving our way through the thick mass of acacia and msasa trees at the bottom end of the vlei. Past the thicket we could now see the compound, and we quickened our pace till we got to Anna's hut.

I was about to knock on the old tin door, but stopped. Someone was in a heated conversation, in Ndebele, with Anna inside.

"Who's in there with Anna?" asked Kathy.

I shrugged. "It must be Simba. Hell, he sounds furious!" We moved closer to the wall.

"Can you understand what they're saying?" I whispered.

She put her ear to the wall and listened carefully.

"Well?" I was impatient.

Kath was hesitant. "I missed most of it but I think Anna said, 'They've done so much for you.'"

I moved against the hut to hear Simba's reply. But he spoke in Ndebele.

"And?" I turned to Kath.

"It's really hard to make out what he's saying," said Kathy. "He's so angry. Sounded like: 'They treat us like children.'" She paused. "Doesn't make any sense."

"Ja, probably some family argument."

We turned and made our way back to the house.

Bruce came round for drinks that night. We chatted politely with Mum and Dad for a few minutes, but the conversation drifted back to the army and Comrade X. It was all we spoke about. We were still talking about Comrade X when we caught the train back to Salisbury two days later. I missed Laurel so much, and this was the man who'd taken her from me. But, unlike the previous ops I'd been on, I had a bad feeling about this raid.

## sixteen

We caught a taxi from the station.

"Fancy a beer?" Bruce asked.

"No, I'm off the booze. Want to be hundred per cent sharp for this op. We're gonna nail this bastard."

"Good idea. Only a few days to go, anyway."

When we arrived at barracks, Conway tried to persuade us otherwise. "Just one beer, fergodsake?" But we held firm. He shook his head in disgust and spat out of the canteen window. "You're a bunch of girls."

A walk through town, a pie, chips and a pint of Dairibord milk, then we turned in for the night.

When the sun peered through the window the next morning, I got up fresh and raring to go. After a quick breakfast, I went looking for Waters. I found him in the officers' mess.

"Briefing session at oh-eight-thirty, Carter," he said.

Waters, Dixon and Simba were in deep discussion in the corner of the ops room when Bruce and I arrived. Young and Conway came in soon afterwards.

"Right, lads. It's a hell of an honour to be chosen to take out the most important terr on the face of this planet. We've got a Special Branch officer assigned to us: Inspector Pettigrew. An obnoxious son of a bitch, but he knows his stuff. He's been working on Comrade X for the past year. He'll be here at nine."

Pettigrew arrived ten minutes early, knocked loudly, and marched straight in.

"Good morning, inspector. You know Trooper Dixon and Private Ndlovu, I believe. This is Sergeant Young and Troopers Carter, Conway and Thomas." Pettigrew shook each of our hands in turn, a limp, disinterested handshake. Apart from Waters, he didn't even bother to look at us. He stood in front of the blackboard and put on a pair of black-framed glasses. I had never seen anyone so pale.

"Looks like Uriah Heep," muttered Conway behind me.

"Now, as Lieutenant Waters has probably told you, I've been tracking Comrade X for over a year. The best piece of intelligence we got on him was from Moses Maduma."

"Speaks like Uriah Heep too," Conway muttered again. I smiled. I wasn't sure what Uriah Heep sounded like, but if he had a nasal, condescending voice, then it would have been just like Pettigrew's.

Uriah continued, "Now, a lot of what he told us has been confirmed as accurate by Trooper … uh …"

Waters came to his rescue: "Trooper Dixon."

"Yes, that's right." He waved in Dixon's general direction, but didn't bother to look at him. "And …"

"Private Ndlovu," said Waters, pointing at Simba.

"Yes, that's right. They'll be briefing you on the camp next, but I'm here to first give you some insight into Comrade X."

I strained forward to listen.

"He grew up in Rhodesia. We don't know where. But he speaks

English like an English professor. Ndebele too. His Shona's not as strong, but he's fluent in that as well."

"How old is he?" asked Conway.

"Mid-twenties. He trained in Moscow. Was top military student among everyone, including the KGB elite."

"What does he look like?" Young asked.

Uriah picked up his file and carefully pulled out a photograph. I grabbed it from him; I had to see the bastard who'd killed Laurel. X was standing in the middle of a group of five others, wearing shorts and a green camouflage T-shirt. Powerfully built, fit, must have stood about six-two. What was most striking was that he looked just like an everyday, normal black man. Smiling, cheerful … *how could this be the same monster who'd gunned down those women and children?* I held the picture closer.

"Pass it along, Carter," said Waters impatiently, so I reluctantly handed it to Bruce.

Uriah's face took on a serious expression. "X is the most sadistic, ruthless soldier in the war. A hard-core of ten loyal gooks in his troop would follow him to hell and back. Die for him. So you've got a tough job ahead of you … that's why an elite squad has been chosen for this operation." He turned to look at us for the first time, then turned away, a disapproving sneer appearing on the side of his face. He couldn't hide what he was thinking.

Waters got to his feet. "Thanks, inspector." He turned to us. "Now grab yourselves a coffee and meet back here in ten minutes."

"What an arsehole," grumbled Conway as we walked across to the canteen. "Hey, let's do the typewriter joke on him."

"Hell, you're childish, Conway," we chuckled. But it would be fun. As feeble as Conway's tricks were, humiliating Uriah would be worth a laugh.

We sat ourselves in the canteen and waited for Uriah. Simba, Young, Conway, Dixon, Bruce and myself.

"Just laugh when we laugh," I told Simba.

"Excuse me, inspector ... will you join us?" shouted Conway. Uriah fixed him with a haughty stare, grabbed a coffee and sat down next to Young.

"Inspector, have you heard the typewriter joke?"

Uriah frowned.

"Well, inspector, there's a duck on a boat in a bath. Now the duck says to the boat, 'Please pass me the soap.' So the boat turns to the duck and says, 'What do you think I am—a typewriter, or something?'" This was the cue for us all to laugh. And we howled with laughter, including Simba. It'd been years since I'd seen Simba laugh like that. Whenever we played Conway's typewriter trick we would always start off pretending to laugh. But it was so silly that we normally ended up rolling around in stitches, for real. It was good to laugh again.

Uriah watched us closely, a puzzled expression on his face. Seeing our reaction, he thought he must have missed a really good joke. He obviously didn't want to appear stupid, so he too started laughing—tentatively at first, and then with a deep throaty awkward roar. Conway clicked his fingers. Our next cue. We all stopped laughing and stared blankly at Uriah who was in false hysterics.

"Inspector, what's so fuckin' funny?"

Of course there was nothing remotely funny about the joke, and Uriah sat there speechless, trying both to explain his false laughter and hide it at the same time. But there was nowhere to hide. He'd been humiliated. He went bright red, and swore at us: "How dare you? Who do you children think you are?" Then he stormed from the canteen.

There was no sign of Uriah when we got back to the ops room. Waters asked, "Where the hell is Pettigrew? Was he at the canteen?"

"Yes, sir, he was there drinking coffee," answered Conway innocently.

"Well, we can't wait any longer. Let's get cracking, Dixon."

"Yes, sir." Dixon brought a large *papier-mâché* model to the centre of the room.

"Dixon, is it as camouflaged in real life?" Young pointed at the model of the camp, which blended perfectly with the surrounding rocks and trees.

"*Ja*, for sure. The real version's almost invisible."

He handed over to Simba, who gave us a detailed description of X's secret camp. The layout, the guardhouse, the garage, the parade ground, the mess hall. He pointed at a small enclosure to the right of the parade ground.

"And this is where they keep the baboons."

"What for?" I asked.

"As an early-warning signal for aircraft," Simba explained. "On the second day we were there, the baboons went ballistic, made a helluva racket. Then, about ten minutes later, some aircraft flew past."

Waters interrupted. "It's interesting. Looks like the terrs are using baboons for early warnings in a lot of camps. Intelligence reports have confirmed it. But not to worry. We'll be going in freefall, so we'll be too high for the baboons to hear us, anyway."

Simba continued with the camp. "That's the eating hall, this is the canteen, and the secret rooms are over here. And finally … here's Comrade X's quarters."

Waters stood up. "Now, if X is so important, why aren't we just doing what we did at Chimoio? Sending in the bombers?"

"Well, you obviously don't want to nail the Russians, sir," Young answered.

"Exactly—if we take out any of the Russians, we're in big shit."

"Sir, what if we shoot one by mistake?"

"You can't, Carter. That's why we're sending in a small hit-squad." He looked at us pointedly. "It's a massive risk to go in while the Russians are there. But we have to. It's our only chance to take out Comrade X. Right?" He looked around to see if we had any more questions before continuing. "On the last night of the meetings the Russians generally like a good bender. The guards tuck into the booze as well. This gives us the perfect opportunity to sneak into camp and neutralise X."

"You want us to take him prisoner, sir?" asked Bruce.

"No, he's too dangerous. Shoot to kill. We're gonna be dropped from the Dakotas at seventeen-hundred hours, fifty-five minutes before sundown. That'll allow you to get to the camp in daylight and read your altimeters on the jump. But the light won't be great, so they shouldn't spot you in the air. You'll land here, about five kays south of the camp." He pointed to the model, then to a map on the wall. "Then move down towards the camp. We watch and wait—here." He pointed to a small koppie overlooking the camp. "Once the party is finished and X has gone to bed, we sneak in through the guards. Over there." He pointed to the camp model again. "X will be fast asleep, and we whack him."

Waters went through exactly what was expected of us, giving each a typed sheet of paper outlining our precise responsibilities. Then he told us what we needed to do in any possible situation.

That afternoon we practised our drills, methodically going through each routine.

"Scott, you must be excited! I bet you're dying to get your

hands on Comrade X," said Bruce as we made our way back to our quarters.

Bruce was right. But I still had a bad feeling, and as the day of the op drew nearer, the feeling grew worse.

We continued rehearsing, drill after drill after drill.

By the last night, we had every movement of the raid planned and practised to perfection.

But I still didn't feel good. I went to Bruce's room to say goodnight. I sat down on the bed next to him and buried my head in my hands. I had to say it out loud to someone. "I'm scared, Bruce."

He sat up and put his hand on my shoulder.

"It's just ... I've got a really bad feeling about tomorrow."

Bruce studied me closely. "I'll tell you, man. I get a bad feeling before every op. And you know what scares me the most?" He looked down at the floor.

"It's poor old mum. She wouldn't cope if I was killed. Kelly's death tore her apart." We both sat silently.

"Scott, do you think it's all because of the *Ichithamuzi?*"

I thought back to that morning four years ago. Simba and I'd run over to Bruce's farm. The wind was howling and whipping into us with force, so we took shelter on the veranda. We looked out at the lands in front. A commotion was developing. It looked like one of Dad's old colonial paintings: the white *baas* addressing an assembly of blacks who'd gathered round a tree in the centre of the field. Above the tree a hover of crows were circling, beating their wings and screeching. Dark clouds loomed on the horizon.

"Come on," I said to Simba. "If they can handle it, so can we." Shielding our faces from the wind, we ran over to join Bruce.

"It's an *Ichithamuzi,*" Simba shouted as we drew nearer the tree. Some of the blacks were making angry clucking noises. Others shook their heads and spoke anxiously in Ndebele. One old man was frantically throwing his hands in the air as the wind blew into his thin grey hair. He was pleading with Bruce's dad, shouting to be heard above the wind and the screeching of the crows.

"What the hell's going on, Simba?" It looked serious.

"They don't want him to cut the *Ichithamuzi*. It'll bring tragedy to the farm."

Bruce's dad turned. "Hey, Simba, you're an educated *munt*. Talk to these boys. Tell them the farm isn't a fucking charity. I need to clear this land to plant crops so I can pay their wages."

"Please, *Baas* Nick," begged Simba. "*Ichithamuzi* means destroyer of homes in our Ndebele language. Don't cut it." Still the crows were beating their wings as they circled closer to the tree.

"Leave it, dad," said Bruce quickly.

"Fergodsake, boy, you're as bad as the rest of them." He grabbed the axe from the boss-boy, pushed him out of the way, and swung at the tree. Ten strong swings, and it fell to the ground in ominous silence. "There," he said. "Job done. Now back to work."

The wind had slowed, but was still blowing the dry dust across the lands towards us. I sheltered my face from the sand and the wind as I stood there looking at Bruce's dad over the *Ichithamuzi*.

"Do you think it's all because of the *Ichithamuzi*?" Bruce repeated.

*Yes it is. They pleaded with your dad not to cut it, but he went right ahead.*

But I didn't say it out loud, just stopped and looked across at Bruce. "Can you imagine what it would've been like if we'd been born somewhere far away ... in a beautiful city like San Francisco or Cambridge? We'd be at varsity now. Share rooms near the river. Before classes we'd get a coffee, just you and me. Oh, and Simba too—they take blacks at Cambridge. Hey, at night we'd go to bars and listen to live music ... laughing, dancing, singing. With Laurel and your bird, who'd be stunning. Then we'd party at our flat afterwards. All night." I stopped ... I was running away with myself, but I couldn't help it.

"Hey, Scott, are you okay?" He put his hand on my shoulder. "Never seen you like this, man."

"*Ja*, I'm fine, Bruce." I quickly wiped my cheeks with the back of my hand.

I could see I was making him feel awkward. Then he brightened. "Hey, let's do it. When this is over, let's go to varsity. Cambridge, and we'll get those rooms near the river."

I started to pull myself together. "Hell, Bruce, that's a great idea. I'm in."

We shook hands goodnight. Then I hugged him.

"Don't worry, Scott. I'll be fine. We both will. Tomorrow's going to be huge."

I knew I was going to have difficulty sleeping that night, so when I lay down to sleep I thought calm thoughts. Fishing in the Impali with Simba, Shoko and Bruce.

That night I dreamed Simba, Bruce and I were at the Baboon Pool. Same old dream I'd been having for years. We were gazing into the water ... the reflections of me, Bruce and the blood lilies looked up at us. Simba's reflection was still nowhere to be found. I glanced across at him, then into the water. No reflection. The baboons were standing on the rocks under the *mahobohobo* trees, barking at me.

"What is it? What is it?" I asked. They were trying to tell me something, but I didn't understand. Then Grey jumped down from the rocks and stood on the water's edge next to me. I'd known him all my life. "What is it, Grey? What are you trying to tell me?"

He looked at me, shaking his head ... his brown eyes seemed sad and troubled. Then he turned, still shaking his head, and made his way up the rocks.

It was a restless night, and I felt sluggish when I got up the next morning. So I made sure that I did everything methodically. There was no room for error. I ate a good breakfast, a solid lunch, and drank plenty of water. After lunch we carefully fitted our parachutes and strapped in our rifles. Then we climbed on board the Dakota and were off. Conway and I were both reflective, and sat on either side of Bruce. Simba sat in the corner and didn't look up. Probably in one of his moods again.

Bruce was full of beans. "Hey, I'm looking forward to the freefall. Shit, they're dropping us from twelve thousand feet and we only open our chutes at two and a half—that's a helluva long way to drop!"

"*Ja*, that's right. The higher the better. Then they can't hear us," said Conway.

"But, Conway, imagine if you fainted before it opened," added Bruce. Neither of us replied. I'd often worried about that.

The flight went quickly. I was thinking of Laurel for most of the trip. *Her blue eyes would go a brilliant bright blue when she was angry.*

"Scott," Conway rapped me on the shoulder. "We're nearly there."

We checked and rechecked our equipment. Then the dispatcher came and rechecked everything again. About five minutes to the drop.

"Stand in the door!" he shouted, as Waters stepped forward. *Green light on.*

"Go!" shouted the dispatcher, and Waters leapt into the evening air.

"Go!" and Bruce jumped out over Zambia.

"Go!" and Simba was falling after him.

"Go!" and I was falling from the African sky.

It was still light enough to read my altimeter, and I watched it closely as I fell through the sky. Two and a half thousand feet and I pulled the ripcord. It opened. Relief. I turned to see where Simba and Bruce were. Simba was floating next to me. Bruce was still falling. My heart was thumping—one, two. Then his parachute opened.

I kept falling. *Right, time to focus.* I went through my pre-landing drills.

*Landing spot* ... yes, fine. Great spot. Dispatcher had done a good job.

*Head tucked ... knees bent ... elbows in*—and I was on the ground.

I released my parachute harness, rose to my feet and quickly looked around. In front of us a mopane forest; to our left and behind, thornscrub and an open vlei. Simba was already on his feet, looking around him. Bruce was still on the ground, trying to release his parachute harness. I counted four others—*yes*, we'd all made it. I was wrong to have felt negative earlier. Things were going well ... it was going to be a successful op.

Waters called us, "We need to move quickly."

We set off at a fast trot, following Simba through the dense mopane forest. Simba suddenly stopped and took three steps backwards. An olive-brown snake with dark-edged scales slithered across the path.

"Spitting cobra," I mouthed to Bruce.

He nodded grimly.

Twenty-nine minutes later, we were at the camp. We advanced cautiously to our observation point. Disturbingly quiet, but we kept creeping forward.

Finally, we reached the koppie.

The camp was deserted.

"What the fuck?" said Waters.

A silence hung over the camp, over the bush. No birds. Dead still, apart from the wind, which was slowly starting to blow.

Something was horribly wrong.

## seventeen

*Magdalene College, Cambridge University, 1983*

"The bus is here."

"Thanks, Lewis." I slung the kit-bag over my shoulder, sprinted from my room and jumped into the minibus outside the Magdalene porters' lodge. It was raining; never stopped in England.

The two coaches sat up front, while the rest of us spread out on the back seats.

"Finn, how many of us are matched tonight?" I asked.

"Only four: you, Kyle, Lewis and Brett."

"Scott, your first fight as captain of Cambridge—are you nervous?" asked Kyle.

"No, looking forward to it." I was in a positive mood. The day after tomorrow I was flying home. Couldn't wait. It was over a year since I'd been back.

We turned off the M25 and drove to the boxing club on the outskirts of Chigwell. As we got off the bus and walked into the spartan changing rooms, I could hear the screaming next door. The fights had started and the dinner audience was in a raucous mood.

We changed and walked through to the doctor's room for our medicals.

"Scott, who'd you think I'm fighting?" Brett asked nervously. It was his first fight.

"You're at welterweight, so ..." I looked around the changing room. My eye settled on a shaven-headed beast covered with tattoos and muscles. An angry young man.

"Brett, I think that's your man over there ... the Beast," I joked.

"Nah, he's more like a light-heavyweight. Your man?"

"Shit, I hope it's not him." Straight after my medical I went looking for our head coach. "Hey, Finn, who'm I matched with?"

"One of the local guys from Chigwell." He looked around. "Over there," he pointed to the Beast. My stomach tightened—it was going to be a tough night.

I was only fighting at ten o'clock, so I sat down in the changing room and began wrapping the bandages over my hands. Kyle sat down next to me doing the same.

"What're you studying?" he asked in his broad Northern Irish accent.

"Political Science, my third and final year."

"Oh, right. So ... did you come straight from school in Zimbabwe?"

"No ..."

"Hey quick, Lewis is on!" Brett called. We moved through to the viewing gallery. I looked down at the ring where the lightweight bout was about to begin. Around the ring were neatly laid-out dinner tables. The spectators were tucking into their starters— lots of shaven heads, a rough-looking bunch. As the fight started most of them put down their knives and forks and hurled abuse at Lewis.

"Nail that fuckin' Cambridge toff," someone shouted in a strong Essex accent.

"So, Kyle, I was saying … I finished school in Zim, then army, then I went back to college to get some good A' Levels. Then here."

"Did you see any action?"

"*Ja*, a bit. I was fighting for Rhodesia against the terrorists—Robert Mugabe and Joshua Nkomo's lot. Anyway, the war ended in 1979 and they had elections in 1980 which Mugabe won by a mile."

"Go, Lewis!" we shouted as Lewis went on the attack with a double-jab. He was scoring with his clean, snappy jabs, using his reach advantage to good effect. After the third round he was named unanimous winner, much to the disappointment of the partisan crowd.

Brett was up soon afterwards, and a smattering of boos broke out across the crowd as he stepped into the ring. He fought bravely, but was no match for the more experienced boxer from a London club. Kyle won on points against a tough, durable lad from Harlow and couldn't stop grinning. As time for my fight drew nearer, the familiar gallows-type dread set in. Like parachuting … waiting for the jump. When the bell rang it was like the chute opening—the dread disappeared and excitement took over.

I climbed into the ring and was greeted by hostile jeering from the crowd. Out of the corner of my eye I could see them hitting the port. Dinner was over. As the announcer introduced the Beast, they cheered wildly.

*Should I attack immediately?* I asked myself as I waited for the bell. Yes, I decided, and as soon as the bell went I launched a vicious attack on the Beast, pounding a series of straight punches at his head. He staggered backwards into the ropes and I charged forward, scoring solid blows to his body and jaw. The ref gave him a standing eight count. *Move in close, throw your punches hard and fast. Use your strength to drive him backwards. Crowd the taller boxer …* my strategy was what Dad had taught me on the lawn so many years ago. It'd served me well: fifteen wins from seventeen fights.

But Beast was no pushover. He'd won twelve of his fifteen fights, and after each of my attacks he'd come back at me like an angry bull. After two rounds it was really close.

Finn was worried in the corner. "I think it's dead even. Lots of work in this round."

Beast's corner must have told him the same thing. He came tearing towards me, immediately trying to back me into the ropes. But I circled to his left, away from his powerful right. He swung his right, but couldn't reach me. So he used his jab. I was waiting for it, blocked it firmly with my right then stepped forward, throwing a left-right combination at his stomach and a straight left at his head. Off balance and going backwards, he tried to swing his right, but couldn't. Then I moved out on my toes, shifting to his left.

The Beast was panting heavily now, so I stepped up the pressure, hammering punches at his head, his ribs, his jaw.

"Ten to go," shouted Finn, and I drove forward, smashing punches into the Beast—straight left, right, left hook, right uppercut—until the final bell rang and the ref raised my arm in victory.

We drove back to Cambridge in good spirits. Even Brett was happy, pleased to have the first fight under his belt. As soon as we got back to Magdalene, I packed my case for home. I was so excited. Then a quick letter to Bruce to tell him about the fight with the Beast—he'd be chuffed.

After that I took a walk to The Eagle to join Kyle and Lewis for a celebratory drink. They were in festive spirits when I arrived.

"Tequilas all round," shouted Kyle to the barman, pointing at me and four pretty American tourists.

"Hey, Kyle, I was only going to join you for a quick beer."

"And a pint of IPA," he called out again to the barman, and then turned to me, "Three good wins. We've gotta celebrate." I knew I wasn't going anywhere quickly, so I tried to relax. We chatted briefly about the fights, but the others were more interested in the American girls. One of the girls came over to the bar and sat down next to me. I bought her a drink, and we chatted awkwardly. I hadn't had a girlfriend since Laurel.

"Man, this Cambridge is one cute little place. I can't believe DNA was discovered in this bar."

I smiled at her. Her name was Natalie. She was attractive: long blond hair, dark green eyes and a bright smile.

"You don't come from Africa. You're just shitting me, right?"

I assured her I did.

"Then why aren't you black?" I told her there were lots of whites in Africa.

She put her hand on my chin and looked into my eyes. "You've got the saddest eyes I've ever seen. What happened to you?"

*Was it that obvious?*

"Barman, tequilas all round!" I shouted. After The Eagle closed, we stumbled back to Magdalene. First some beers with Kyle, then cheap German wine in Lewis's room.

Finally Natalie and I ended up in my room. I poured her a glass of Baileys as we sat on the edge of the bed listening to the Beach Boys.

"Hey, Scott, these are great shots." She got up to look at the pictures hanging on my wall.

Bruce, Conway and I stared proudly at the camera on the day we got our SAS berets—three young men ready to take on the world. Then Bruce and I as eight-year-olds, clutching our prize certificates after the cross-country race where I'd carried him. He was beaming at the camera, I was looking at my feet. Then a picture of me holding a baby boy: Brian. Next to that a picture of me and Brian, now four years older. Handsome little fellow, with a cheeky smile. At his feet was a rugby ball.

Finally, Laurel on our lawn in front of the mango trees, resting her hands on Shoko's magnificent, twisted horns. Her blue eyes sparkled up at me.

"Is he yours?" she asked, pointing to the boy.

I didn't answer.

"And who's she?"

"Laurel." I didn't want to talk about the pictures with her.

She walked back to the bed and sat down next to me. Gently, she slid her hands across my face, cupping my neck on both sides at the back of my head. Then pulled me closer to her, her mouth warm and inviting.

I pulled away. "Sorry, Natalie."

"Because of her?"

I looked out the window. "But it's late, you're welcome to stay." I poured her another Baileys and we chatted into the night. I was grateful for the company.

"Scott, you've been such a good host, let me give you a massage." I guessed she may have had ulterior motives, but I didn't want to be alone with my thoughts and memories.

I lay face down. She sat on my thighs. Starting at the lower back, she applied pressure with both thumbs on either side of my spine. Then moved her way up the back, all the way to the base of my neck. Sliding her palms down either side of the spine to the pelvis, she scooped her hands around my hips and back up the sides to the shoulder-blades. It felt fantastic. Gently, she slid her hands down my back, resting them on my buttocks. Softly she pressed downwards. Then leaned forward, grabbed my shirt and pushed it over my head and onto the pillow in front of me.

"Oh my God … what happened to you?" she cried out, pointing at my back in horror.

I hurriedly put my shirt back on.

"Hey, dude, you've gotta tell me, man—what happened?" She looked shaken.

"It's late, Natalie …"

She grabbed the bottle of Baileys, poured herself a shot, downed it—and quickly poured herself another.

"Come on, tell me."

"It's getting late. It's probably best you go."

She sat down on the bed next to me, sipping at her Baileys. "Come on, mystery man … you've gotta tell me."

"I said you should go!"

She put her hand on my shoulder and looked into my eyes.

Grabbing the glass from her, I opened the window and hurled it outside. I could hear it smash against the wall in the courtyard. Then I picked her up in my right arm, took her bag with my left, and carried her to the door. I dumped her outside, slammed the door shut and locked it. Breathing heavily, I stood leaning against the door.

I arrived early for work at the Baron of Beef the next day. The job was important for me, providing pocket money and paying for all of Brian's expenses back in Zimbabwe. Every month I would send him fifty pounds, a princely sum for me as a student, and a lot of money in Zimbabwe.

Soon the manager, Paul, arrived and we opened the bar

together. The customers began to trickle in. A cheerful-looking guy dressed in veldskoens came up to the bar.

"Lovely day outside," I said politely.

"Is it?" he said in a broad Zimbabwean accent.

"Haven't heard that expression in a while," I smiled. "Where're you from?"

"Nyama ..."

The music started playing. "Turn it off!" I shouted. Then turned back to the Zimbabwean. "Sorry, where did you say you were from?"

"Nyamandlovu, near Bulawayo." Except for us, the bar was now silent.

"So, what can I get you to drink?"

"Pint of lager, please." I poured him his beer and he moved away quickly to join some friends in the corner.

A couple walked into the bar and sat down in front of me.

"What can I get you, sir?"

"Two pints of beer please, mate." He had a broad Aussie accent. "Not this warm shit you drink over here. Proper beer."

"Lager?"

"Yeah, that's right. You don't sound like a Pom, mate. Where you from?"

"Zim."

"What colleges would you recommend we see?" his girlfriend asked.

"Well, Trinity is the richest Oxbridge college," I told her as I passed them their lagers. "It's impressive—six British prime ministers have been educated there. They've had twenty-eight Nobel Prize winners ..."

There was a tap on my arm. "Scott ... can we have a chat?"

"Sure, Paul." I turned to the Aussie couple. "I'll be right back."

I followed Paul to a quiet corner of the bar and sat down.

"Listen, Scott, I'm very happy with your work, but there've been a number of incidents now, and … well … some of the staff and even some customers are uncomfortable with you around. I'm afraid I'm going to have to put you on final warning. One more complaint, and I'll ask you to leave. Okay?"

"Really, Paul?" I was surprised. This seemed a bit out of character for him. Anyway, I couldn't afford to lose the job, so I told him that it wouldn't happen again.

I gave the Aussie couple directions to Trinity and poured them another two lagers.

"A pint of bitter and a gin and tonic," called out one of the regulars.

"Yes, sir." I quickly poured the drinks and passed them over the counter.

"Another lager for me, too, please." It was the man from Nyamandlovu.

"So how are things in Zim?" I asked as I poured his drink. "Mugabe seems to be doing a reasonable job."

"Not a chance. He's an evil bastard."

"Why?"

"Well he's murdering the Matabele in their thousands."

"I've heard a few stories about the Fifth Brigade," I told him. "But I didn't think it was that serious."

"*Ja*, it is. Mugabe's Fifth Brigade are North Korean trained. Bad bastards. Make the Nazis seem like choirboys."

He stopped as I handed him his lager, then took a deep gulp and continued, "Anyway, these Fifth Brigade have been murdering, starving, raping, beating and torturing the Ndebele in Matabeleland on a massive scale. They're calling it the *Gukurahundi*."

"Gukurahundi?"

"Ja, in Shona it means 'the early rain which washes away the chaff before the spring rains'."

"So why's he hammering the Ndebele?"

"You know Mugabe's terrs and Nkomo's lot, ZIPRA, have never really got on. Since Mugabe came to power they've had a couple of battles. And a lot of the ex-ZIPRA terrs have gone back into the bush as dissidents. They're effectively terrs again. So the Fifth Brigade are chasing these dissidents, but in the process are murdering thousands of innocent Ndebele."

It all sounded a little hard to believe. Perhaps the man from Nyamandlovu was embellishing the truth.

"Another pint, sir?" I called out to one of the regulars ambling over. He nodded, and I poured.

"Vodka and Coke, please," called out another customer.

"Sure," I said, passing the pint to the regular. After serving the vodka and Coke, I went to help Paul pack crates of beer in the storeroom. When I got back to the bar a familiar voice boomed out at me. "Two lagers please, mate."

I turned to face the Aussie couple with a smile. "How was Trinity?"

"Yeah, mate, it was awesome. What else do you recommend?"

I handed them each a lager. "Hire a punt below Magdalene Bridge and make your way along the River Cam behind the colleges. It's beautiful."

After closing I cashed up and walked quietly back to my room. As I arrived, the phone rang.

"Hi, Dad, can't wait to see you all."

"Looking forward to seeing you too, son." He sounded tense. "Listen … I've got some bad news."

"What?"

"They've taken Anna."

"Who?"

"The Fifth Brigade."

## eighteen

*For God shall bring every work into judgment, with every secret thing, whether it be good, or whether it be evil.* Ecclesiastes 12.14

Dad met me at the airport in Salisbury, now Harare. It was great to be back, great to see Dad.

"How're things?" I asked as we made our way to the car park.

He didn't answer.

"When did they take her?"

"Last week," he told me as we climbed into the bakkie and drove off.

He slowed down and hooted at a couple of donkeys strolling across the road. "Last week, this big army truck pulled up outside the house. Fifth Brigade asking for Anna."

"Why Anna?"

"The boys on the farm think it's got something to do with Simba."

I wound down the passenger seat window. *It would have been because of Simba, but I didn't want to discuss it with Dad.* "Did you try and stop them taking her?"

"Damn right I did. I held her by the arm. Wouldn't let her go. Until they put three AKs against my head. Mum was screaming at me to let go. I didn't have a choice."

"Have you told Simba?"

"*Ja*, I briefed him a few days back."

"I heard he got a bursary for Oxford."

"That's right," Dad said, as he stopped to fill up with petrol.

"Full tank please, *shamwari*," he called out to the attendant as we pulled up at a grubby service station. A portrait of Mugabe stared out at us from the wall above a kiosk where they were selling Cokes and stale meat pies.

"All right, *baas*, it's full now. Thirty-five dollars."

"Is Anna gonna be okay?" I asked as Dad started the engine.

"They've taken her to Bhalagwe Camp near Kezi. It's like a concentration camp." He hesitated as he stared at the road in front of him. "We need to get to her quickly. I'd like to go in and rescue her. I know it's a lot to ask you, son, but will you come with me?"

"Jeez, Dad, are you sure about that? Two white guys?"

Dad had that look in his eye—the same one I remembered when he was teaching Simba and me to fight. "I grew up in Kezi. Grandpa's farm is close to Bhalagwe. I know the bush there like the back of my hand. We'll drive in and tell them we're visiting Grandpa. If it's too dangerous to drive, we walk to Bhalagwe."

"Hell, Dad, I'll think about it … but are you sure you want to risk your life?"

"For sure. Anna's been with us twenty-six years … if we leave her, she'll die. I'll go whether you come or not."

The same old welcoming committee … except Anna … was there to meet me on the lawn when we arrived home. I'd almost forgotten Shoko wouldn't be there to greet me. But I barely had time to settle in and catch up with Mum before we were off again. To Kezi, early the next morning, in the bakkie.

After filling up with petrol at Nsiza we drove on, through Bulawayo and through Matobo Hills, where they'd buried Cecil John Rhodes and Mzilikazi, the famous Ndebele warrior and father of Lobengula. And it was just after Matobo Hills that we were stopped by two lines of green metal spikes across the road. A Fifth Brigade roadblock. To the right of the roadblock was a machine-gun post, covered with sandbags. A soldier had the gun pointed directly at us, and he looked dead keen to try it out. Wearing the distinctive red Fifth Brigade beret, a sergeant marched over to the vehicle.

"Get out," he barked. He stank of Chibuku beer. His puffy red eyes didn't bother to look at us.

Dad scowled.

I gestured towards the machine gun. "Hey, Dad, don't say anything." We stepped from the car. The sergeant took a cursory glance in the back of the bakkie.

"Open, now!" he shouted, pointing at our two suitcases. He tossed the contents onto the road, then sauntered back to the machine gun, where he grabbed his carton of Chibuku and took a deep gulp.

The machine gun was still pointing at us as we repacked our cases and began driving off. Through Kezi, then on to Grandpa's farm.

As we drove up the koppie leading to Grandpa's house, Dad asked, "When did you last see Grandpa?"

"Just before Granny died—about three years ago."

"Well, he's aged a lot since Granny died," Dad warned.

He was standing on the veranda when we drove into the yard. His hair and beard were now completely white, his face lined and gaunt. He walked with a stoop, but his green eyes were still bright and alert. Quickly we shook hands as he ushered us inside. I stopped on the veranda to admire the magnificent view right across the Kezi farming district.

"How are things at Cambridge?" he asked me as he made us some toast and a pot of tea.

"Fine, thanks, Grandpa."

"And all okay with you, Peter?" But he didn't wait for Dad to answer. "Things are bad here—really bad." He turned to Dad. "Where's the picture of Anna?"

Dad pulled out an old photo of Anna and Simba on our front lawn.

Grandpa carefully studied it. "Good, 'cos a few of the farm boys have just been released from Bhalagwe. They might recognise her." He passed us a plate of toast and the pot of tea. "Eat up quickly. Then we'll go and see these boys."

He led us down a narrow bush path to a small compound, with about fifteen huts.

Silas was sitting outside his hut and got to his feet, a big smile on his face once he saw Dad. When Dad was a young boy growing up on the farm, Silas had been the herdboy. Over the years he'd worked his way up the ranks on Grandpa's farm, finally rising to boss-boy, a position he'd held for the past fifteen years.

They were good friends, and Dad shook his hand firmly. "Hey, Silas, you've gone grey."

Silas laughed. "*Baas* Peter. You also, *eh?*" I looked at Dad. I hadn't noticed the patches of grey which were sprouting through his once-black hair.

"Hello, *Baas* Scott," he greeted me.

"Hi, Silas, nice to see you." I'd known him since I was a child. He was a warm, likeable man.

"*Baas* Scott, my girl is here. She go school, she like talk English. You talk to her?"

"I'd love to, Silas."

He shouted, "Violet!" and a pretty young girl came running from the other side of the compound.

"She's really thin," I noted to Grandpa.

"*Ja*, it's terrible what these Fifth Brigade are doing. They're starving these blacks. All the stores are closed, and they've cut off their food supplies. Their houses are constantly searched for food. If they find any, they get a good beating and the food is destroyed."

"Very nice to meet you, *baas*," said Violet after Silas introduced us.

Grandpa was clearly in a rush, but didn't want to offend Silas. "Scott, why don't you and Violet have a chat in Silas's hut? The rest of us will meet with the boys who've just got out of Bhalagwe … see if they've got news of Anna. I'll give you a full briefing afterwards. Okay?"

"Sure."

"*Baas*, would you like a cup of tea?" Violet asked as I followed her into Silas's hut. In one corner was an old, ragged-looking mattress. In the centre was a wooden stool. I sat down on it.

"I'd love to, thanks, Violet." She put the kettle on the fire outside and came back into the hut, standing at the doorway.

"Violet, please call me Scott. You don't need to call me *Baas* Scott."

"Okay, *baas*."

"No, not *baas*, just Scott. Say Scott."

"Scott."

"That's it, perfect. Your English is very good. So much better than my Ndebele." She smiled proudly.

"How old are you?"

"Fourteen."

"And where do you go to school?"

"In Matobo. My favourite subject is science." She had an intense expression in her watery brown eyes as she looked down at me. I could tell she enjoyed practising her English.

"Scott, would you like milk and sugar in your tea?"

"Yes please, Violet, one sugar."

She brought me a chipped green enamel mug that had lost most of its paint. "My father tells me that you go to university."

"Yes, I go to university in England," I told her, speaking clearly so she could easily understand me. "Do you want to go to university?" I took a sip of tea; it tasted terrible.

"Yes, Scott." Now she was comfortable with just Scott, she couldn't stop using it.

"I'd like to be a doctor, Scott."

"That'll be interesting."

"Yes … my father has been saving money to pay for my university since I was three. He said that even then he could tell I would be the clever one in the family."

We chatted for a while. Then I stood up and gulped down the rest of my tea. "Well, good luck, Violet. I hope to meet you again."

Grandpa and Dad were walking out of the next-door hut, as Dad waved over to me. "Let's go. We'll brief you at the house."

I went over to say goodbye to Silas. "You have a wonderful daughter," I told him.

"Thank you, *Baas* Scott. Very clever, *eh?*" he said beaming proudly.

Dad and Grandpa were striding back purposefully, and I jogged to catch up.

"How'd it go?" I asked Dad.

"One of the boys who's just come out of Bhalagwe recognised her photo. Says she arrived about five days ago. An officer has taken her to be his *wife*, which means she'll probably be raped, but at least by only one person ... for now."

He frowned. "We need to get to her quickly."

We arrived at Grandpa's house and went straight to his study. He locked the door behind us. "Peter, I think it's important for Scott to understand what we're up against here."

Dad sat down in a chair next to me.

Grandpa continued. "These Fifth Brigade are savages. In Silas's home village in northern Matabeleland, they beat the whole village. Then forced some of them to dig a mass grave and climb into it before shooting them. Some were still alive when they were buried." He stopped and closed his eyes. "The villagers were made to dance on the graves singing songs praising Mugabe and ZANU-PF."

I was shocked. It was my varsity vacation. My fellow students were partying on Mykonos, and I was about to take on the Fifth Brigade.

"Your dad is hell-bent on rescuing Anna." Grandpa walked over to where Dad was sitting. "Peter, my personal view is that you shouldn't go. These are dangerous, evil men."

"I agree, Dad," I added.

"Sorry, I'm not going to let Anna down."

Grandpa looked across at me. "Your father's always been like this—stubborn. Anyway," he continued, "there's a curfew. No one is allowed to enter or leave the area, and if they catch you moving around between six at night and six in the morning, they'll shoot you." He put his hands behind his back, made his way to the study window and looked outside.

"Just before sundown I'll take you on an old farm road to within ten kays of the camp. You can make your way on foot from there. Silas isn't happy about it, but he'll be your guide … you have to take someone you can trust."

We left in Grandpa's bakkie at five-fifteen, in time for Grandpa to get back before the curfew started. Silas and I sat silently in the back as we drove quickly along the old farm road. I took in the view on all sides, looking for signs of army trucks. To my right and in front of us was an open plain, dotted with acacias and watering holes; to my left a range of koppies covered with acacia and mangwe trees. We arrived at our drop-off point at five-thirty-five. My stomach tightened with excitement as I reached under the bakkie and pulled out an FN rifle, a .303, spare mags, hunting knives, binoculars and torches. It reminded me of my army ops.

"Good luck, boys," Grandpa said, shaking our hands firmly before driving off.

Silas led the way as we followed him quickly through the bush. The wind was starting to pick up. After about fifty minutes we heard the sound of trucks and hid behind some trees. It was three cattle trucks followed by an army truck. The cattle trucks were packed with men, women and children. I could see their faces … wide-eyed and terrified.

"Going to Bhalagwe?" I asked Silas. He nodded. I tightened my grip on the .303.

After the trucks had gone, Silas pointed to an old broken gate. "Antelope Mine."

"I've heard some terrible stories about that place," said Dad. "If they're true, I'd rather not see it."

We followed Silas through a broken fence and past an old overgrown mineshaft towards another shaft about fifty metres ahead. Before we got there Silas stopped, refusing to move any further. So Dad and I continued alone. Around the shaft were tyre tracks from the army trucks. Cigarette butts, cartridges, Coke bottles. On the edge of the shaft was a makeshift loading bay.

"What happens here?" I asked Dad.

He shrugged.

At the edge, we peered down the shaft and the smell hit me: rotting meat with a tinge of sweetness. We walked over to where Silas was standing—unmoving, staring solemnly at his bare feet in the dry brown sand.

He spoke softly without looking up. "*Baas*, at night they bring the bodies from Bhalagwe. My people. Many people."

I looked across at the mineshaft in disbelief. So this was a mass grave for Mugabe's victims. The word hit me: genocide.

The sun was making its way down, a bright red glow over the black granite koppies. The wind was sweeping into my face and with it the brown dust from Antelope Mine. I covered my eyes. Through the open fingers of my hand I could see an African black eagle perched on a mopane about sixty metres from where we were standing. A beautiful black bird nearly a metre in length, he must have been one of the few living witnesses to the genocide at Antelope Mine.

I put my arm around Dad's shoulder. "Let's get Anna."

The lights from the camp lit up the dark evening sky as we got closer to Bhalagwe. The camp was at the foot of a koppie.

Silas suggested that we first climb the koppie to study the camp. Then we could plan our rescue. It was thick bush and heavy going, but we were walking quickly. Each of us alert, on guard. Antelope Mine was a stark reminder of what we were up against.

"All right, *baas*." Silas motioned us to a stop. It was the perfect viewing gallery: a thicket about half way up the koppie and behind a rocky outcrop.

Activity was starting to build up on the parade ground below.

"*Aiee, hayi, hayi* … " Silas muttered under his breath and looked away. "Too bad men, *eh. Too* bad."

The Fifth Brigade's evening entertainment had started. They'd assembled a large crowd of the prisoners to watch. I pulled out my night-viewing binoculars and focused on the rows and rows of prisoners. No sign of Anna.

"Dad, you and Silas look out for Anna. I'll do a quick recce to check out the camp and make sure there's no one following us."

I slipped into the bush and carefully made my way down the mountain towards the camp. Even in the dark I could see how well hidden the camp was, allowing these monsters to carry on their evil deeds in private. It was covered on three sides: Bhalagwe Hill, on which we were hiding, Zamanyone Hill to one side and then Antelope Dam.

There was no sign of life on the mountain; no one following us. I tucked in behind some rocks, pulled out my binoculars and looked out over the camp. Dominating the view were rectangular holding sheds. Around each block of a dozen sheds was thick barbed-wire fencing. This must have been where they packed the prisoners. To the right of the prisoners were lines of neatly parked army trucks, and directly behind them were rows of green tents and more rectangular sheds, where the soldiers probably slept. Silas said they'd about two thousand prisoners in camp at any given time. It looked big enough to hold double that.

A whooping call rang through the night. Hyena. I imagined a group of yellow-grey hyenas with their sullen dark eyes and large, pointed carnassial teeth scavenging at one of the mass graves.

Then I climbed back up to where Dad and Silas were hidden.

They were waiting anxiously for me.

"We know where she is," whispered Dad. "Let's move!"

## nineteen

"Where?" I asked as we climbed down the koppie. Dad pointed at a small rectangular shed on the western perimeter of Bhalagwe. I took a mental snapshot of the location.

"She was on the parade ground," Dad explained. "Then one of the soldiers marched her across the camp to that shed."

"What were the Fifth Brigade doing to them on the parade ground?"

"You don't want to know, son."

When we reached the bottom of the koppie, I called Dad and Silas into a huddle.

"Okay," I pointed to the soldiers on the parade ground. "Let's wait for these guys to go to bed. Then we go in and get her. Her shed is on the edge of the camp, so it'll be easy to get to."

We waited patiently for hours. Finally, as they started to turn the lights off across the camp, we made our way downwards. There was a sentry-box about eighty metres from Anna's shed. The light was on but there were no signs of activity. We circled round the camp and waited in a clump of acacias about a hundred metres from the shed. More lights went off as we crept towards

Anna's shed. Hell, I hoped she was still there.

We dived for cover as we heard two soldiers starting up a conversation. Must be the guards—all the rest had gone to bed. Shit, they were walking straight towards us. I thought of the Frelimo guards at Cabora Bassa. I wished we had silencers on our rifles. If we fired now, we'd wake the whole camp. My grip tightened on my hunting knife. They carried on walking towards us. We lay dead still. I tried not to breathe. Then they were four metres from where we were lying. I was ready to spring. But they walked right past.

When they were out of sight, we crawled forward. I bumped into Silas. He was soaking wet, sweating heavily. Matabele thorns were sticking in my palms, but I kept going. Thirty metres away, twenty metres, ten metres … and then we were there.

I gently opened the door and looked inside. The officer was lying on his own, fast asleep, snoring. Anna was on the floor, tied to the wall with either a chain or a rope, I couldn't tell. She was whimpering like a wounded impala, her head against the concrete floor.

"I'll look after him. You get Anna," I said quietly to Dad. We needed to move quickly before the guards saw us. I crept to the officer, silently stood up and held the knife over his head, in case he woke up.

"Anna, it's *Baas* Peter," I could hear Dad whisper.

"*Baas, baas,*" she cried softly. The officer stirred.

"*Shhh*, Anna, *shhh!*"

Then the officer turned over and went back to sleep.

I could hear Dad cutting. Good, she was tied with a rope. The cutting stopped. I could make out the three of them crawling to the door. So far, so good. I held my breath.

Then a thud as one of them bumped into a chair. It was a faint sound, but the officer had been well trained. He sat bolt upright.

With my right hand I rammed the knife into his temple, twisting and twisting the blade into his skull. I held my left hand over his mouth to stop him screaming. I kept on twisting and ramming until all movement stopped. I looked down—my shirt was soaked in blood and brains. I thought of my varsity mates on the beach. No time. I walked to the door and crouched down next to the others.

"Good work, Scott! Are you all right?" asked Dad.

"Fine. Let's get out of here before they find him."

We crawled on our hands and knees all the way out of the camp. All I could smell were the blood and brains on my shirt, a dull metallic smell, like old coins. We reached the edge of the camp safely. I looked up at Dad and gave him a quick thumbs-up. So far so good.

Then four flashlights, could have been more, lit up the darkness. "Drop your guns, now!" At least five soldiers surrounded us and were pointing their AKs directly at us. We placed our weapons on the ground and rose to our feet.

Their leader spoke. "And what do we have here? Ahhh ... some white men. Now tell me ... what is a white man doing rescuing one of our prisoners? Very, very silly, *eh?*"

They got us to stand in a straight line with three of them at the front and two behind, their AKs pointed at our heads. Silas was called forward, and the leader smashed the rifle butt into his head. He went crashing to the floor and the two on either side of the leader rushed forward and swung their boots into him.

"On your feet," the leader hissed.

Silas got to his feet. Even in the dark I could see he was bleeding badly from the head.

"Now sing!" the leader ordered.

"*Pamberi ZANU-PF, Pamberi Mugabe*," shouted Silas.

"Louder!" screamed the leader, ramming his boot into Silas's groin.

Silas fell to the ground, crying out in agony. He struggled to his feet, "*Pasi ne ZAPU, Pamberi Mugabe*."

Then they opened fire at point-blank range, the bullets tearing into Silas's leg. All their AKs had silencers attached. I looked around me. Two guards had their AKs pointed directly at our heads. If we tried to help him or make a run for it, we'd be shot down in seconds. To my left, Anna was sweating heavily. To my right, Dad stood upright, glaring at the Fifth Brigade leader.

He turned to us, ignoring Silas rolling on the ground, clutching his blood-splattered leg.

"Okay, who's next?" he asked, a big smile on his face.

I looked around. There was no point in making a run for it. Rather be proud. I stepped forward. "It's me."

"No," said Dad, stepping in front of me.

"He, he, he," laughed the leader in mock delight. "Don't worry. You'll both get your chance."

If our time was up, I'd go down fighting. "How can you do this to your own people? Some day Mugabe will pay for this. And so will you, you murdering bastard!"

The leader swung his rifle butt and I went flying through a thorn bush into the soil, where I lay still, the sand sharp against my face.

"Get up," he barked.

I got to my feet. He slapped me with his open hand and waded in with his boot, kicking me hard in the groin. I stumbled onto my knees.

"Get up," he repeated. Again I got up. "First, I kill the old man, so the cheeky one can watch and enjoy." He cocked his weapon and held it at Dad's head.

"Get on with it, you coward," growled Dad.

I closed my eyes. Then I heard the bullets thudding into flesh. Fearing the worst, I opened my eyes and looked across at Dad. But he was still standing. Lying on the ground in front of him were three Fifth Brigade soldiers. I turned to look behind. Both soldiers were motionless on the ground. Someone was gently comforting Anna in Ndebele. A familiar voice. Simba. With him were two others, also carrying AKs.

He called us together. "We must head for that koppie over there. Quickly," he said, pointing at a grey shadow about eight hundred metres away. Silas was still on the ground, whimpering in pain. Dad picked him up and carried him. I was shaking as I collected our rifles. Both the narrow escape from death and seeing Simba again had really thrown me. I didn't want to follow him, but it was life or death. When we arrived at the koppie Simba motioned us into a thicket. He turned to one of the men with him, "Tuli, from here you must cover all tracks. We disappear." Then he turned to the rest of us, "It'll be light in about an hour. We're gonna hide you in underground caves about two kays from here. When it's dark again we'll get you back to Kezi."

"Thanks, Simba," said Dad before we set off.

Simba looked at me, waiting for me to say the same. But I didn't even look at him. Tuli broke off a leafy mopane branch and did his best to cover our tracks and the blood that was dripping from Silas, as we set off quickly after Simba. Almost immediately we heard the Bhalagwe siren going off—a piercing sound. They'd found the dead soldiers. We quickened our pace.

After about half an hour, Simba called a halt and led us to a small koppie behind a clump of mopane trees. We squeezed through a narrow gap between two large boulders, and then crawled through a thin channel in the rocks for almost fifty metres. At the end of the channel we slid down through more rocks into a tiny cave. Dad climbed in first, and gently laid Silas on the rocks. Then grabbed his torch and shone it first on Silas's leg, then at his stomach.

"Doesn't look good. He's got a nasty gut wound."

Simba called over to Tuli. "Bring the bandages."

Tuli brought over a small first-aid box. Simba opened it, pulled out some bandages and wrapped them round Silas's leg and stomach. Silas was doing his best not to make any noise, but he was in so much pain that he couldn't stop himself from crying out in agony.

"Okay, nobody makes a sound," said Simba, putting a finger to his lips. "I'll guard the western entrance. Tuli, you take the eastern side." He pointed at the other man. "Roger, you take the northern side. *Baas* Peter, Scott. Cover this entrance and keep an eye on Silas."

He kissed Anna on the cheek and held her hand as he spoke gently to her in Ndebele. Then he leapt out the cave. We all manned our stations, while Dad sat with Silas. His breathing was becoming more ragged—short, pained gasps. Dad kept talking to him in Ndebele, a gentle soothing sound.

The morning light drifted into the cave. We had the perfect hiding spot. The entrance to the cave was covered by a thicket of thorn trees and mopanes, completely invisible from the outside. To get to the entrance you had to crawl fifty metres through a narrow strip of rock, the opening of which was similarly camouflaged from outside.

I went over to Silas and put my hand on his pulse. It was fading. "Goodbye, Silas," I said sadly. He was barely conscious.

Dad put both his arms around Silas's head and hugged him tightly. "Goodbye, Silas … and thank you." Then he held his hand as his life drifted away from him.

There was a rustling outside. My grip tightened on the .303. It was Simba. "We've got to move," he told us when he saw Silas's body. "Now that it's light, you can see the trail of blood behind us. Tuli covered most of it, but there's enough there for the Fifth Brigade to track us."

We jumped out of the cave and made our way back along the channel through which we'd come. Simba gently helped Anna to her feet and followed us, then moved to the front and led us quickly through the bush while Tuli moved behind, covering our tracks. This time there was no blood to give us away.

Anna was in a state of shock after all she'd been through. So I picked her up and carried her. After about thirty minutes, Simba called us to a halt. We were standing outside a group of three granite koppies packed tightly together. Squeezing through the rocks, we found a large thicket of vegetation and clambered into the centre. Inside was a small clearing, completely screened from the outside. Simba had found us another excellent hiding spot. I thought back to our days in the army. As our guide he'd always managed to find us great spots in which to take cover.

I forced my mind back to the present. Simba was gently stroking Anna's head on the side of the clearing, his back to me. My grip tightened on the .303. All I had to do was cock the rifle, aim and fire. And he'd be gone. But he'd saved us. Without his intervention, both Dad and I would be dead, and I was confident he would now guide us to safety. My grip loosened.

Simba got to his feet and pulled out our breakfast: a can of bully-beef and a packet of Marie biscuits. He waved to Tuli and Roger, and the three of them went to take up their guard positions at the foot of each koppie outside. I thought of Silas. He hadn't wanted to be our guide; we'd as good as killed him ourselves.

Dad and I took turns sleeping. In the morning I slept, but woke when Simba entered the clearing.

"All okay, *Baas* Peter?" he asked Dad. I watched them through half-closed eyes. I didn't want to speak to Simba.

"Fine, thanks, Simba. Please drop the 'baas' ... just Peter is fine." Simba nodded, but I noticed he never addressed Dad by name after that.

"Beautiful bush around here," said Dad.

"*Ja*, north of here are the Matobo hills which are sacred for us Ndebele. That's where the Oracle for Umlimo was killed," he told Dad as he sat down beside him.

"Umlimo?"

"He was the spiritual leader of the Ndebele in the 1896 uprising against you white settlers: the First *Chimurenga*. Umlimo is a god and the Oracle, his human voice."

Dad looked at him. "Interesting. What happened to him?" I strained my ears to listen.

"Well, you whites were in serious trouble. At one point we had you under siege in Bulawayo. Legend has it that an American by the name of Frederick Burnham, with a young commissioner called Armstrong, made his way at night into the Matobo Hills. They tied their horses to a thicket, like this one. Then they crawled on their hands and knees through the thick bush to the Oracle's sacred cave. And waited. The Oracle appeared and started to dance. That's when Burnham shot him, just below the heart."

Dad rose up and squatted on his haunches. "Did your warriors catch him?"

"No, he and Armstrong escaped. Dealt a major psychological blow to the Ndebele. A few months later Rhodes negotiated an end to the fighting."

In the afternoon, I took guard. Anna lay on her side without moving, staring into the rocks. As soon as the light began to fade, Simba was back again talking to Dad, finding out exactly where Grandpa's farm was.

"Tuli knows the Kezi area well. We'll get you there quickly and safely. No longer than nine hours. Mother shall go with you as they won't be expecting white men to be involved. They'll be looking out for me."

Once the sun went down Simba and Tuli led the way to Grandpa's house. After about an hour's walking I heard the sound of army trucks. We must have been next to a road. The lights came into view and Simba motioned us down behind a group of mopanes. But they drove past, the sound of drunken laughter carrying in the still evening air.

"Fifth Brigade, coming back from the shebeen," explained Simba.

We kept a fast pace but reached Grandpa's farm well after midnight. Simba hugged his mother and shook hands with Dad. "Goodbye, thanks for coming to get my mother."

"No problem. You saved us. Thank you."

He held out his hand for me. But I turned away and knocked on Grandpa's front door.

Grandpa was devastated at the death of Silas. "I feel responsible," he said miserably. "I insisted he go with you as guide."

"Show Anna the shower," he called out to me as he forked rashers of bacon into the frying pan. When Anna appeared from her shower wearing Grandpa's faded blue track-suit, he dished out the bacon and eggs. Anna grabbed her plate and went outside. Dad called her back in, and we all sat at Grandpa's dining-room table. It was pretty basic; probably had been since Granny died. As we ate, we briefed Grandpa on the rescue.

He listened carefully while he finished his breakfast. Then he poured us Tanganda tea from a big old teapot. "They'll be searching everywhere. Here, too … there aren't many white farmers left in Kezi." He looked at me and Dad. "We're not going to be able to get you home until this has all blown over. You should stay here for at least a week. They'll suspect dissidents, perhaps someone connected with Anna's son, to have rescued her. So they won't be looking for white men."

He turned to Anna. "But they'll be looking for you, in a big way. You've got to hide here. In the cellar. No one must know you're here, not even Lois, my maid." Rising to his feet, his cup of tea in one hand, he walked over to the window. "When those bastards come looking for you, there's a little trapdoor in the corner of the cellar. They'll never find you there."

He walked back to the table and bent down to look at Anna. "You've eaten nothing, Anna."

She was sitting at the table, her face a sickly yellow colour. Her food was almost untouched. Grandpa grabbed a slice of hot toast, buttered it and then spread a healthy layer of honey onto it. He cut it in four pieces and offered it to Anna. "Please, Anna, eat this. You'll feel a lot better."

She picked up a slice and took a small bite.

We set up Anna's bed in the cellar. I showed her the trapdoor, where she should hide. "So, Anna, when the soldiers come, you pack the blanket in the cupboard and the mattress on top. There must be no sign of anyone in the room. Okay?"

"Okay, *baas*." She sat down on the bed. When I reached the door I turned to look at her. She sat huddled in a little ball, her arms tucked under her knees. I locked the door after me.

"Boys, get some sleep. If they come, I'll wake you. You guys don't need to hide."

I gave Grandpa the key to the cellar.

As I climbed into my bed, there was a knocking on the door. It was Dad. "Scott ... Simba saved our lives. You didn't thank him, didn't even look at him. Why?"

"Dad, there's history between us."

"What history?"

"Sorry, but I don't want to talk about it."

He left the room muttering under his breath. Antelope Mine, the officer I'd killed, Silas and Violet. I forced them all from my mind and pretended I was fishing on the Impali with Shoko and Bruce. Finally I drifted into an uneasy sleep. I woke up with someone standing over me.

It was Grandpa. "Are you okay, boy? You've been crying out in your sleep."

I got up, made myself a cup of tea and chatted to him. He'd heard from the boys in the compound that the Fifth Brigade had been burning huts on the farm next door. They'd be with us soon so I went to keep watch outside. Sure enough, about twenty minutes later, I heard the drone of army trucks. I walked quickly inside, grabbed the cellar key, woke and hid Anna, closed the trapdoor after her and packed away her bedding. Then I went upstairs, a feeling of dread clawing at my stomach.

# twenty

Grandpa met them at the door. They pushed him aside and did a quick tour of the house, helping themselves to his bar along the way: KWV brandy, cane spirits, Cokes, Lion Lager—whatever they could find. Then they hit the compound. Lois told us later they'd been asking about Simba, certain he'd been involved in the rescue. But no information was forthcoming, so they gave everyone a beating using an assortment of knobkerries, cattle whips and mopane branches. Then they set the compound alight before leaving. We'd saved Anna, but what price would these poor villagers across Kezi pay for it?

"*Aiee*, too sad, too sad," concluded Lois miserably.

"Look, thank God you're alive, that's the main thing," Grandpa told her. "In Nyamandlovu and Tsholotsho the Fifth Brigade have been burning the huts, with all the villagers locked inside. You guys are lucky."

We stayed with Grandpa for five more days, then made our way to Bulawayo. Dad and I went first in the bakkie. We were stopped and searched by the Fifth Brigade, but they found nothing. So, after 'confiscating' a carton of Dad's Madison cigarettes, they let us through. Grandpa followed five hours later. He hid Anna beneath some compost in the back of his farm truck, and drove into town. They knew Grandpa well, and after he pulled out a bottle of cane spirits for them, they waved him on.

We met up with him at the Eskimo Hut ice-cream parlour in Bulawayo. Anna quickly swapped cars as we hugged Grandpa goodbye and drove off. On the way Dad explained to Anna that we'd be dropping her at a farm in Kadoma. He'd found a new job for her with friends of ours, the Wilsons. Good people—they'd look after her. It wasn't safe for her to come home. He warned her that she shouldn't keep in touch with any of her friends, that she'd have to start a new life. When the problems with the dissidents and Fifth Brigade were over she could come back, but only then.

"*Baas, eh* … Simba?"

"Don't worry, I've spoken to him. He knows where you'll be."

After dropping Anna in Kadoma, we made our way back home.

I briefed Mum over a cup of tea, then walked down to the Baboon Pool with Dad and the dogs. I was curious to see the baboons again in real life, having seen them so often in my dreams. And sure enough, they were there on the rocks … Grey and the rest of them, eating *mahobohobos*.

"Hello, boys, nice to see you," I called out. It was like seeing old friends again. But they didn't see it that way. Grey gave me a brief glance; the rest didn't even bother to look. We sat by the river's edge where Simba and I had stood so many times in my dreams, and looked up at the baboons. Behind them the koppies were a fresh green with the summer leaves of the msasas.

Dad smiled, "So it's been some vacation for you, hey?"

"It certainly has." I paused. "Why do you think the rest of the world lets Mugabe do this to his own people?"

"Do they know it's happening?" asked Dad.

"Of course they do. The church is all over Matabeleland, and would've told them what's going on. The world leaders are just ignoring it. For some reason it's acceptable for a black leader to murder tens of thousands of blacks. But if those were whites he was murdering, or if he was a white murdering blacks, the world would be up in arms."

"Ja, you've got a point," agreed Dad.

I got to my feet, picked up a stone and skimmed it over the water's surface. "Do you think they'll ever punish Mugabe for this?"

Dad stared into the water. Finally, he spoke. "Ja, I reckon they'll punish him, someday. I mean the Nazis were all tried. And if they don't punish him in this life, his reckoning will come. You can't get away with that."

"I hope you're right." I bent down and scooped a handful of water into my mouth. "Let's make a move."

Early the next morning I set off for Kariba in Dad's bakkie, stopping in Harare on the way to pick up Brian. We arrived at our campsite on the shores of Lake Kariba in the early afternoon.

We pitched our tent, grabbed our rods and cool box, then made our way down to the Caribbea Bay Boathouse where we hired a boat.

"Can we go tigerfishing?" Brian asked.

"No, it's bream fishing this year. Next year, when you turn six, then I'll take you tigerfishing."

He grabbed my hand tightly and we kept walking to the boathouse where our boat driver, Enos, was waiting patiently.

"Have you got the worms?" I asked Enos as we launched the boat.

"Yes, *baas*," Enos replied cheerfully.

As we sped off towards Sanyati Gorge, I held out an earthworm for Brian, then watched as he pulled it over his hook. I tapped him on his back. "Good boy ... now let's catch some supper." Enos brought the boat to a stop in a small cove.

"Brian, before I show you how to cast, we need to set up the rules for a competition." His eyes lit up—he had a competitive streak in him. "Whoever catches the least fish today makes tea for the whole weekend. Deal?"

"Okay, *ja*," he said with a big smile, and we shook hands.

Then I showed him how to cast, and his fishing line, float and hook went flying out into the water. Almost immediately his float started bobbing up and down.

"Hey, Brian, you've got a bite!" He jerked his line out of the water.

"No, no ... not like that!" I told him as I helped him put another worm on his hook. "Give it time. The fish needs to feed on the worm. Normally he'll nibble a bit first. Then he'll get greedy and take a big bite. When he does that, you'll see the float go right down. *That's* when you strike!"

He cast again and we both watched closely.

"Scott, he's biting. Look!" The float was darting in and out of the water.

Enos and I stood on either side of him, shouting advice. "Not yet, Brian," I called out as I saw his grip tighten on the rod. It moved to the left, a little to the right, then down, and he struck.

"No! Too soon!"

He put on another worm while Enos and I lectured him on the timing of his strike. He cast again. Again Enos and I watched. Again his float started bobbing and weaving excitedly in the water. But this time he waited patiently—he was a capable little boy, and learnt quickly. Our eyes were all glued to his float. It dashed away from the boat, then back towards us, then towards the bank. Each time the movements were getting more urgent, more pronounced. And then it dropped ... quickly, deeply. And Brian struck! Enos and I cheered with delight as he pulled his line from the water. On his hook was a half-pound bream, his first catch.

I showed Brian how to remove the hook from the fish's mouth, then took out my camera. It was a special moment for both of us, so I took several shots. He was a handsome fellow, with his large brown eyes and tanned, healthy skin. A massive grin covered his face. Always happy, always smiling, I was so proud of him.

We put the bream in the keep-net. I picked Brian up and hugged him. "You're a champion, my boy. Your first catch!" It was hard to believe that a week earlier I'd been running for my life in Matabeleland.

"That will make a delicious supper," I said, rubbing my hands together.

He gave me a strange look. "We can't *eat* him! Look what a nice little fish he is."

I laughed and ran my hand through his short dark-brown hair. Already I had a strong suspicion that we wouldn't be eating any of the fish. It could be Enos's lucky night.

Once Brian's line was back in the water, I cast my own rod. But my eyes were glued to Brian's float.

"*Baas, baas!*" Enos was pointing at my float, which had plunged deeply below the surface. I struck and pulled out a three-quarter-pound bream.

"Brian, I think you're going to be making me tea all weekend."

"No ways! Watch ... I've got another bite!"

But I made sure Brian stayed ahead of me, and when Enos told me we needed to head for shore, he had three bream in the keep-net against my two.

Enos turned the boat and aimed for the boathouse.

"Scott, can I ask you something?"

"Anything you like, my boy."

"Are you my dad?" I was stunned at the question and didn't respond, so he asked me again.

"What does your mum say?"

"Nothing. Whenever I ask her, she changes the subject."

I didn't say anything as we sped back past the branches of the half-submerged mopane forest, the wind strong in our faces at the front of the boat. The sun was setting, a bright red glow spreading over the horizon. A herd of elephants on the banks were pulling down branches with their trunks.

Eventually Brian broke the silence. "Can we come fishing again tomorrow?"

"Of course, it's your weekend. We'll do as much fishing as you want."

When we got back to the boathouse I handed him the keep-net. "Brian, do you want to eat these fish?"

He crinkled up his nose. "No, we can't eat them."

I winked at Enos, who took the fish from the keep-net and put them in a plastic bag.

Hand in hand, we walked back to the campsite.

"Scott, I think I'd like a cup of tea," he said with a cheeky grin.

I laughed. "A bet is a bet," and I made a fire. While we waited for the kettle to boil we got out the rugby ball. "Have you ever played RAT?" I asked. He shook his head.

"Okay, well, you pass the ball back and forth. Each time you drop it, you get a letter. If you drop it three times you are a RAT. Then you go up against that tree over there and the other player throws the ball at you." We passed the ball between ourselves. This time I made sure Brian didn't win; he had to learn to lose as well. He stood up against the tree and cheerfully took his punishment.

The water boiled. While I made tea, Brian played with the rugby ball.

"Your boy's a real natural," commented another camper as he watched Brian punting the ball ahead, catching it and running through two imaginary defenders.

I had planned on bream and boiled potatoes for dinner, and didn't have anything else. Brian's refusal to eat the bream meant that cornflakes, milk and sugar were on the evening menu. After the cereal, I took him for a shower. Then we snuggled up in our sleeping bags inside the tent and I read *Winnie the Pooh* to him, by torchlight. Soon he was fast asleep and not long afterwards, so was I.

"Wake up, wake up, Scott!" Brian was peering over me. It was pitch dark. I sat up with a start.

"What's up, my boy?"

"You've been screaming." He looked frightened.

"Come on, my boy, you're imagining things."

"I promise, Scott. You were screaming and screaming."

I pulled him close and gave him a big hug. He didn't often camp in the bush. It was no wonder he was nervous.

"Who's Bruce?" he asked me.

"What?"

"You were shouting out his name."

"I'm sorry, Brian. Let's try and get some sleep." I turned over and closed my eyes. I'd never mentioned Bruce to Brian before.

"Scott, I can't go to sleep now."

I couldn't either, so I turned on the torch, picked up *Winnie the Pooh* and read into the early hours of the morning.

Finally, he fell asleep and I turned off the torch.

"Wake up, Scott."

I wiped my eyes. The early morning light was starting to creep into the tent. "What now, boy?"

"I'm ready for my tea, please."

I grabbed him by the neck and pulled him towards me, laughing.

He was chuckling, a naughty expression on his face. "That's the bet."

"It certainly is." I got to my feet and went to start the fire.

As I waited at the fire for the water to boil, he walked down to the water's edge. "Please can we go canoeing?" he shouted, pointing at a spare canoe on the shore.

"Of course." After breakfast we pulled the canoe into the water and paddled along the banks of the lake. In the afternoon we went fishing again with Enos. Again, he kept all the fish.

The clouds had been gradually building, and back at our tent the rain started, gently at first, then slowly building to a downpour. We walked outside in our shorts and ran across the lawn, laughing loudly as the warm rain splashed down on us. It soon stopped, so we dried ourselves and sat on the lawn, looking out over the lake. With the rain had come the flying ants, and they were streaming out of small holes on the edge of the lawn. Brian jumped to his feet and chased after them in all directions. Immediately he came running back with a handful of the fat, buttery little insects.

"Don't squash them," I told him. "They're flying around to mate."

He looked up at me, puzzled.

I sat him down on my lap. "After the rains, the boy and girl flying ants come out to make babies."

He held out his handful of crumpled flying ants. "These

ones?"

"*Ja.* The boy and girl meet up, break off their wings and go to start a new home, called a colony. Then they make baby flying ants."

"Really?"

"Yes. Later, when the colony is all set up, new flying ants come out and the same thing happens again. Now, they're actually called termites …"

"Can we eat, Scott?" he interrupted.

"Sure." I unpacked the cornflakes. "Hey, I don't want you telling your mum we ate cornflakes both nights," I laughed.

"I won't tell her."

"Promise?"

"*Ja*, I promise."

That night I read *Winnie the Pooh* again. But this time he didn't fall asleep quickly. He knew it was our last night together and didn't want to go to sleep. "Just one more page. Only one more," he would plead whenever I tried to say goodnight.

Finally I had to be firm, so I closed the book and kissed him goodnight. It'd been a long day, and almost immediately I put my head on the pillow, I was fast asleep.

It seemed like I'd only been asleep for a few minutes when I felt a tugging on my shoulder. "Wake up, Scott, wake up!"

I sat up. Brian was looking at me expectantly, his eyes wide open.

"For goodness sake, Brian, I'm not making you tea now. It's the middle of the night."

"No, I don't want tea. You've been screaming again."

"I'm sorry, boy." This time I believed him.

It was only when he held out *Winnie the Pooh*, a sheepish grin on his face, and said, "Please read … I'm too scared to go to sleep," that I realised I'd been conned. I wrestled him out of his sleeping bag, tickling him until he was squealing with laughter. But he got his way anyway, and again we read *Winnie the Pooh* through the night, finishing the book just as the sun peeped through the tent flap the next morning. I let Brian sleep as I packed everything into the car.

He was in a pensive mood when we set off for Harare. On the way, we stopped over in Karoi. I ordered meat pies and we sat in the front of the bakkie eating them. A little boy got out of the car in front of me, a pellet-gun in his hand. It brought back memories: the last time I'd stopped in Karoi was with Conway and Bruce, on the way to Lusaka to take out Nkomo.

"When I'm next in Zim, I'll get you a pellet-gun," I told Brian. "You've got to learn to shoot."

Immediately he brightened up, and we chatted about the pellet-gun all the way to Harare.

"Hey, I'll be back soon," I assured him as I hugged him goodbye.

He stood next to his mother, sobbing, as I turned the car, waved goodbye and drove fast out of their front gate.

## twenty-one

I didn't sleep on the plane that night. There was a lot on my mind. But I had no time to dwell on the horrors of the past weeks when I got back to Magdalene the next day. A day to unpack, write to Bruce, settle back into Cambridge life, and then I was off again. To a training week with the British Army boxing team in Aldershot. I was particularly excited about this trip, as I'd heard that Lieutenant Waters had rejoined the British Army, and was now based in Aldershot. It would be good to catch up; I hadn't seen him in five years.

We took nine boys—the same nine who were likely to represent us in the varsity match against Oxford, our main event of the year. We drove through the garrison town of Aldershot to the army barracks where we were met by Bob, our trainer and supervisor for the week. He showed us to our rooms. "Right, boys, dinner in the officers' mess in fifteen minutes."

After dinner we drank tea and sat around chatting about the varsity match. Kyle's mate from Belfast was at Oxford, and he had briefed Kyle on their team.

"They've got an impressive heavyweight," he told us. "Had five fights so far this year, knocked three of his opponents senseless. Stopped the other two in the first round." He turned to me. "From your neck of the woods."

"What's his name?" I asked.

"Simba Ndlovu."

"Simba?" Hell, I knew he was at Oxford. Didn't know he was boxing, though. This was big news.

"Do you know him?" asked Kyle, surprised at my reaction.

I mumbled a clumsy response that I might know him, and then announced, "Boys, we meet outside the front at five tomorrow morning. No one to be late." I said goodnight and walked back to my room along the grey military corridors of the home of the British Army. I couldn't believe it. Simba in the Oxford team! Dave White was our heavyweight. Simba'd be too strong for him. *What if I fought Simba? Hell, that'd be incredible.* I ran to Dave's room, marched right in and just blurted it out. "Dave, can we swop weights?"

"What?"

"I need to fight Simba, the Oxford heavyweight."

"But you're too light! I mean, you're only eighty-one kilos."

"I only have to weigh over eighty-one kilos to fight at heavyweight. Anyway, at eighty-five you're not much heavier."

"Okay, but to swap I've gotta get to eighty-one kilos."

"Come on, you've got six weeks, you'll easily lose four kilos."

"But why such late notice?"

"I've only found out now that Simba's going to be fighting at heavyweight."

"All right—let me sleep on it."

I went back to my room and paced up and down excitedly. I'd be giving away a lot of weight, but it'd be worth it.

I knew I wasn't going to sleep for hours, so I put on my running gear and off I went. About five kays, and fast. Along poorly lit streets on the outskirts of town. Cold and dark, it was a far cry from the Zimbabwean bush, where I'd just come from. As I sprinted the last one and a half kays on the homeward stretch, all I thought about was Simba. I showered, pulled out a book and read for hours before finally falling asleep. When the alarm rang at a quarter to five I jumped up, changed, and made my way to the meeting point.

Lewis was already there. "Hey, Scott, you've got a spring in your step today."

Bob arrived. "Boys, we're meeting the army team at the corner. Let's get cracking." It was a six-kilometre run. On the way, Dave sidled up to me, "Hey, I've been thinking about what you said. Look, I'm sure there're good reasons for you wanting to fight Simba and I know you're captain and all the rest, but it's not really fair on me."

I had to convince him. "Ja, Dave, look, I fully understand, but this is so important to me. I reckon we do the following: when we get back to Cambridge, we have a three-round sparring match. Full-on. Whoever wins gets to fight at heavyweight. Whoever loses fights at light-heavy. Deal?"

"Deal." We shook hands awkwardly as we ran along. I quickened my pace. I had to beat Dave. I had to fight Simba. Then faster, even faster. There were three army boxers in front of me as we entered the Aldershot athletic track for the final four hundred metres sprint. Straining everything I had, I caught the third army boy as we hit the final hundred-metre mark. The other two came in about seventy and fifty metres ahead of me. *By the end of the week I'll beat them*, I promised myself.

Bob had prepared a busy schedule. Every day it was an early-morning run at five o'clock. Sparring at ten. Gym work at three, and speedwork at five in the afternoon. When I woke up for the morning run on the last day, I was ready for the challenge.

We set off at a quick pace. I stuck with the two army speedsters as we ran in the dark through the pouring rain. An icy wind was blowing right through me. But I just stuck on their shoulders. They picked up the pace with a kay to go, but still I stuck with them. Then we hit the athletics track, the last four hundred metres, and they both started sprinting. So did I, and my lungs were near bursting as I flew past the second speedster. One hundred metres to go, and the leader had three metres on me. I thought of Simba as I pumped my legs. We were dead-even at fifty metres, and I surged clear for a strong win at the end.

"Good fitness," the army speedster shook my hand.

After a quick shower we changed and made our way to breakfast. It was in the canteen that I saw him. I was really excited. "Sir! Lieutenant Waters!" I shouted over the breakfast hall.

"Carter, what the hell are you doing here? Have you joined the British Army?" He made his way over to where I was standing and shook my hand. Then he hugged me.

"No, sir, I'm at Cambridge. I'm here on a boxing-training week."

He grinned. "So you're at Cambridge. Good boy. Well done, Carter. I'm glad it's all worked out for you."

"Thank you, sir."

"Why don't you join me for coffee?"

I walked with Waters to the coffee table, poured myself a cup, followed him to a private table in the corner and sat down next to him.

"Hey, Carter … remember that raid we did on Nkomo's house? When you and I shot up his bedroom?"

"Yes, sir."

"Well, you know we thought it was just bad luck that we'd missed him?"

"Yes."

"It wasn't. The reason why he wasn't there was because he'd been tipped off. Apparently he got a call twelve hours before we hit his house. And you know where the call came from? The Comops building."

"You mean there was a spy at Comops?"

"Yes, right at the top of the hierarchy, in the Comops High Command. He told Nkomo we were coming."

"Hell, sir, how did you find out?"

"It's public knowledge now. After the war, Nkomo and ZIPRA intelligence told everyone. Listen, Carter, you're not in the army any more, so stop calling me sir. It's John."

"Okay."

"Anyway, I'm pleased to see you're in good shape. You've done well to pull yourself together after that Comrade X op." He stared into his coffee and for a long time we were both silent. Finally he spoke again. "Have you ever told anyone what happened?"

"No."

"Be careful. A soldier of mine in Borneo had a similar incident. Never talked, blew his own brains out last month."

"Sometimes I wish I never made it out of there," I whispered.

"Nonsense, you've got a lot to live for."

"Sir, what frightens me the most is that ... after everything, all the dead ... Were we fighting for the right cause?"

"Hell, Carter ..." He stared out the canteen window without saying anything. Finally, he turned to look at me. "I'll make three points with the benefit of hindsight. A minority can't rule a majority like we did in Rhodesia. You can't discriminate like we did against the blacks. And we should have stopped fighting much earlier. In September 1976, after the Kissinger-Vorster talks, Smith agreed to majority rule. If we'd held elections with Mugabe and Nkomo back then, think how many of our friends would be alive today."

He got to his feet. "Sorry, Carter. Am I boring you?"

"Not at all, sir!"

"Then let me ask you a question. This put it all into perspective for me. Imagine you were a nineteen-year-old black growing up in Rhodesia in the seventies. You couldn't vote or go to the same schools, restaurants, hospitals or bars as the whites. Everyone, including the law, regarded you as a second-class citizen. You could either accept your lot or stand up for yourself and join the terrs. What would you have done?"

I took a deep sip of my coffee. "Hell, I'd never thought of it like that."

He looked at his watch. "I've got to go."

"Sir, why don't you come and watch me box? It's the varsity match against Oxford. I'll be fighting Simba Ndlovu."

"Not Ndlovu who used to track for us?"

"Yes, sir."

"I'll come if you promise to give him a damn good hiding!"

"That's the plan, sir."

"Goodbye, Carter, it's been good to see you," he said, shaking my hand. "You were a happy kid when I first met you, but you've lost your smile. Make sure you get it back, before too long."

"Thanks. For everything, sir."

I sat down next to Dave on the way back to Cambridge. "Let's target the bout as soon as possible. I'll talk to Finn over the weekend. Shall we do it on Monday?"

"Sure," he agreed.

Finn wasn't keen for me to fight at heavyweight, especially

against Simba, who was nearly twenty kilos heavier. But he reluctantly agreed, and we gloved up silently after training when the other boxers had left. Poor old Dave had no idea how badly I needed to fight Simba. He was caught completely by surprise as I tore at him with brutal intensity. I had him on the ropes and hit him with straight rights, left hooks, right hooks, uppercuts. He covered his face, doing all he could to defend himself. Then I got him in the stomach—left, right, uppercut to his jaw and he fell.

"That's enough, boys." Finn helped a groggy Dave to his feet.

Kisho, our Japanese coach, had been watching closely. He seemed angry and called me into a private room. I walked over immediately. I had a lot of respect for Kisho, and he'd spent many hours giving me private coaching.

"You sad. No smiling, no laughing, no fun. What wrong?"

I looked at him surprised. "You mean now, or always?"

"Always."

"I don't know what you mean, Kisho."

"When I young man I fight in Bangkok. Underground. There other fighters like you. Empty." He stopped. I could see he was genuinely worried about me. *Hell, what had I become?*

Kisho continued, "You good boy. Be happy, go have fun."

I ran back to Magdalene. That night they'd invited me to join the Wyverns, the hard-partying Magdalene drinking society. I'd said no, but with Kisho's and Waters' words in my head, I knocked on Lewis's door, "Hey, I'm on for tonight."

"Great stuff! See you there."

The initiation was no walk in the park. It started with power-eating in Formal Hall, all of us wearing our black gowns. I and the two others being initiated had no time to enjoy the beautiful candle-lit surroundings of the 16th-century college hall, impressively decorated with the Heraldic Arms of Queen

Anne. Everything on the dinner menu was unceremoniously shoved in front of us by twelve Wyverns, and down our throats it went. Stew, potatoes, cauliflower, cabbage, broccoli, bread—and it had to be eaten quickly. If we showed any signs of slowing, we'd be rewarded with another helping. Then seconds, thirds, fourths—all quickly. Then dessert: a thick, sweet, uncomfortable chocolate pudding. And another and another, and finally the last helping. We waddled out of Formal Hall. Already I could feel the food rising.

Then into the College Bar, where a large group of students had gathered to see us suffer. A bucket was strategically placed next to us, and we were each given three full pints.

"Go!" The stopwatch was counting as we started downing the pints. I got through the first one; started the second. And it all came out, pouring up from my stomach, through my open mouth into the bucket. I carried on downing the pint. Then again, into the bucket. Then the third pint, quickly. Loud cheers from the Wyverns, and the students in the bar congratulated us. The initiation was over.

The mood in the pub was great. The music started, and I hit the rum-and-Cokes. I hadn't drunk in ages and could feel it going to my head, but I didn't care. I was going to enjoy myself. Another rum, a shot of tequila, then more rum, and we moved on to the Pickerel Inn. Another tequila. I was staggering, Lewis propping me up as we left the Inn and made our way into town. To some nightclub. We walked in. The music was fantastic, and the place was packed with old friends.

Amazing.

*Dust In The Wind* started playing—my favourite. Laurel was there right in front of me, dancing. Bright blue eyes, short-cropped dark-brown hair. Still gorgeous.

"Laurel, I'd a nightmare about you. I dreamed you were on the Viscount."

There was a hand on my shoulder, firm.

"Bruce!" I flung my arms around him and gave him a bear hug. "Man, it's great to see you looking so well! Hell, I've missed you."

"Ja, Scott, great to see you, man. Hey, we made it here. Can you believe it? Two farm boys from Selukwe. Always said we would, hey?"

There was another hand on my shoulder. Conway.

"Carter, how the devil are you? Hey, Thomas, have you learned to shoot yet?"

"I beat you, Conway. You know that," Bruce shouted right back.

"Ding-dong, ding-dong," Conway tolled his imaginary bell. We laughed. It was so good to see them again; I couldn't stop smiling.

Then the wind started to blow. We were walking through the Zambian bush, mopane trees on all sides, a range of koppies to the left. No birds. Silence. Then Kariba …

"Don't get on that plane, Laurel!"

The wind was whipping across the airport runway. But she kept on walking, over the runway and onto the Viscount. Then Chimoio …

"*Die, you murderer!*" The girl screamed as she leapt to her feet, her wooden gun pointing at my head. Bruce shot her and she splattered into the wall. Then Antelope Mine … A strong breeze was blowing from the mineshaft, carrying the dust. And with it, the bodies.

Then I saw him. Right in front of me. Simba.

"After everything we did for you. Why?" He stared at me, open-mouthed. I crashed my fist into his jaw. He was on the ground and I dived on top of him, smashing punches into his face. Left, right, left.

He was going to pay!

## twenty-two

I opened my eyes. Lewis was shaking me firmly.

"Are you okay?" asked Kyle. My head was throbbing.

"Do you remember what happened?"

I didn't, so kept quiet.

"It was pretty disturbing, Scott. You beat up some poor black guy for no reason. Lewis and I got you out of there quickly, before the cops came. But you lost it … you were shouting out names, 'Laurel … Bruce,' like you'd gone mad. It's not the first time. Why don't you tell us your problem?"

I poured myself a glass of water from the tap. I hadn't told anyone about my past. Now wasn't the time. But they needed an explanation, so I told them about Laurel, the Viscount and *Gukurahundi*.

Both stared at me wide-eyed. They got up to leave. Later, on their way out, they came over to show their support.

"We're going to win for you," promised Kyle. No one ever mentioned my talk again, but there was a new level of intensity when we arrived at training that evening. After a gruelling session of hill-sprints, gym work and sparring, the boys called it a night.

Kisho called me to one side. "You have more training. Make strong." And we did strength work: weights, squats, press-ups and, to round it off, another set of hill-sprints. I jogged back to Magdalene, took a shower, got a bite to eat, and headed for my room. As I opened my room door, the idea hit me. *What about persuading Dad to come over?* I needed all the help I could get for this fight, and he was the best trainer I'd ever had. Finn and Kisho wouldn't mind.

I called him immediately. Told him the good news, that I'd be fighting Simba. I could tell he was excited.

"Hey, boy, remember? I always said there'd be a third and final decider!"

"Can you come, Dad? I need you. Listen, I'll pay you back for the costs of your trip as soon as I'm working. Just come, please, as soon as you can. This fight, it's important, it's gonna put things right for me."

"All right, my boy, I'll dig into my savings. I'll come."

I put down the phone and punched the air. *Yes!* Five weeks to go! I got out my pad and wrote to Bruce. Told him I was fighting Simba. He would understand how important the fight was to me.

There was a shadow hanging over the front door of Fenner's Gym when I arrived for training. I looked up to see two monsters.

"Will Roberts," the giant introduced himself. He didn't need to. I'd seen him play many times that season. First-team lock, captain of the England under-21 squad and destined for great things. At least a hundred and ten kilos of solid muscle.

"Matt O'Connor," the other giant said, holding out his hand. I'd also seen him play. First-team prop, he'd troubled every front row Cambridge'd played all season. At least a hundred and twenty kilos, although not all muscle. *These guys need to be in the selection frame for the Oxford match*, I thought to myself. Given that there was no upper limit in the heavyweight division, every year the boxing captain would look to recruit monsters like these from the rugby team. They'd win their fights on sheer size. I was captain, and for the benefit of the team I had to make sure we had the best team in the ring.

I called Finn and Kisho to one side as the boys warmed up.

"We've gotta give these guys a chance," I told them. "If they're the best, they must fight."

"But what about you?" asked Finn.

"These guys should spar off today. And I can take on the winner tomorrow. That way we're sure of getting the best guy in the ring."

They agreed, so after training we put Will and Matt in the ring. Matt flew at Will, and walked straight into a thundering right. Down he went. Will was cool, calm and collected, and he battered Matt all over the ring. Finn didn't even wait till the end of the first round before stopping it.

I had a tight, uneasy feeling in my stomach. This guy was really strong, and fighting like a seasoned pro.

"Will, there's one more face-off you've gotta do. That's me. We can either do it now or tomorrow. Which would you prefer?"

"Now's fine. Let's get on with it."

I gloved up quickly. A face-off now would be to my advantage. Will had worked hard at training and pulverised Matt. He'd be tiring soon. This was gonna be a helluva fight. Heavier, stronger, taller, more reach ... it was all stacked against me. But I had experience and fitness on my side.

Kisho called me over and whispered in my ear. "Make him angry. You'll tire him. Then you beat him." I thought of George Foreman and Muhammad Ali, their rumble in the jungle. The bell rang.

I went storming forward, dodging a jab on the way in, and caught him with a right straight on the nose. Then a left jab. He was furious. He'd never taken a step backwards to anyone, and he charged at me. The crisp, straight combinations that'd destroyed Matt were gone. Instead, he swung from everywhere. *Perfect, all going to plan*, I thought. I covered up, took a few shots, then moved around the ring. Still he kept swinging; he'd tire soon. I kept moving. Then I'd step in, smack him with a left-right combination, and get out quickly. He grew angrier, his punches wilder.

After the first round he was panting, completely out of breath. Kisho put a wet towel over my face in the corner.

"Okay, he's dead on his feet. Now you score, lots and lots." And I did. He was out on his feet. I moved in, letting rip with combinations, then moved out again. As the round came to a close, he could barely lift his hands. Left jab, right cross, left hook, and he staggered backwards. He turned and marched straight at me. Left, right, I hit him, and moved. And again. He staggered backwards.

"That's enough, boys," said Finn, quickly stepping between us.

I was singing in the showers after training. My fight with Simba was assured, and Dad was coming that night. When he arrived, I took him for a celebratory drink at the Pickerel Inn, near Magdalene Bridge, and ordered a real ale for him and a Coke for me.

"Warm beer," Dad gave me a strange look as he took a sip.

"*Ja*, real ale, or bitter. It's been part of the English culture for centuries."

He took another sip and pulled a funny face. "Not too sure about this, son. What's the difference between this and proper beer, like our Castle?"

"The big difference is that this beer's still alive." Dad gave it a suspicious look, and I carried on. "It's fermenting in the barrel as it's sold."

We sat down in front of the fire.

"This is one of the oldest pubs in Cambridge," I told Dad. "Dates back to the sixteenth century. They say it was a brothel, gin palace and opium den before it became a pub."

"*Jeez*, man." Dad looked around him, shaking his head.

"So what news from home?"

"All fine. Your mum's well, sends her love." He stopped. "Look, son, why don't you join me for one beer. Your fight's still over a month away."

"All right, Dad." I went to the bar, bought a pint of real ale and walked back to join him by the fire.

"You were saying?"

"As we expected, the Fifth Brigade came looking for Anna."

"No!" I looked around me. The fire in front of us was burning strongly. At the bar a group of students were comparing notes from a party over the weekend. The band in the corner had just started playing *Handbags and Gladrags*. It was hard to believe that, as we sat there, the Fifth Brigade were busy murdering the Ndebele in their thousands. Dad kept going.

"Anyway, they arrived in an army truck packed with these murderers, all wearing their red berets. A captain got out from the front. Evil bastard." Dad stopped, then smiled. "As he stepped from the truck, Dixie bit him."

"Oh, no!" I guessed what was coming.

Dad put his hand on my shoulder. "No, don't worry, Dixie's fine. As soon as it happened, Mum grabbed Dixie and rushed him inside."

"Good old Dixie," I laughed.

"The captain was furious. They marched into Anna's compound. When nobody could give them any info on her whereabouts, he went ballistic. Gave them all a hiding. Especially the poor old boss-boy, who spent ten days in hospital afterwards."

"Anyone killed?" I asked anxiously.

"No, all alive, all okay."

"And Anna? how's she settling in Kadoma?"

"Fine. I stopped by to see her on the way to the airport. She's doing okay."

After we'd finished our pints, I walked Dad back to his B&B.

"Goodnight, Dad ... run at six o'clock tomorrow, Magdalene Bridge. See you there."

We set off at a cracking pace the next morning—the nine boys who were fighting in the varsity match, plus Dad. He'd been training hard, and kept up with me at the start. Down Magdalene Street, then right past St John's.

"Hey, Dad, look!" I pointed across to Trinity College as we ran past. "Remember *Chariots of Fire*? Well, the Great Court Run, before the clock finishes striking twelve, is in Trinity, right over there."

He was impressed, and as we ran down King's Parade, I looked around for more things to show him.

"Hell, that's amazing," Dad called out as we ran past King's College with its beautiful gothic-style chapel.

"Yes, founded in 1441 by King Henry VI," I told him proudly. "Can you believe it? Five hundred and forty-two years ago."

Kyle joined us at the front as we turned right down Mill Lane, then over the River Cam and across the fens to Grantchester.

"So were you also a boxer, Mr Carter?"

"*Ja*," said Dad. He was starting to breathe heavily.

"It's also in my family," Kyle told him. "My great-grandfather fought in the first varsity match against Oxford back in 1897. I can't wait to get my Blue ... keep it in the family."

As we turned for home, I could see Dad struggling to keep up.

"Dad, I'm gonna pick up the pace. Just follow the boys at the back." As I hit King's Parade I sprinted, with all I had, all the way to Magdalene Bridge. I put on my track-suit, did some warm-down stretching with Kyle, and waited for the others.

Later that morning, I helped myself to a huge breakfast: porridge, bacon and eggs, sausages, tomatoes and toast. The nice thing about fighting at heavyweight was that I didn't need to worry about what I ate ... the heavier I was, the better. As I crossed Magdalene Street on my way back to my room I saw a copy of the previous day's *Cambridge Evening News* being blown across the street by a strong wind. The headline read: 'When will Magdalene open its doors to women?' I smiled to myself. Magdalene was one of the few remaining all-male Oxbridge colleges.

"Scott." I looked up. It was Dad, walking towards me over Magdalene Bridge. He was with someone. Looked like Bruce's mum. Yes, it was. *What was she doing here?*

I kissed her on the cheek. Hell, she looked like an old lady now. Wrinkles everywhere.

"Nice to see you, Scott."

"This is a nice surprise, ma'am. What are you doing in Cambridge?"

"I came to see you."

"Well that's great, ma'am. Can I show you around Magdalene? Dad hasn't seen it either."

"Sure."

I took her for a guided tour. "Built in 1428," I told her proudly. First I showed her the Pepys Library. She didn't look terribly interested, so I told her the diary of Samuel Pepys, Magdalene's most illustrious old boy, was in the library. That normally got my visitors excited. Still she wasn't interested. So I took her to our famous Formal Hall, which held candle-lit dinners most evenings.

"Scott, I need to talk to you." She looked around. "In private."

"Ma'am, can I show you King's and Trinity first?"

"No, thank you." She was looking at me, her eyes melancholic. Something was going on. I looked at Dad. He too had a sad, anxious look on his face.

"Remember when I came to see you off at the airport?" she said.

I nodded.

"And you promised that if I ever wanted to know what happened, you'd tell me."

I shook my head. "Some things are best left alone, ma'am. Please."

Dad wrapped his arm around my shoulder and spoke softly. "Come, my boy. Let's go to your room." He led me through the quad, past the porters' lodge and over Magdalene Street to my room near the river. He sat me down on an armchair and placed his hand gently on my shoulder.

Mrs Thomas sat down next to me. "Please, I need to know what happened."

I got to my feet, feeling trapped. "Ma'am, I really don't want to go there."

"I'm afraid you have to. Not for me, not for Bruce. But for yourself." She leant down, picked up a small suitcase she'd been carrying, and opened it. It was filled with letters.

I took a closer look. My handwriting.

"Scott, you've been writing to Bruce for years now."

I nodded.

"Every week."

"Yes, ma'am."

"Why?"

"Well, he's my best friend." I looked up. Dad had his face buried in his hands. Mrs Thomas was staring at the floor.

"Scott, he's been dead for five years."

## twenty-three

*All go unto one place; all are of the dust, and all turn to dust again* .... Ecclesiastes 3.20

"*Booo!*" jeered the crowd. Simba must've entered the ring. I didn't look, didn't want to see him. I climbed through the ropes, and the packed Cambridge Guildhall erupted with cheers. It felt as though the roof was about to lift off. I looked around me, soaking in the atmosphere. The students were chanting rhythmically: "Cam*bridge*, Cam*bridge*," and stamping their feet on the floor.

Dad was trying to tell me something, but I couldn't hear above the noise. Still I didn't look at Simba. There was no gallows feeling tonight. I simply had to win, and would pay any price to do so.

Dad tightened my head guard and checked my gloves. *Move in close, throw your punches hard and fast. Use your strength to drive him backwards. Crowd the taller boxer.*

The ref called us to the middle of the ring.

Finally I looked up at Simba. He ignored my gaze.

He'd avoided all eye contact over the last three days. Probably in one of his moods again. We'd arrived outside Comrade X's camp. A silence hung over the camp, over the bush. No birds. Dead still, apart from the wind which was slowly starting to blow. Something was horribly wrong.

Dixon was visibly angry and walked over to Simba. They were arguing. Then Dixon indicated to Waters and slipped off into the bush with Simba. Waters pulled us in behind some bushes, where we took cover and waited.

I looked around me, quickly taking in as much detail as possible. We were on a small koppie with mopane trees on all sides. To the left, a range of koppies led into the distance. In front, the camp, camouflaged against the bush with two huts visible. No one in camp. *Where were they?*

Then movement behind us. I turned my AK. It was Simba. On his own. *Where was Dixon?* He tapped Waters lightly on the shoulder.

"Dixon's waiting for us. We've found them."

"Let's go, boys," said Waters. Young was up first. In a half-crouch, he went after Waters. Conway rose about two seconds later. Bruce got to his feet after Conway. He turned to look at me.

I was trying to get a mopane fly from my eye so was slow in rising.

"You okay?" he asked quietly.

I quickly mouthed a reply, "Yes," and followed them.

Simba ushered us behind a group of rocks and quickly drew a map in the sand with a stick. "We're at the front of the camp now … here," he said pointing at the sketch. "This is where they all are … gathered round the back."

I watched Simba closely. Beads of sweat were trickling down his face. His eyes were darting from left to right.

"They're having a meeting. Perfect for an ambush … but we've gotta move quickly," he told us.

"What about the Russians?" asked Waters.

"No Russians. They must have gone. There're eleven of them, including X. If we get a good position, we can take them out. All of them."

"Okay," agreed Waters.

"Right, we move from here," said Simba, pointing to the map in the dark-brown soil. "Along the left flank of the camp, at the bottom of that range of koppies. To here, it's about six hundred metres." He pointed again with his stick. "Then we cut straight up the koppie for about sixty metres." He tapped the sketch lightly with the stick. "That'll be the best spot to hit them."

Simba checked his watch and led us towards the range of koppies. At the foot of the range he took us through the thick bush. Lots of thorn trees and mopanes. They wouldn't see us. We followed him in single-file. He was on edge, kept checking his watch as he crept forward in a half-crouch. Next was Waters—calm, experienced, ready. Then Young, also calm. Then Bruce, taking short sharp breaths and looking nervously from side to side. Then me, and at the back, Conway.

A silence still hung over the bush. *Why so quiet?* I thought. *What about the noise from X's meeting?*

Simba stopped and called us back into a little huddle. "There's an open ten-metre strip right in front of us. We need to move quickly through it." He checked his watch again. Something wasn't right.

"Let's move … fast." And he led us into the clearing. I looked around me as we entered the open space. It was covered on all sides by koppies, like a theatre. Perfect for an ambush. Then the air erupted with gunfire—AKs. Out of the corner of my eye I saw Young drop, bullets tearing into his body. Waters was rolling his way out of the clearing and into the bush. Bruce fell too, clutching his leg in agony. To his left was Simba. Bruce held out his arm for Simba to grab. Simba didn't hear him, so I screamed, "Simba, grab him! He's been hit!"

Simba looked down at Bruce and me. Then turned and ran into the bush.

*What the hell?* No time to think about it. I was on the ground, rolling, searching for cover.

Then the shooting stopped and a loud voice called out: "You're surrounded on all sides. Put your weapons on the ground. Hands on your heads. Now!" The voice was clear, precise.

I looked around. Bruce was on the ground holding his leg, in a lot of pain. Conway was at his side. The three of us were in a clearing. Waters was nowhere to be seen. No sign of Dixon. Young was dead. I lowered my rifle to the ground and raised my hands above my head. Bruce and Conway did the same.

"Now take three steps towards that big thorn tree," the voice shouted. We stepped forward.

"Get on your stomachs. Hands on your heads." We lay still on our stomachs for at least fifteen minutes. They didn't come out of the bush.

*Where had Simba gone? Where was Waters? And Dixon?*

"On your feet."

We rose, keeping our hands firmly on our heads. I searched the surrounding koppies, all covered in mopanes and acacias, looking for the voice. But the light was fading fast, and I couldn't see anyone.

Then something hard was rammed into my temple: the barrel of an AK. I could hear heavy breathing right behind me.

"Hands behind your back," shouted the clear voice.

I shifted my hands from my head to behind my back, where they were immediately grabbed and tied tightly behind me.

"Right, move!" They marched us down a narrow bush path towards the camp. Bruce hobbled in front of me, one leg covered in blood.

I hadn't even caught a glimpse of our captors. There must have been at least five of them marching behind us. There was a noise that sounded like Conway stumbling, then a loud crack—probably a rifle butt to his head. I heard a quiet moan.

The narrow path was covered with thorn trees. Bruce was struggling with his leg, so progress was slow. After we'd walked about fifty metres, one of the terrs overtook me and zeroed in on Bruce. "Faster!" he hissed, and swung his boot into Bruce's buttocks. Bruce went flying into a thorn-bush on the edge of the path, and lay there, unmoving. The terr bent down, grabbed Bruce by the hair and yanked him to his feet. I stood there unable to defend my friend, with my hands tightly bound and a gun at my head.

Bruce somehow kept walking, and the terr moved to the back again. I didn't get a chance to look at him; all I could see was that he was wearing a dappled green-and-brown camouflage uniform. Within five minutes we entered the camp. Our five guards were all wearing the same camouflage uniforms. They didn't even look at us as they chained us by our ankles to a pole in the centre of a large, well-lit clearing. Once we were all tied up, three of the group left, leaving two to guard us.

I sat down on the dark sand. "How's your leg?" I whispered to Bruce, seeing that he was in real pain.

"*Shhh*," he said. He was straining to hear what the guards were saying—unconcerned about us, they were speaking in Ndebele.

We sat quietly. Bruce had been fluent in Ndebele since he

was a little boy. From where I was sitting, I could see nothing of the camp. It was tucked away in the bush. In front of me was the range of koppies from where we'd come. To the edge of the clearing was a small enclosure, with four baboons inside. The light around them was good and I could clearly make out each baboon. I thought back to our pre-op briefing: they were used as an early-warning system against planes.

Both guards got up and walked over to us. They kicked each of our ankle-chains in turn, checking the ropes were securely fastened. They lit cigarettes and sauntered off, stopping to stand and chat about fifty metres away.

"What'd they say?" I murmured to Bruce.

"It's gonna start in about twenty minutes. The show. We're the entertainment. They're saying ... God, you don't want to know what they were saying." He didn't need to tell us ... his eyes said it all.

"Shit," said Conway. We sat silently.

"No, I'm not gonna die in a gook camp in Zambia." Conway's voice had a desperate edge to it. "Man, I've still got so much to do. I'm gonna do one of those round-the-world trips when all this is over. Hey, why don't you boys come with? We can party, big time. Oktoberfest, and the Running of the Bulls in Pamplona. It's awesome, the town just goes wild. We'll have a blast."

We didn't look at him.

"And my little boy," continued Conway. "Sure as hell, he's gonna play rugby for Rhodesia. And the Boks. I'm gonna see him do it."

Bruce turned to face Conway, then me. "Boys, we don't let these murdering bastards get any satisfaction from us. Don't show any pain, and if they threaten to kill us, we tell them to get on with it."

"Okay, Bruce," I whispered. Hell, he'd grown up. Just a few years back he was a chubby little teenager, scared to take on the Millers.

Bruce lowered his voice and kept speaking. "They were talking about Simba too." Then he paused and sat staring into the dark sky above.

"And?" asked Conway.

Still, Bruce sat there, saying nothing.

"What'd they say, Bruce?" I insisted.

He looked across at me. I could tell it was hurting him to say it. "Simba betrayed us. They were expecting us. He led us into a trap."

"Williams was right," said Conway shaking his head in disgust. "He warned us at Cabora Bassa that Simba wasn't to be trusted."

I could hear the bitterness in my voice as I spoke. "We gave him everything he needed. Why?"

Bruce didn't look up. "He was like a brother and best friend to us."

There was the sound in the distance of a crowd arriving. The two guards took a deep puff of their cigarettes, then crushed the butts under their boots and came quickly back to stand over us.

The group drew closer. Most were wearing the same camouflage kit. I stiffened as I saw the tall, powerfully built X striding purposely towards us. Laurel's murderer. I recognised him from the photo, and there was nothing I could do.

The guards rushed to grab chairs. X and a handful of others sat down about twenty metres from us.

"That one first." It was the same clear voice. X's voice. He was pointing straight at me. One of the guards came rushing to unlock my ankle-chain.

A group of five came forward and stood over me. None were dressed in uniform. *Probably the cooks and cleaners,* I thought as they dragged me to the centre of the gathering.

I was made to strip naked, then drop down to my knees, my hands still bound tightly behind my back. They put a bowl in front of me and told me to eat; it looked like impala entrails. As soon as I took my first mouthful, the woman in the group came forward and kicked the offal into my face. I lashed out with my feet, and immediately one of the guards stepped forward and bound my legs tightly together.

Then everyone in the group had a go: kicking, punching and spitting at me. One boy even tried to set my hair alight with matches, while the soldiers looked on, laughing.

Spurred on by the applause, the woman decided to do some role-playing. Pretended to be the white *medem.* Stood there screaming at me, the supposed black cook, for burning her dinner. "It's burnt, kaffir ... what the hell am I gonna eat?" She grabbed me by the hair, "Answer me, you stupid fuckin' *munt.*"

I stared up at her; couldn't believe what was happening.

She took a few steps back, then ran at me, swinging her boot into my ribs. I could hear ribs cracking. I went flying, landed face-first in the dirt, then lay in the soil, spitting sand and blood. Then she pulled me by the hair back onto my hands and knees. The soldiers were cheering and clapping. Encouraged by the applause, she decided to take it a step further.

"Hey, kaffir, would you like to fuck the white *medem?*" The soldiers burst out laughing.

"Kaffir, I hear you *munts* are big. Are you going to make me happy?" She rolled me onto my back and slid her hand down to my groin.

"*Aiee* ... very, very small, *eh?*" she complained, swinging me around for the crowd to see. They screamed with laughter. Then she swung her fist into my balls. I wanted to scream out in pain but forced my mouth shut as the crowd cheered.

Then she took off her green T-shirt; there was no bra underneath. The soldiers went wild, cheering and clapping. Her breasts were like two enormous pumpkins. She held me down on my back and lay on top of me, smothering my face with her breasts.

"Suck it, kaffir," she ordered, trying to force her oversized nipples into my tightly closed mouth. "Get the white *medem* excited."

Now I could smell her for the first time. "Come, on my little *munt*, I can tell you want me," she said loudly for the crowd to hear, then bent down and ran her breasts against my chest. Slowly her huge nipples started to tighten. Then she stuck her tongue into my left ear. It was wet and warm.

Her stench was on top of me, all over me, overwhelming me.

"Come on, kaffir, don't be scared. Your *medem* wants to make you happy," she shouted, leaning her breasts into my face. She slid her hand across my face, then grabbed my hair tightly. Then she ran her hand down over my chest, letting it rest at the base of my stomach.

"Now you kiss the *medem*, kaffir," she taunted me, before gesturing to the crowd who rose to their feet, cheering and shouting more abuse at me.

I tried to roll away but she grabbed me by the hair and pulled me towards her. I held my mouth tightly shut, but she forced it open with her left hand. Then her tongue was inside me. Wet, warm, darting in and out of my mouth. She tasted of *sadza* and smoky fires. Still the stench. Her other hand was moving down my leg. Then she wrapped it round my buttock and turned me to expose my genitals to the crowd. Again the crowd were on their feet applauding my humiliation. Her grip on my mouth weakened, and I chose my moment. As her tongue dashed into my mouth I bit her. With all my strength, with everything I had. She screamed, a high-pitched wail, while I spat the blood from my mouth.

Furiously she pulled me back onto my hands and knees, as one of the soldiers tossed her a large branch from a thorn tree. She swung the branch into my back. Ten times. Each blow smashed into my flesh, my muscles, my bones. But after each blow I got back onto my hands and knees and stared straight ahead. No one saw my pain.

"That's enough," called out X. "On your feet."

I struggled onto my knees, then fell back into the sand as my body gave way. The guards dragged me by the arms to Bruce and Conway, and chained my ankle to the pole.

"I'm proud of you," mouthed Bruce.

"You've had your fun. Now go," X told the group. They walked away quickly, not stopping to look back.

X rose to his feet and approached us.

I had never been in such pain. But there was no time to think about it. He was going to kill us now; of that I was certain. Dixon had probably been murdered by Simba. Waters was our only hope. They hadn't caught him. If they had, he would either be chained up with us, or they'd be parading his dead body for all to see. On his own he'd be no match for this lot. But he could call in reinforcements. Perhaps the Hunters. I looked across at the baboons. They were still relaxed.

X carefully studied each of us with his narrow brown eyes.

"You." He pointed at Conway and walked back to his seat.

"No, no," Conway said quietly. Then he shook his head and

rose quickly to his feet, his shoulders squared. As the guards untied his ankles he looked at the two of us.

"You'll look out for him ... my boy ... Brian."

I looked into his eyes. There was a look, an emptiness there that I'd never seen before. I knew Conway was going to die. And he knew it too.

He turned to Bruce; a flicker of a smile crossed his face. "Hey, I don't want *you* to teach him to shoot!" and then he rang his imaginary bell for the last time, loudly, from his shoulder, "Ding-dong, ding-dong." He waited for Bruce to say something. But Bruce was choking, breaking up.

Then he turned and marched right up to X.

Almost immediately there was a burst of gunfire. Three shots.

## twenty-four

The bell rang to start the fight.

"Go, Scott! Four-all ... it all depends on you!" shouted Kyle. This fight would determine who won the varsity match. But I needed no extra motivation. I'd dreamed of this moment for so long.

I marched straight at him. Through his left jab, his right cross ... I didn't bother to duck, I was so angry. I threw a left jab, straight right, and then a crunching left hook. He fell back against the ropes and I smashed a right to his jaw. His legs were wobbling, so I waded in with left-right combinations to his face. Then an uppercut, straight through his guard to his chin. He dropped to the canvas. The crowd were on their feet, roaring and stamping and shouting.

Simba got up while the ref gave him a standing eight count. He looked at me with expressionless eyes. I thought of Conway marching to his death. I'd make him pay. He moved away from me while his head cleared, dancing on his toes. But I stalked him down. As he flung a straight right, I slipped to my left and crashed a left hook into his ribs. Down he went. I could see he was in pain. Not enough pain. Not enough pain for what he'd done to Bruce.

"I haven't even started, you bloody traitor," I swore through my gum-guard.

He heard, and was back on his feet. I tore into him again, but this time he held me in a clinch, leaning his weight on me. The ref broke us apart and I went at him, hammering a heavy right to his body. He winced and I flung out a left jab, catching him beneath the eye. Then left-right, left hook to the body, and he staggered back against the ropes. Again he was in trouble, but the bell went.

I went back to my corner, breathing heavily. The crowd were still on their feet, still cheering, still stamping. As Dad passed me the water, I looked across at Simba's corner and I was back in Zambia.

Bruce's leg was badly damaged. It was caked with blood and the dark-brown sand was sticking to it. But Conway was still alive. And when I next looked up he was staring impassively at X, unflinching.

"How could Simba have betrayed us, Bruce?"

"God knows. He knew what X would do to us. You and me've been his best mates since we were kids." He paused. "You remember the Miller boys? We always stuck by him."

"He must've known he was going to do this when we went home together, released Shoko together. I can't believe it."

I looked up at Conway. Then looked away quickly. X had a knife in his hand. The baboons were still quiet.

"Remember that cross-country race? You would have won by a mile, but you stopped to pick me up."

"This is the first time you've ever mentioned it."

"I'll never forget it. Just wanted to make sure you knew."

"Bruce, there's still time. Waters'll come through for us."

Then another burst of gunfire. Four shots. We looked up. Blood was pouring from Conway's feet. Instead of being with Claire for the birth of their baby, he'd come on this raid. For me. I'd have to live with that.

"Hey, Scott," Bruce was talking quickly. "We're still gonna make it to Cambridge."

"*Ja*, of course, Bruce."

"And if one of us doesn't make it out of here, the other one must still go."

"We'll both make it."

"Just promise me, Scott. That if I don't, you'll get there."

I looked at Bruce, into his eyes. He knew.

"Bruce, I'll go. Whatever it takes. I promise."

Another burst of gunfire. Six shots, maybe more. Conway was on the ground, blood pouring from both his legs.

"Tell mum I love her," said Bruce quickly. I looked up at the baboons, willing them to show a reaction. Still relaxed.

Another burst of gunfire. I looked up warily. Conway was lying motionless on the ground.

The guards were approaching. They walked over to Bruce and unlocked his chains.

"Goodbye, Scott."

They led him to where X was standing. It was almost as if he relaxed once they took him. The uncertainty had gone.

I turned my head away, couldn't bear to look. Sat there staring up at the baboon cage. And, in front of my eyes, they were going mad.

"Bru ..." I stopped myself. I couldn't draw attention to the baboons, otherwise X would see them. None of his terrs had noticed, they were so focused on us. "Bruce, delay as long as you can," I screamed.

X swore in Ndebele and barked instructions to the guards. They came to me. One of them kicked me in the leg, the other unlocked my chains, then hauled me over to where Bruce was standing. I'd blown it, just as the planes were about to arrive.

X stood about a foot away from me. "You speak when you're spoken to." A loud crack as he swung his fist into my open jaw. I dropped to the ground but quickly stood up again, urgently trying to clear my head. X's punch would've given us precious seconds for the Hunters to arrive.

They were coming, they had to be.

*Please, God!* I prayed.

"Now you watch," said X. He walked over to Bruce, then bent down and grabbed his knife. It was covered in sand and blood, Conway's blood. X dangled it in front of Bruce's face. His words were precise, clear. "You saw what happened to your friend." He pointed with the knife at Conway. "Now I want you to tell me everything that Madumo told the Rhodesians about me. Everything."

"Fuck off, you murdering bastard!" Bruce spat with contempt. And X hit him. Twice, a right uppercut to the solar plexus and a left hook to his cheek that sent him flying into the sand. I looked up at the baboons; they were still frantic. The planes could be here soon. I needed to play for time.

"Hold on, hold on," I cried out.

X smiled, a satisfied smirk on his face. I could tell he was enjoying this.

"If you let him go," I nodded at Bruce, "then I'll tell you everything."

Bruce'd been lying face down in the sand. But when he heard

me he rolled over onto his back. "No, Scott, he's gonna kill us both anyway. Tell him to fuck off!"

Bruce was right, but there was a chance the Hunters were coming. Every extra second was precious.

"I'll let him go. Now tell me everything." X was impatient.

"No," I said firmly. "I want proof that he's been released and is safe. Otherwise you'll kill us both as soon as I've told you."

X spat into the sand. "No, it doesn't work like that." He turned to the guards and pointed at Bruce. "Pick up this piece of shit." They stood Bruce up in front of X. One of the guards handed X a pistol which he pressed against Bruce's foot, then turned to me. "You tell me, or I shoot."

"Don't tell him, don't!" Bruce was shouting at me.

"Trust me," I told Bruce. I called out to X, "Okay, I'll tell you." I told him all the obvious stuff which I soon realised was all we knew. We were the foot soldiers; we'd only been told what we needed to know for the raid. I told it to him slowly, pausing for effect and taking up as much time as possible.

Still no sign of the planes.

Bruce was watching me, a puzzled look on his face. I hoped he realised what I was doing.

X tightened his grip on the pistol. "You're wasting my time. I want proper information, *now!*"

He fired two rounds into Bruce's left foot. Bruce let out a cry of pain, then cursed himself for showing weakness. He was desperately trying to grab his feet, but couldn't. The guards were holding him up, his hands still tied behind his back.

"Don't shoot him. I'll tell you," I shouted.

But he turned to Bruce's other foot and hammered two rounds into it.

Dad kept it brief at the end of the first round: "Don't let him lean on you. He's trying to wear you out. Take a breather. If you carry on at this pace you'll tire in the third. Keep it up, boy, you're ahead."

I charged forward at the start of the second and smashed a straight right through Simba's gloves, sending him crashing into the ropes and onto the canvas. Another standing eight count. I thought of the bullets ripping into Bruce's feet. And I was onto him, hitting him as hard as I could. I crashed a right hook into his ribs. I saw him wince, bend over, and I came through with uppercuts to his chin—left, right, and then a left hook. He staggered, as I hammered a combination of straight punches at his face. He dropped.

Waiting for the ref's standing eight, I thought of Conway. He'd never seen Brian. And I was onto Simba again, smashing into him with everything I had. But I was breathing heavily now, panting. He pulled me towards him in a clinch, leaning his weight on me, before the ref pulled us apart. The bell rang to end the second.

The crowd was celebrating, "Cambridge! Cambridge!"

"He's gonna have to knock you out to win," said Dad. "So stay away from him. No more brawling, okay?" I nodded, but as soon as I saw Simba at the start of the third, I thought of Bruce, of Conway, and I went rushing forward, pounding left-right combinations to his body and his head. But I'd worn myself out; the punches had lost their force. And Simba knew it.

He strode forward, ramming out powerful left jabs from behind a tight guard. I was up against the ropes, and he smashed a straight right into my jaw. Then a left to the body, a right to the chin, and I was flat on my back. The crowd was stunned into silence. It wasn't going according to the script. I got to my feet and danced away from Simba, flinging out tired left jabs to keep him at bay while my head stopped spinning. I could see his eyes, watching, waiting, as he moved smoothly in and out of my range.

He struck: a crunching right to my nose, left jab to my cheek and a punishing right hook to my jaw. I dropped. My head was dizzy. I was in trouble. The crowd was quiet. All I could hear was Dad: "Only twenty seconds to go ... hold on, boy."

I got up onto shaky legs. If I was going down, I'd go down fighting. I marched straight at him, firing tired, empty punches.

Then he caught me. A right hook smashed into my jaw, through my jaw. I was floating ... at the start of the race. Bruce next to me.

*Bang*, the starting-gun rang out, and we were off. I tripped and tumbled to the ground. Bruce stopped, bent down, picked me up and carried me. Effortlessly, fast, down Impala Vlei. It was peaceful. Impala were dotted over the vlei, grazing calmly. Some lifted their heads as we ran past, others kept on grazing.

"Thanks, Bruce, thanks ..."

Then I looked up, waking from a deep sleep. Dad was peering over me. "Are you okay, my boy?"

I nodded hazily, then sat up and looked around. A boxing-ring, spectators.

"Was I knocked out, Dad?"

"I'm afraid so," he said, putting his hand on my forehead. "The main thing is you're all right, son."

The crowd was dead quiet. Slowly I took in the seriousness of my failure. My chance to pick myself up, to put my miserable life back on track, was gone.

Inside the ropes, the Oxford coach was arguing with the ref. Then the ref beckoned me to the ring. I stepped through the ropes and waited for the announcement. *And the winner by a knockout is ...*

But it never came. Instead: "Ladies and Gentlemen, we have a majority decision …"

I looked up at Dad, puzzled. A spectator at the edge of the ring turned to his friend, "Lucky bastard, he fell after the final bell." The fight had gone to the judges. I was in with a chance.

"And the winner is …" The packed hall stopped breathing.

I was waiting desperately for my name to be called.


Waiting desperately for the Hunters to come. *Where were they?* The baboons were going mad.

"Right, talk!" yelled Comrade X at me. I didn't have anything else to tell him, so I hesitated. He turned back to Bruce.

"No!" I yelled back. "Leave him alone. I'll tell you everything!" He didn't stop, walked right up to Bruce, and grabbed a knife from one of the guards.

"Scum!" shouted Bruce at him. He leant forward, grabbed Bruce's ear and sliced it off, holding it up for me to see.

"Leave him! I'll tell you everything I know!" I shouted.

Bruce was screaming in pain. I was panicking. I had to save him. *Where was Waters, where were the Hunters? What could I tell X?* So I started repeating what I'd already told him.

He didn't even look at me but turned to one of the guards, grabbed his AK and opened up. The bullets tore into Bruce and threw his body backwards. But X kept on firing, as round after round splattered Bruce across the sand.

He swung his boot into my groin and I stumbled to the ground. Then my face. Again and again he kicked me. I lay on the sand waiting for it all to end. It didn't matter any more. Bruce and Conway were gone.

Then, like the thunder and lightning before a storm, the Hunters erupted across the sky. X and his guards, his soldiers …

all of them turned and fled. I was lying on my stomach under a mopane tree when Waters found me. I knew he'd come.

"And the winner is … Scott Carter from Cambridge!" Dad, the crowd, the team, the coaches, Waters in the front row … everyone went wild.

That night the same old dream came back to me. Simba, Bruce and I on the rocks of the Baboon Pool. The sun was shining; it was a beautiful spring afternoon. We looked into the water, reflecting a light burgundy from the leaves of the msasas. From the smooth, molten surface, the blood lilies, my face and Bruce's looked back at us, like they always had. Simba's reflection was nowhere to be seen. Grey and the other baboons were under the *mahobohobo* trees, barking at me, trying to tell me something I had never understood. Then Grey jumped from the rocks and stood on the water's edge next to me, as he often did in the dream. But this time he pointed at the blank space in the water that should have reflected Simba's face. He barked at me … and, for the first time, I understood everything he said.

I woke with a start. *What had he said?* There was a knock on the door. "Coming," I called, and went to open it.

"Simba," I stopped, shocked, and stood there looking at him. His right eye was closed, his cheeks swollen.

"Scott, can we talk?"

I didn't want to talk to him. What he'd done was something I would never forget. I grabbed my wallet and walked out the door. He followed. I ordered two coffees at Quayside. We walked back over Magdalene Bridge down to the courtyard outside my room and sat on the banks of the River Cam.

"I've never thanked you for saving mother," he said calmly as we sat down.

I didn't say anything. He'd saved Dad and me from certain death. I took a sip of the hot sweet coffee. "So all that's happening in Matabeleland ... is this what you fought your war for? Is this what you betrayed your friends for? Betrayed the people who cared for you? Is Mugabe really a better alternative than Ian Smith?"

Gazing into the river, he grabbed a small twig and tossed it into the water. "Hell, I don't know. What's happening in Matabeleland is genocide. Mugabe's an evil man. Smith wasn't. But his politics were wrong: you can't discriminate like he did. We were right to make a stand."

He took a sip of his coffee, got to his feet and walked towards the bridge. Below Magdalene Bridge a college rowing team were climbing into their boat, practising for the University Bumps. He stopped at the river's edge and turned to me. "I had a deal with Comrade X. He gave me his word he wouldn't kill any of you, that you'd be kept as prisoners of war for propaganda purposes. I believed him. I was young, naïve."

I stood up and looked out over the river. Then up at Magdalene Bridge, with all the students and tourists bustling past. There was one thing I needed to know. Something I'd agonised over and couldn't comprehend.

I walked over and stood next to him. "Simba, the three of us ... Bruce, you and me. We were best friends. How could you have betrayed us?"

"You Rhodesian whites," he said, looking away, "you never understood us. I tried to explain to you many times. Then I remember one afternoon at the Baboon Pool. We were standing on the rocks, skimming stones over the water. You stopped, turned, and told me that if the blacks were allowed to vote, they'd vote for Ian Smith anyway. That's when I knew you'd never get it."

"But Simba." I stopped him. "Put politics aside. Bruce and me, my parents, we were good people, decent human beings. Mum looked after you; we all did. And Bruce and I were your best friends. We grew up together. How could you have betrayed us?"

"Best friends," he shook his head, staring into the River Cam. "You still don't get it. There was nothing to betray. We were never even friends. You were the white *baas*, I was the little *piccanin*."

He turned and looked me directly in the eye. "Scott, what is my name?"

I looked at him as if he'd gone mad. "Simba."

"No, not the name you whites use. My real name. The name my mother gave me, the name she calls me at home."

I stared at him blankly.

"You won't know, so I'll tell you. It's *Mlilo*. Means *fire* in Ndebele. You thought we were best friends. But you didn't even know my name. Couldn't even speak my language."

The dark clouds were opening above us. I stood still, gazing at our clear reflections in the river. His expression was thoughtful. For a long time I didn't say anything; just stood there staring into the water. Then his reflection disappeared, as it had done so often in my dreams.

I looked up and he was gone.

# twenty-five

*Harare, Zimbabwe, 2009*

The office door opened.

Mlilo stood in the doorway.

"Scott, it's been a long time. Too long." He was smiling, looking genuinely pleased to see me. His hair was still jet black, but lines were starting to appear on his once-smooth face. The years had slipped by. Like me, he was now fifty.

I walked over to him and shook his hand firmly. "Thank you, Mlilo."

"Don't mention it." He stopped. "Would you like some tea or coffee?"

"No, thanks."

"You can't catch cholera from boiled water," he chuckled. "How about a Coke? Made and bottled in South Africa."

I laughed as he passed me a Coke from the fridge in his office. His secretary made him a cup of tea and we sat in his office talking. It'd been nine years since I last saw him—the day Dad lost his farm.

I had been working for Lehman in Tokyo in February 2000, and was following the Zimbabwean news closely. It really bothered me that Zimbabwe, which had so much to offer, was starting to fall apart. Back in 1997 Mugabe had paid his war veterans the equivalent of about 300 million US dollars, a payment which the country simply couldn't afford to make. I remembered when Dad had called me at the end of 1999. He was furious.

"Mugabe's losing the plot. The IMF have had enough, and they've just suspended funding for Zim. But what really annoys me is his war in the Congo. It's costing us over a million US dollars a day. He's got about eleven thousand troops fighting there. Not for the country, but to protect his personal business interests. It's a disgrace."

He called me again in February 2000. This time he sounded quite pleased with himself. "You'll never guess what he's done now. There's going to be a referendum on amendments to our constitution."

"Oh really, Dad?" I was quite busy at work and wasn't terribly interested in a referendum to be held thousands of miles away.

"Ja, it'll allow him to give white farms to blacks without compensation. Also, to stay on for another two terms, and it'll give his government immunity from prosecution. Remember what he did in Matabeleland?"

"Will he win, Dad?"

"No, we'll beat him. A lot of us white farmers have been campaigning. Our farm workers should vote against him."

A week later I read that fifty-five per cent had opposed the motion; the first defeat of Mugabe's political career. *Well done, Dad,* I said to myself, a big smile on my face. But I'd underestimated Mugabe. Everyone had. Almost immediately, his thugs were on the white farms.

When they first arrived on our farm, Mum phoned. I could tell she was upset and I offered to fly back immediately.

Dad got on the line. "Don't worry, boy—just a few drunken kids calling themselves war vets. Nothing I can't handle."

But I wasn't so sure, and when news came through that some farmers had been murdered, I booked my flight to Zimbabwe.

At Harare airport I hired a car and sped through to Selukwe, now Shurugwi. I smiled when I saw the magnificent gum trees at the farm turn-off. As I bumped along the dirt track in my hired car, I noticed little grass huts had sprung up everywhere. Groups of noisy young Africans sat outside the huts, beating drums and drinking Chibuku beer. *Must be the war vets*, I thought. But apart from the huts, the farm was untouched, the bush even more beautiful than I'd remembered. Mum, Dad and Anna were thrilled to see me, but they were guarded, tense. Mum made the tea while Dad sat me down and briefed me on the so-called war vets. They'd arrived ten days earlier, and were insisting the farm was theirs and that Dad should leave forthwith.

"Have you called the police?" I asked.

"It'll be a waste of time."

"Well, let's call them," I suggested. "I mean, these guys are squatters. They've got no right to be here."

He shrugged, so I thumbed through the telephone directory and dialled the Shurugwi Police Station.

"May I speak to the Member in Charge?" I asked.

"All right, hold on."

I waited for at least ten minutes while they put me through.

"Hello …"

"Hello, good afternoon. Is this the Member in Charge?"

"It is he."

"I would like to report the presence of squatters on the Carter farm."

"I am very sorry, sir, but I cannot help you. This is a political matter, and there is nothing we can do."

"Look, man, we've got a group of hooligans illegally squatting on our farm. Can't you do something about it?"

"I am very sorry, sir, but this is not a matter for the police. It is a matter of politics."

Finally, realising the futility of my call, I put the phone down.

Dad was shaking his head. "You can't blame these guys. Mugabe is the president, and he's put these war vets on the farm. What can the police do?"

"Ja, it's one big mess." I looked up at Dad. "You don't look concerned. Aren't you worried?"

"You know, son, Mugabe's an evil bugger, but he's not stupid. He knows the country relies on us farmers for food. Surely he won't kick us off?"

After tea I excused myself and took a walk through the bush to the Baboon Pool. After many years living abroad it was a relief to be able to walk through my beloved bush. The pool was still nestled among the msasa-clad koppies, more private and picturesque than it had ever been. The bright yellow and orange of the flame lily petals appeared as I neared the pool. Fresh, clean and inviting, the water beckoned, so I stripped down to my shorts and dived in.

A troop of baboons was perched on the rocks above me, feasting on *mahobohobos*. Grey was nowhere to be seen. *Where was he?* Then I realised with sadness that he would have died of old age by now. I was forty-one; he would have been the same age as me and would have died at least fifteen years ago. But the other baboons were in festive mood and nonchalantly tossed *mahobohobo* pips at me, just as their parents had done so many years before. I lay on my back in the still water and gazed up at them. The troop leader was a powerfully built animal who looked just like Grey. He studied me curiously, then turned back to the *mahobohobos*.

Pulling myself onto the rocks, I lay on my back under the warm summer sun, admiring the koppies covered with their green canopy of msasas. This was heaven. Then the crack of a rifle shot shattered the afternoon silence. The baboons scampered off into the bush on all fours.

I quickly put on my clothes and walked in the direction of the gunfire. The sound of laughter drifted towards me. I moved behind a clump of msasas and waited. Soon a group of about ten young men emerged from the bush, drinking Chibuku beer and talking in Shona. Their leader had an AK-47 rifle slung carelessly over his shoulder. Mugabe's war vets. They must have been poaching. Thank goodness they were empty-handed.

I waited until they were out of sight before I slipped home through the bush. This was disturbing: they were poaching on our farm, killing animals which were a special part of the land.

As I drew closer to the house I could hear the sounds of drumming and chanting coming from Anna's compound. But this was not the cheerful sound of beer-hall partying. This was sinister: the drums of war.

When I got home, I told Dad about the poaching.

He buried his head in his hands. For the first time I could see real concern on his face. "Hell, son, that's bad news." Then he turned and looked out the window in the direction of the noise.

"Listening to the drums and the activity over the past day or so, I think they're building up to something big. They've yet to confront me. Since they arrived, the only contact I've had with them is a message through the farm manager that they want me off the farm."

I looked up at him questioningly.

"I'm going to scout around the compound tonight, see if I can find out what's going on. Will you come with?"

"*Ja*, of course, Dad. It's just as well one of us can speak Shona and Ndebele."

He smiled. "I'm surprised you never learnt. Mlilo and I tried to teach you."

Mum asked Anna to sleep at our house that night, but she wouldn't have any of it. "No, they can't stop me sleeping in my own home," she said stubbornly.

"All right, Anna, but then go home early. I'll cook. You don't want to be out late with that lot around."

I ate little of Mum's scrambled eggs. I had an uneasy feeling about these war vets. Dad seemed to be taking both them and Mugabe a little too lightly.

After supper, Dad and I got changed into our old camouflage gear.

"What rifles do you have now?" I asked, pulling on my jacket.

"The .303 and .22," he told me. "But I'd rather leave them behind. There's not going to be any shooting tonight."

Staying off the path, we walked through the bush towards Anna's compound, where the drums and chanting were getting louder. Fortunately it was a dark night. There was only a half-moon, and it was well covered in the thick cloud.

We made our way through the large thicket, then edged our way to the compound where we hid behind a clump of thorn trees. The war vets were busy searching everyone in the compound, swearing loudly in Shona.

"They're asking our guys for their ZANU-PF cards to prove they're Mugabe supporters," Dad whispered.

"Do any of our staff support Mugabe?"

"No, they're all MDC supporters."

The ringleader dragged Anna into the centre of the interrogation circle, where he cursed her in Shona. She glared straight into his eyes as he screamed at her. Then he slapped her, sending her crashing to the floor. Dad tensed, and immediately I put my hand on his shoulder.

"Not now, Dad."

About a hundred and fifty farm workers, half of whom worked on our farm, were made to stand in the centre of the clearing outside Anna's hut. Fifteen war vets, armed with whips and knobkerries, patrolled around them.

"*Pamberi ZANU-PF,*" the war vets shouted.

"*Pamberi ZANU-PF,*" the crowd mumbled.

Immediately the whips cracked.

"*Pamberi ZANU-PF,*" shouted the crowd.

"This is a re-education camp," explained Dad. "They're doing this all over the country. The intention is to pump the farm workers with propaganda to make sure they vote for ZANU-PF in the June elections."

Then the ringleader started bellowing at the farm workers in Shona.

"He says that the British want to rule Zimbabwe again," translated Dad. "To vote for the MDC is to vote for white power, to vote for the British." One of the war vets dragged an old man out of the crowd, laid him in the sand at the front and lashed him on his back.

"What did he do?" I asked Dad.

"No idea."

An ominous tone crept into the ringleader's voice as he continued in Shona.

"He's saying that the ballot papers are not secret. ZANU-PF

will know from the numbers printed on the paper exactly who voted for the MDC. Those people will be hunted down and punished."

Then he called Dad's farm manager, Enoch, to the front and berated him. Enoch was arguing with him. This incensed the war vet, who screamed at him, grabbing him by the ears and smashing his head into the wall of Anna's hut.

"He's telling him that he and the workers should beat me up tomorrow and kick me off the farm. Enoch refused."

"*Pamberi Mugabe*," the war vets screamed.

"*Pamberi Mugabe*," the workers shouted.

"Pamberi ZANU-PF!"

"*Pamberi ZANU-PF!*"

"*Pasi ne MDC!*"

"*Pasi ne MDC!*"

The whips cracked again as the farm workers were made to march around the perimeter of the compound chanting slogans and singing revolutionary songs. Dad and I quickly leopard-crawled toward home. Finally, once we were on the other side of the thicket, we rose to our feet and hurried back to the house.

Back inside, Mum made us a cup of tea. We sat in silence as the echo of chanting voices carried on the still evening air.

"These guys mean business," warned Dad. "This is a professional job. These re-education camps are just like the *pungwes* Mugabe's terrs used to hold during the war."

"Kathy should be here tomorrow," said Mum, changing the subject. We didn't say anything.

I went to bed at midnight and closed the windows tightly to try and shut out the noise. But I couldn't shut it out and as the hours ticked by it grew louder. Finally I drifted into an uneasy sleep. And, for the first time in years, my old dream came back to me. No Bruce, but Mlilo and I on the rocks of the Baboon Pool. I gazed down at our reflections in the red of the blood lilies, as I had so many times before. My hair was turning grey, my face lined with wrinkles. The tragedy and stress of my early years, coupled with the relentless life of a workaholic more recently, had taken its toll. But it was a distinguished face, the face of someone who'd really lived, who'd seen it all. I cast a disapproving glance at my physique. Gone were the tightly packed muscles of my youth. Instead I saw the fading body of a forty-something executive struggling to find the time to work out.

Next to my reflection was Mlilo's, looking up at us. I could see it clearly for the first time in my dreams, see him for who he really was.

I woke with a start. The light was streaming through the window.

I put on my trainers, shorts and T-shirt and walked out onto the front lawn, where the sun was peeping over the mango trees. After five minutes' stretching I went for a run, sucking in the beautiful clean farm air as I jogged through Impala Vlei. A couple of reedbuck drinking at one of the water-holes dashed into the bush when they saw me. The impala raised their heads. I reached the Impali and was thrilled to see it in full flow. Flinging aside my T-shirt and trainers, I dived into the water and lay on my back, letting the Impali carry me downstream, as I'd done so often as a child. *It's time to get yourself fit*, I told myself, did a crawl-sprint upstream and then let the strong current carry me back down again. Panting loudly, I swam to the side and pulled myself up onto the grass bank.

As I lay back on the grass, letting the warm early-morning sun soak into my body, I heard the familiar call of the grey lourie. "Go-*whay*, Go-*whay*!"

"Bloody Go-Away bird," I laughed. "Hey, listen, I'm not hunting anything, so you can shut up."

But it didn't keep quiet. Instead it kept on calling. "Go-*whay*, Go-*whay*!"

My peaceful morning was ruined, and to make matters worse, the sun disappeared behind dark clouds that were starting to gather.

I got to my feet. Still the lourie was calling.

"Listen, you stupid bird! I'm not trying to shoot anything!" I bent down to pick up a stone to chase it away. As I felt my fingers on the stone, I stopped. Perhaps I wasn't the hunter.

He was sitting on a big msasa about a hundred metres from the river. I walked towards him.

"Go-*whay*, Go-*whay*!" he kept calling.

As I made my way through the bush, I looked around me in all directions. A herd of impala was drinking from the river a few hundred metres upstream. In the distance, one of the farm workers was herding Dad's cattle.

Then I saw the blood.

# twenty-six

Following the trail, I soon found it. A dead kudu, oozing blood from a nasty AK-47 gut wound. The war vets hadn't even bothered to track the suffering animal. There was no time to bury or cover the body. I pulled on my shirt and trainers and ran as fast as I could.

The sun had disappeared completely now, and dark clouds continued to gather as I dashed for home. When I hit the home-stretch I was still sprinting, sweat pouring down my face. I raced onto the front lawn and stood there, hands on knees, gulping deep breaths.

Kathy jumped up into my arms as I walked through the door. "It's so good to see you, Scott!"

Anna brought the breakfast through while Kathy and I caught up on our news.

"Are you okay, Anna?" I asked. She had a black eye, her face badly swollen. She nodded, and went back into the kitchen.

"Tell me about life in Tokyo," urged Kathy.

I looked out of the window. The drumming and chanting had started again. But there was a new intensity to it, and it was growing louder and more threatening by the minute.

"Sorry, Kath, I'm a bit distracted," I said, pointing in the direction of the compound.

We got to our feet and walked outside. There, lying on the veranda, was a dead dove, soaked in blood, and a stick rammed through its heart.

I picked it up and looked in the direction of the drumming. "No prizes for guessing who put this here."

"Scott!"

"What's up, Dad?" I shouted back.

"Do you have a second?"

"Sure." I turned to Kathy, "I'll be right back."

He ushered me into his study and closed the door behind him. I told him about the dead kudu and the dove. I could see his mood visibly darken.

"I think they're going to make their move today. We should get the women into town as soon as possible."

I nodded.

"If we have to fight, you take this, son." He passed me the .303 rifle. "I'll use this," he said, tapping the barrel of the .22.

I put the .303 back in the cabinet. The house was silent.

"Mum, Kath …?" I called. No reply.

"Anna?" Again, no reply.

We looked in the lounge, in the kitchen, in the bedrooms. No one. The sound of chanting was closer, much closer.

"Oh, my God," shouted Dad. Well into his sixties, he was still in fine shape and his arms pumped from side to side as he scrambled for the door.

I reached it before him, flung it open and tore outside onto the front lawn. They were there. Ten of them wearing felt hats, armed with whips and knobkerries.

It was almost dark outside, the black clouds low and threatening.

"*Pamberi Mugabe, Pamberi ZANU-PF, Pasi ne MDC!*"

Two of them at the back were holding AK-47s. There was the sound of a car pulling up in the driveway. But I didn't look, and focused on the vets circling around Kathy and Anna. "Dance!" the ringleader shouted at them.

"No!" responded Kathy firmly, her face grim. She must have been terrified. Thank goodness I couldn't see Mum with them.

I looked at the driveway. A new Land Rover had parked in the drive and a large African man was climbing out. The ringleader turned his sullen, red-rimmed eyes on me and Dad. "Your *gel* is not doing what we tell her," he growled. "If she don't, there will be *too much* problem, *eh?*" He stank of Chibuku beer.

"Let her go!" I shouted.

"*Aiee*, you are *too* cheeky. We have come to take our land back. We are the veterans of the armed struggle for liberation."

"You're not war veterans!" It was the voice from the Land Rover. A voice from my childhood. Mlilo. I'd heard he was a lawyer in New York—*what on earth was he doing here?*

I turned to face him. He had changed very little since that day in Cambridge so many years ago. Unlike me, there was no grey in his hair, and he stood tall and broad-shouldered on the lawn behind me.

He walked towards the ringleader. "How old are you? Twenty-two? You were still in nappies when we were fighting the war."

"Old man, you talk too much!"

Mlilo ignored him. "Back then the Rhodesians called us terrorists. To the rest of the world we were freedom fighters."

"*Pamberi Mugabe,*" shouted the ringleader, taking two paces towards Mlilo.

"We had a cause, we were fighting for our freedom," Mlilo continued. Then he stopped, took a few paces towards the ringleader and stared him in the eye. "And what's your cause?" The ringleader glared at him.

"A drunk, paid by Mugabe to steal land!"

"The people of Zimbabwe, we want our land back," shouted out the ringleader in a hoarse voice.

"*Hayi!*" shouted Mlilo. "Twenty years, and he's done nothing about land. Why now, *eh?* To punish the people who voted against him."

The ringleader's red eyes glazed over. "*Eh*, you are a puppet of the British."

"*Uh-uh.*" Mlilo snorted. "Ian Smith declared independence from Britain thirty-five years ago! Mugabe rants about the British to stir up racial hatred. This is a Zimbabwean matter."

"*Aiee*, this is not right. Mugabe is the father of Zimbabwe. You are a traitor." He turned to me and Dad. "This is my farm. You must leave now!"

The war vets formed a circle in the centre of the lawn. Kathy and Anna were shoved into the middle.

"*Pamberi Mugabe! Pamberi Mugabe!*" they shouted.

"*Pamberi ZANU-PF. Pamberi ZANU-PF!*"

"*Pasi ne British! Pasi ne British!*"

Kathy and Anna stared down, silently.

Dad called out to their leader. "Please, let the women go. You can take me prisoner instead."

They stopped chanting and came to us, waving their knobkerries and whips. The AKs were pointed at Dad's head.

"The land must go back to the people. You must leave!"

Mlilo started to talk again, but Dad stopped him. His voice was quiet and firm. "For fifty years I've been farming this land, helping feed the people of this country and the people who work on this farm."

He was standing to my right, his grey hair blowing in the wind. He'd lost most of the muscle from his younger days, but none of his determination. Mlilo was on my left.

"Old man, if you don't want to go, we make you go!"

I looked at Dad. Heavily outnumbered and unarmed, we were helpless.

"Mudiwa!" I turned to the veranda to see Mum standing tall, looking over us. She stepped down onto the lawn and walked straight towards the war vets.

"Fergodsake, Mary, what are you doing?" Dad was furious.

But Mum kept on, and only stopped once she was standing right in the centre of our tormentors.

"What are you doing here?" Mum asked, looking at the war vet standing directly behind the ringleader. Her head barely reached his densely muscled chest.

He turned away.

"Mudiwa, I had high hopes for you," she said sternly. Still he didn't look at her. "So did your mother." She paused. "You know I taught her, too?" Still he didn't turn his head. "And the week you were born, she brought you to the school to see me."

He nodded, head bowed.

"She told me she had a feeling you were going to be different. Special. Made me promise her I would teach you. I kept that promise, Mudiwa."

"Ah, I am sorry, Mrs Carter." He wiped his nose with the end of his thumb and put his hands in his pockets.

"Mudiwa, do you know how many years I have been teaching at the school?"

Still he didn't look up.

"More than forty years. I always felt that in some small way, I was making a difference."

Mudiwa mumbled to the vets behind him. "This old lady taught me. She taught all my family. Let them go." The circle opened for Kathy and Anna.

"I am very, very sorry," said Mudiwa.

"You should leave now," Mum told him.

"We must leave," Mudiwa said softly to the others, and the war vets drifted away. But before the ringleader disappeared from sight he turned to Dad and shouted, "I will come back to get my land!"

Then they were gone.

I held Mum's hand which was shaking slightly. As we walked to the house, the skies opened and warm rain began to wash down on us.

Dad pulled out a bottle of red wine. "I think we need a drink." He poured us each a glass.

"A toast to Mary," said Dad, holding his glass up to Mum. He went over to her and in a rare moment, he put his arm around her shoulder and kissed her on the cheek. We all toasted Mum. She didn't say anything.

"When did you get back from New York?" I asked Mlilo.

"Three months ago. I came to join the MDC ... to give something back to my country."

"Peter," said Mlilo, turning to Dad, as we sipped our wine in front of the fireplace.

"Ja." The rain was crashing into the front windows.

"This is one battle we're not going to win. We're up against Mugabe and behind him you have the full might of the Zimbabwean army."

"What do you mean?" I asked.

"This is a shrewd campaign that Mugabe is running. If any white farmer beats back the war vets he will simply send in the big guns. And Zimbabwe has a powerful, battle-hardened army from the Congo."

"Are you saying I should move off the farm?" Dad asked.

"No, I'm *pleading* with you to move off the farm," he said rising to his feet. "If not, they will send in a hit team. Not officially— they'll be posing as war vets—but they'll be armed to the teeth, and they'll destroy you."

Dad stared out at the rain still beating on the windows.

"Scott," Mlilo explained. "One Bulawayo farmer had a reputation for being a tough character. Wouldn't tolerate any nonsense from Mugabe's gangsters. So Mugabe sent in his top soldiers, pretending to be war vets. Twelve truckloads of heavily armed soldiers against one man with a shotgun."

He stopped speaking while Dad filled our wine glasses.

"So what happened to him?" I asked.

"He fought them off for hours, but eventually they smoked him out of the house with petrol bombs. As he crawled out the house to get some air, they shot him."

"Mlilo, I appreciate your concern, but I think I'd rather die than give my farm to Mugabe's hired hands."

"Dad, if you stay and fight, I'll stay with you."

"Me too," said Kathy.

But after several hours of persuasion, Dad finally agreed to move off the farm. He knew that if he stayed to fight, we'd stay with him, and he didn't want to risk our lives.

"Anyway, Dad, you've got the title deeds," I told him. "If they come to their senses, then you can come back and farm."

When the storm was over, Dad, Mlilo and I took torches and walked along the path through the thicket of msasas and acacias, and on to the compound. Our legs were soaking from the wet grass by the time we arrived. We knocked on the tin door of the hut next to Anna's. It opened, and out came the farm manager, wiping the sleep from his eyes.

Speaking in English, so that I could understand, Dad briefed him on our plans. We needed to get everything we owned off the farm as quickly as possible. If the war vets knew what we were up to, they'd stop us. We'd be storing everything on a friend's well-hidden plot about five kays away. They had a storeroom, stables, cattle pens, garage, everything we needed. Tonight we would ferry the household possessions in the two cattle trucks. As early as possible, a team of farm workers would round up the horses and cattle; another team would load and transport the farm equipment. Before the vets were out of bed tomorrow, everything we owned would be off the farm.

The farm manager was devastated. "*Aiee*, no! No! You leave us?"

Dad put his hand on Enoch's shoulder and spoke gently. "I'm sorry, Enoch. I have no choice."

When we got back, Dad erected two makeshift lamps on the veranda. We parked the two trucks on the lawn as we feverishly loaded our household possessions. When the first truck was full, I drove to the plot with Kathy and a team of workers. Quickly we offloaded, and sped back for the next load. By the time I got back to the house, the second truck was already roaring off, with Mlilo at the wheel.

Before four o'clock the next morning, the house was completely empty and we started on the tool shed. Then the remaining farm equipment, and soon all our possessions were off the farm.

It was still dark when Kathy and I drove down to the stables, each with a horsebox in tow. Enoch's team had the horses ready.

We shuttled back and forth to the plot and, within an hour, our sixteen horses were safely away. Dad and Mlilo were arriving to pick up their last load of cattle when we arrived at the pens.

Dad climbed out of the truck. "Scott. You and Kath, take this load."

After the cattle were all safely penned, we parked our trucks and tractors in the garage and drove off in the bakkie. First we dropped Mlilo and Anna in town, then Kathy and I headed back to pick up Mum and Dad. As I drove up the farm road at first light, I saw the war vets ambling out of their huts. Little did they know that their loot was gone.

When we got back to the house, the farm workers had gathered on the lawn, waiting for Dad. I walked inside. He was sitting on the floor, staring into the fireplace. Mum was next to him, holding his hand.

"Dad, they're all waiting for you."

"I know." His voice was choking up. "What do I tell them?"

"Hell, I don't know, Dad." I put my hand on his shoulder. I'd never seen him cry before. I couldn't bear to look at my parents as they walked out onto the veranda.

The farm workers were distressed, most of them sobbing openly and pleading with Dad. "Please don't go. What will we do, eh?" Some had their wives with them, babies strapped to their backs. They depended on the farm. *How would they survive?*

Dad was firm. "As soon as Mugabe lets us back onto the land, we'll be back. I promise you!"

One by one Mum and Dad hugged all the workers, giving each of them an envelope of cash.

"Give us a moment, son," Dad said quietly after the workers had gone.

Hand in hand, he walked with Mum onto the lawn, where they

stood without moving. This was where they'd had their wedding, my first birthday, Kathy's twenty-first. They were still standing hand in hand as they watched, for the very last time, the sun rise over the mango trees.

## twenty-seven

*Zimbabwe, 2009*

"Are we nearly there, daddy?" Sidney had heard so much about the farm, and couldn't wait to see it.

"Yes, darling, we've just passed through Gweru. We'll be there in less than half an hour."

I turned to Mlilo. It'd been more than thirty years since the betrayal. I was still uncomfortable talking or even thinking about it, but I wanted to understand why he'd done it.

"When did you decide to change sides?"

He sat up straight in the driving seat. "As you know, I'd always been conscious of the fact that we Africans were subjugated, but I still joined the Rhodesian Army to earn as much money as possible for university." He paused, staring straight ahead. "I still remember that day, like it was yesterday. We were driving back from your mum's school, and she said to you: 'You might want to see things from Simba's perspective. There he is, fighting for us. For his country, yet he's not allowed into the same schools, hospitals, bars and restaurants.' You know, Scott." Mlilo looked at me, shaking his head. "Your mother saying that really hit home for me. There

I was, risking my life fighting for people who wouldn't let me into their schools and hospitals. I decided then that I had to change sides."

He put his foot on the accelerator.

"I still didn't do anything about it," continued Mlilo. "Until after that weekend in the Falls with Conway. That Danish girl made a move on me. I did all I could to get away, yet you all shunned me as if I'd done something disgusting. After that weekend I made contact with ZIPRA."

I'd heard enough and changed the subject. "Only fifteen minutes to go, Sidney."

"Daddy, will we see your pet deer?"

"Darling, Shoko was a kudu. We won't see him, but there'll be other kudu. We'll see lots of animals you can tell your mommy about when we get home."

"When did you get married?" Mlilo asked.

"Seven years ago. Kristin was working with the UN in Tokyo when we met. She would have joined us on this trip, but her mother is staying."

I looked out at the bare, unused farm lands as we drove. "Have any of the land-grabs been a success?"

"They've been a disaster. He gave most of the farms to his cronies, who either looted them or used them as holiday homes for weekend braais. Zim has gone from being the breadbasket of Africa to a starving beggar nation."

"So how is this power-sharing government of yours doing?"

"Okay." He didn't sound convinced and paused before continuing. "What alternatives did we have? Set up an opposition government outside the country? That would've been a waste of time. At least this way we can try to change things from the inside."

I squeezed Sidney's hand. "Darling, we're here."

Mlilo turned off onto the farm track. Immediately I noticed that the beautiful gum trees on either side of the turn-off had been chopped down. They were lying in a wasteful heap on the ground, not even used for firewood.

He drove carefully up the farm road which was now covered in potholes. Through the window, I looked out at my cherished bush. The grass had been badly overgrazed. A veld fire smouldered in the distance. We parked near the house.

I held Sidney's hand. "Look, darling … this used to be our beautiful front lawn."

"Why have they dug it all up?"

"No idea. There's nothing even planted here." I looked down to where the bottom of the lawn used to be. My rugby posts, the mango trees, were gone. "Oh, no!" I cried out loud. "Why chop down mango trees?"

We looked to the house. Very little remained of the impressive thatched roof. The once-spotless white walls were now a filthy brown. I took Sidney by the hand and led her into the house. Everything we'd left behind was broken. The windows were all smashed, the built-in cupboards were torn apart, the old table in the pantry had been gutted.

I walked into my bedroom, as three squatters looked up at me, surprised.

"Eh, hello," they said politely.

"Good afternoon," I replied. The walls of my room were a filthy black from their fires. In the centre their clothes and blankets lay in an untidy heap. There was a strong smell of smoke but something else, too. My nose crinkled up in disgust as I recognised the stench: sewage. All the bedrooms were packed with squatters, so I went to my favourite room: the lounge. I sighed with relief as I noticed that the orange stone of the fireplace still stood proudly in the centre. But that was all that remained. Squatters were spread out across the room. Again the stench of smoke and sewage, so I picked Sidney up and quickly went outside.

Mlilo suggested we go to see his hut. Sidney and I followed him and Zandile round to the back of the house. We looked down from the house. The compound was like it always had been; the syringa tree was standing in the centre of the clearing, but the path that wound its way down from the house was completely overgrown and the thicket between the house and the compound was gone. We walked through the grass to the syringa tree.

"There's the hut that me and grandmother built," Mlilo said proudly to Zandile. He grinned at me. "Sorry—Scott helped with the floor."

Zandile saw a little car made from fencing wire outside the hut, and ran to play with it. Sidney was right behind her, and the two played in the sand while Mlilo and I smiled on.

Afterwards, the girls on our shoulders, we walked through the bush, first to Impala Vlei. I looked out for the impala and reedbuck to show Sidney, but there was no sign of life anywhere.

"All poached," said Mlilo solemnly.

"Zandile, this is where your Dad rode bareback for the first time," I told her. We walked onward to the Impali River, stopping on the way to show Sidney where we'd found Shoko.

"You'll love the Impali," I told Sidney as I quickened my pace. "We can swim there, if you like."

As we came over the rise to the Impali I walked even faster. But it had changed. Gone was the crystal-clear, strong-flowing river. Instead, the water was a dirty grey and stank of sewage. Coke bottles, crisp packets and plastic floated down the river. I closed my eyes and rolled back the years, remembering myself as a young boy lying on my back, letting the strong current pull me downstream.

"Don't go near the water," I called out, thinking of cholera. The wind was starting to pick up, and one of the plastic Coke bottles blew across the water onto the river bank.

"I'm sure the Baboon Pool will be fine," I said to Mlilo. "Let's take a look at that. We can cut straight through the bush."

"Wait for us," called out Mlilo.

But I quickened my pace. I needed to see the pool. To see it like it used to be. As I got closer I walked even faster, till finally I was running, with Sidney clinging to my shoulders. When I came in view of the beautiful msasa-clad koppies, I looked up expectantly. But they were bare, the msasas gone.

"No!" I cried out aloud. Every single msasa had either been cut or burnt down.

I approached the entrance to the pool, filled with a deep sense of dread. The blood lilies were nowhere to be found. The now-familiar stench of sewage was everywhere; sewage and Lifebuoy soap. Empty packets of crisps and Surf washing powder suds floated on the slimy surface of the pool.

"Don't worry, daddy," said Sidney, concern on her face as I quickly wiped my cheeks on the back of my arm.

I sprang up onto the rocks above us where the baboons used to sit eating mahobohobos. The mahobohobo trees were still standing, but there were no baboons. I looked around frantically. No baboons. Then, in the far corner of the rocks, I found them. Their bones. It was all that was left of them. Horrified, I sat looking out over the waste. On the rocks below, Mlilo stood near the pool, holding both Sidney and Zandile firmly by the hand to make sure they didn't touch the water. A strong breeze, carrying the dust of the soil where the msasas had been, was blowing across the valley. Shielding my eyes from the sand and wind, I climbed down to join the others.

I didn't say anything as we walked back to where we'd parked. Nor did I say anything as we drove from the farm to Mopane Park, where we'd stay the night.

At Mopane Park we took the kids to see the lions. Then, later, we sat on the lawn watching the elephants bathing. After the excitement of seeing the elephants had worn off, Zandile and Sidney were ready to play again.

"Let's play hide-and-seek," said Zandile, taking command.

"Okay," squealed Sidney, as she ran to hide behind a thorn-bush on the edge of the lawn.

As I stretched back on the grass I thought back to my childhood, playing with Simba. I didn't remember ever allowing him to decide what we'd play.

Slowly my dark mood began to lift. Then a familiar face loomed in front of me. Coming back to Zim, I was always bumping into people from my past. This guy was showing guests around. He saw me staring at him and gave me a friendly wave. Then I remembered. It was Jim Brook, who'd taken Shoko all those years ago.

"Hey, Jim," I interrupted him. "I'm Scott Carter. You took care of a kudu for me back in the seventies?"

"*Ja*, I remember." He turned to the tourists he was with. "Back in the late seventies, we rehabilitated a pet kudu for Scott here. Did very well, old Shoko. We kept him in the small park for about six months." Then he turned back to me. "You know, every day he came back to where you dropped him off, looking for you. Then we let him into the wider park, and he took to it like a duck to water. Was very happy. Must have died of old age years ago."

"Fantastic, Jim!" A big smile creased my face. "Did he breed?"

"Absolutely. If you like, I can take you for a drive later. I'll show you his territory—we might even see some of his family."

While Mlilo and I waited for Jim outside reception, the kids played hide-and-seek, Zandile still in charge. I was excited for the trip with Jim. To see where Shoko had spent his latter days. It was the first positive thing I could show Sidney. I'd told her so much about the farm where I'd grown up, but all she had seen so far was the waste and decay of Mugabe's rule.

Sidney and I sat up front with Jim. I didn't want to miss a word of the story.

"Over there," he said, pointing at a range of koppies in front of us. "That's where he lived."

"Must have reminded him of the hills at the Baboon Pool," I told Sidney. "He loved it there."

At the foot of the koppies I asked Jim if I could get out. The others stayed in the car, while I walked briskly through the bush. When I was sure I was out of sight of the truck I leaned back against the granite boulder and closed my eyes. I wanted to imagine Shoko living here. To see him cantering past the koppie, his ears raised alertly to the sky, his brown eyes looking across at me. I opened my eyes and kept walking. There was a rustling sound in a clump of acacias near a group of large granite boulders. I edged forward. Then I saw him. A beautiful kudu bull.

"Shoko," I called, expecting him to come to me as he'd always done.

But he turned and scampered into the forest of msasas nearby.

I was still smiling when we drove back to camp.

As we were putting the girls to bed, the rain started and pattered steadily against the tent. But the girls were exhausted, and soon they were both fast asleep. When the rain stopped, Mlilo and I moved the camp chairs onto the lawn, where we sat watching the black clouds drifting over the thorn trees and msasas on the far side of the dam. On the near side, a grey heron stalked through the shallows, looking for food. Then it rose onto the bank on its spindly yellow legs and took flight over a flock of yellow masked weavers, hovering over their nesting site in the reeds.

"Mlilo, the war. The sadness ... the lives lost. When you look around the country today ... at the desolation, the ruin, the destruction ... what was it all for?"

He looked to the front of the dam, where a herd of kudu had appeared. Eight of them. We watched as they drank at the water's edge. All around the camp, flying ants were still swarming out of their holes, their wings glimmering in the evening air.

"You know, Scott. When I look at our children playing together, it gives me hope. The boundaries have gone." He poured himself another glass of beer, and we sat silently for ages, watching the kudu.

"I'll never forget what you did," I said quietly. "But the Ndebele message you left for me when you transferred the money. What did it mean?"

His voice was calm and assured. "We come and go. Fortunes and friendships are made and lost. The war we fought, Mugabe's ruin—it's all transient. Only the land is forever. Your friend, Mlilo."

I slept well that night.

My old dream came back to me. I was on the rocks with Mlilo at the Baboon Pool. Next to us were Sidney and Zandile, holding hands. The water was a slimy grey, littered with Coke bottles and plastic. The stench of sewage was everywhere. Then a light breeze gently swept through the valley. Our reflections, all four of them, smiled up at us from the now crystal-clear water. It took on a crimson hue, and I looked up to see that the msasas were back on the koppies, their glorious red spring leaves striking against the blue sky above.

I turned my head to the higher rocks, where the blood lilies were bursting into flower and the baboons were eating the ripe yellow fruits of the *mahobohobo*, nonchalantly tossing the pips in our direction.

*finis*

CPSIA information can be obtained at www.ICGtesting.com

262738BV00009B/31/P

9 780958 489195